ABOUT THE AUTHOR

K.T. Rose is a horror, thriller, supernatural, paranormal, and suspense author based in Detroit, Michigan. She shares her passion for spine-chilling stories with readers through flash fiction on her blog. Her works include *Trinity of Horror*, *The Haunting of Gallagher Hotel*, the *Netted* Series, and *The Trish Vampire Series*.

ABOUT MONSTER

Blood. Family. Secrets. In the quiet suburbs, a mother's darkest instincts threaten to destroy everything she's built.

Trish has spent centuries perfecting her disguise—the devoted wife, the caring mother, the ideal neighbor. But beneath her suburban facade lurks a bloodthirsty vampire struggling to contain her true nature. When a horrifying accident exposes her secret to Victoria, a college student who becomes an unwilling witness, Trish's carefully constructed world begins to collapse.

Now suspicious neighbors circle closer, her husband Randel's trust wavers, and Victoria's desperate search for answers threatens everything Trish has worked to hide. As human and supernatural threats converge from unexpected directions, Trish faces an impossible choice: reveal the monster within or watch her family burn.

Some secrets run deeper than blood. Some monsters are closer to home than she ever imagined.

Monster is the second installment in K.T. Rose's supernatural thriller series. Perfect for readers who crave the domestic tension of *Big Little Lies* meets the dark mythology of *Let the Right One In*—a chilling exploration of maternal love, ancient hunger, and the lengths we'll go to protect those we love.

CONTENTS

About the Author iii
About Monster iv

Part 1: Her
Chapter 1: Demands...3
Chapter 2: Liar 8
Chapter 3: Cover 12
Chapter 4: Derelict 16
Chapter 5: Accepted 22
Chapter 6: Attention 28
Chapter 7: Teresa 33
Chapter 8: Sultry 41
Chapter 9: Parade 46

Part 2: Care Plan
Chapter 10: The Burning Twilight 55
Chapter 11: Lucid Crimson Waters...60
Chapter 12: Conscious 64
Chapter 13: Notes 68
Chapter 14: Elephants 74
Chapter 15: Key Takeaways 77
Chapter 16: Mr. FBI...85
Chapter 17: Flight 94

Part 3: Gone Mad
Chapter 18: Worry 105
Chapter 19: Feelings 113
Chapter 20: 1924 117
Chapter 21: Zoom 123

Part 4: Steve's

Chapter 22: Crush 133
Chapter 23: Lists 138
Chapter 24: New Aches 141
Chapter 25: Hungry? 146
Chapter 26: Night Walk 153
Chapter 27: He Shed 161
Chapter 28: Passenger 166

Part 5: The Set

Chapter 29: Consider a Car 173
Chapter 30: Across the Street 176
Chapter 31: Empty Nest 180
Chapter 32: Security 185
Chapter 33: The Set...189
Chapter 34: Jag 194
Chapter 35: Electrode 197
Chapter 36: Teeth 203
Chapter 37: Tatters 206
Chapter 38: Garbage 213
Chapter 39: Favors 217

Part 6: Store and Go

Chapter 40: Cigarettes 225
Chapter 41: Visitors..230
Chapter 42: Duck..233
Chapter 43: Where? 238
Chapter 44: Boyfriend 244
Chapter 45: Die..247
Chapter 46: Friends 252
Chapter 47: Little One 255

Excerpt From Books 3: Watcher 257
More from K.T. Rose 263

THE TRISH VAMPIRE SERIES

MONSTER

TRISH

BOOK 2

K.T. ROSE

PART I

Her

CHAPTER 1

Demands

November 7, 2024

How dare she? How dare *she?* Trish growled to herself as she stood in her son Darwin's doorway, staring Victoria down. The girl was alive, but not well. She bawled her eyes out as she sat on the floor, her arm draped over the top of Darwin's toy box, and her back settled against the light blue wallpaper. She watched Trish with narrowed eyes, hateful slits full of disdain. Her sunken cheeks may have huffed with her exasperated breaths, but her face looked tight and tired. No longer smooth and youthful, her once brown skin had a gray tint to it.

She looked thirsty.

"Liar," Victoria said, a tight scowl spreading across her thin face.

Blood dripped from Trish's nose after Victoria struck her with the shovel. The throbbing aches in her face were easy to ignore. Instead, she imagined choking Victoria to death. Or even shooting her in the face and telling the police that she was a home invader. Trish's feet told her to move, put some plan—any plan—in motion, but her mind demanded that she stayed still.

What if Victoria can't die? Trish thought. *What if choking her doesn't work—what if shooting her doesn't work?* A flash from the past reminded her that shooting Victoria would not work and would inevitably result in another failure, just like she failed to end her the night they first met. No. Victoria wasn't dead. She was there, and her fangs were long and sharp, pulling all the attention in the room when she spoke.

Then another thought moved across Trish's mind. If Victoria could die, Trish would have to kill her in front of Darwin. The uneasy realization made her recoil. She opted to do nothing. Nothing but study.

Victoria's dark, thick hair was pulled back into a low ponytail and her dark brown eyes were wet with tears—no longer hazel as they had been in the photos shared all over the internet, no longer honey-eyed like they were the day Trish had bitten her. Victoria looked frail in her stained light blue hoodie. The stain was a coppery splotch, situated over Victoria's left side. It looked like blood, but Trish wasn't sure. Despite the ring, she should have smelled the blood. But when she sniffed, she smelled nothing of the sort. Alarm tightened her chest. Since when could she not smell blood? Trish made a note to jot the strange phenomenon down in her journal right after she'd gotten rid of Victoria.

Trish started, "I—"

Victoria interrupted, seemingly impatient for a response. "I know what you are," she said, tears still spilling down her face. "You can play everyone else, but don't pretend like you don't know who I am."

"I'm calling the police," Trish said.

"*Tsk*. No, you won't. You're not stupid."

"I don't know what you're talking about, and you're scaring my son. Leave, or I'll—"

"You are such a *fucking* liar," Victoria quipped. "You might not look as young as you do when you're killing people, but you are a murderer. A *monster*," she said, and when she said it, Trish's gut churned. *A witness.* Trish was so struck by Victoria's existence that she'd forgotten that Victoria did, indeed, know what Trish was.

Victoria shook her head. "Why did you do this to me?"

Trish didn't speak. She took small steps toward Darwin, who, surprisingly, didn't seem upset anymore. He gazed at Victoria from between the wooden rails of his bed, uninterrupted. Victoria didn't seem to care that Trish was moving to shield Darwin. In fact, she didn't seem very scared either, which was baffling to Trish. Victoria knew Trish's true nature, but she didn't flinch or cower. She only talked.

"You destroyed my life when you bit me—when you *killed* me." A pregnant pause, then she wiped her face and pushed herself up to her feet. Her abrupt movement pushed Trish to her final spot just in front of Darwin. She felt his small hands pull on her yoga pants as he groaned and grumbled, as if telling her to move out of the way.

Once Victoria stood, she stopped and looked Trish in the eyes. "But you can change me back. I mean, you look real. You..." She trailed off as her gaze fell onto Trish's belly.

Deny, Trish's thoughts roared. *She needs to leave.* "I don't know what you're talking about. Just please leave."

Victoria's face crumbled. "Don't talk to me like I'm crazy—I'm not crazy!" she roared.

"Keep your voice down," Trish said through her tightening jaw as she strode toward Victoria, a step away from standing toe to toe with the girl.

"Demons are real..." Victoria muttered as her eyes moved up the length of Trish's body.

No, they're not, Trish thought. "I need you to leave."

But Victoria stood there with pursed lips.

Had she drunk anything or anyone? How many bodies has she had? Trish thought.

"I'm not leaving until you change me back."

"Victoria—"

"No! How can you say you don't know what I'm talking about when you somehow know my name? I *saw* you kill Chad!" Her pointed words rolled off her tongue in quick succession.

Trish shuddered. The bodies that she'd left at Miller on different occasions were unquenchable, and the fact that one of those bodies bled over to her front step...

She swallowed as an invisible vise gripped her neck.

Another vampire. Steve's voice.

"I don't know—"

"Patricia Weston," Victoria announced. Trish's name sounded like venom rolling off the scorned girl's tongue. "I know what you are."

Chills shot through Trish's body. Victoria was going to reveal what Trish was if she wasn't handled appropriately and fast. But how could Trish handle her? *How does she know my whole name?* She tried to think of how, but panic stopped her. *One thing at a time. Get... her... out of here.*

"So, what are you going to do?" Trish asked, accepting that she'd have to deal with Victoria in another place at another time.

Victoria knitted her brow. "I'm not *doing* anything. You're going to turn me back." She looked over Trish's shoulder and directly at Darwin. "I can't live like this anymore."

"I wish I could help, but I—"

"I can't eat," Victoria said.

Trish tilted her head, wanting to know more.

"I haven't held food down in over two months, and I feel like I'm starving to death." Her voice cracked when she said *death*.

Trish wanted to ask Victoria how she felt. Were their hunger pains alike? But no. Trish said nothing.

"As soon as you change me back, I will leave," Victoria said. She wasn't yelling, but her voice carried. Her proposition boomed in Trish's ears.

Trish thought back to how Victoria ended up in Darwin's room in the first place. She caught Trish off guard with her speed and strength, something that should have been impossible on an empty stomach. *Wow*, Trish thought, encompassed in envy. Victoria wasn't missing anymore; they stood in the same room, and Trish couldn't smell a thing. She sighed.

Victoria stood there for a bit, her breathing getting heavier by the second. "Where are your fangs? Huh?" she finally asked.

"What?" The question caught Trish off guard.

"You used your fangs. I saw them. I felt them."

Trish said nothing.

"You're going to change me back," Victoria demanded.

Darwin cried, and Trish's blood boiled. "You're freaking my kid out! Now leave!"

Victoria frowned at Darwin, a genuine sense of concern crossing her face. Then she looked at Trish, and her face tightened. "I guess you want to make this hard. Okay. I expected that—I mean, why would you help me with anything?" she said facetiously. She walked toward Trish and stopped short, her face blank and wet with drying tears. Her voice shook. "I'll leave, but you *will* change me back."

It sounded more like a desperate plea than an obscure threat.

Trish followed her up the hall and out the front door she had forced her way through. Then she watched Victoria take off, running up the street. She darted, feet barely touching the ground as she sprinted. She was out of sight within seconds.

CHAPTER 2

Liar

Vicky ran, tennis shoes slapping the pavement.

Since she was little, she'd always moved the fastest when she was angry. Like when Mom yelled, "*Victoria Syleste Scott, clean your damned room,*" or whenever Dad went fishing without her. Or that time when Moody skipped Christmas dinner with her and their parents to hang out with his rude, bitchy girlfriend. Vicky moved fast to get things done and decompress. It had always worked. She'd burn off the stink from whatever had pissed her off and move onto enjoying something that never changed throughout her state of rage, like playing *Zombie World* with Moody or watching *Family Feud* with Mom and Daddy.

But this was different.

Vicky bolted across yards, bypassing opossums and a few raccoons digging their way through a dumpster.

As an invisible chill tried to freeze her features, it only dried rogue tears. She couldn't feel the icy air, and for a second, as she tried to remember what chilly autumn nights felt like on her skin, her mind veered, acknowledging the familiar dire warning from her achy, empty stomach.

When Vicky made her way to Lakeshore, she secretly hoped that she'd be running to Burger King just outside of the monster's neighborhood after their meeting. She planned on using the little money she had to stuff her face and get a ride to the police station.

But no. Instead, she was running on empty, and her side stung as her wound pulsed, reminding her that it was there, and that Steve hadn't stitched it up well. Vicky shook her head, banishing him and all his angst into the back of her mind.

She picked up speed, lighter on her feet. Then her brow furrowed. That *thing* wasn't what it was pretending to be. It wasn't human. It wasn't a suburban woman with a nice big house and a newish Jeep. It for *damn* sure wasn't a mother. Nothing as sweet as a baby could have formed in the womb of such a creature.

Nah, Vicky thought as she veered into the street. There were no streetlights on this part of her route, and the farther away from the houses she remained, the better. She didn't want to deal with the smell of sleeping people lying peacefully in their beds. The blood coursing through their veins begged her to steal it for her own fulfillment. *Never…but it would be easy,* she relented; her stomach turned in agreement. The pangs from her opening wound weren't helping either. She could break into the next house coming up on the right, and gorge on the very new cravings that she'd spent months fighting. She could even loot the home's bathroom for more bandages along with some needle and thread to weave the gaping hole in her side closed.

But instead, she ignored her body and kept running.

The monster had taken control of Vicky, robbing her, taking her breath and time away, as if that were its job all along: to steal and sacrifice for its own existence.

Fucking abomination, Vicky thought. She was sure that was how her parents and Paster Otis would describe it…if she ever saw them again. She shoved that thought away too.

After she turned the corner, she sprinted across the row of front yards on her toes, not stirring any motion sensors or pissing off any backyard dogs. She was too fast and too quiet. As she moved toward the curb and back to the street to avoid an obnoxiously bright porch light, she thought about the map she'd studied of that very neighborhood. Her heart slammed into her chest as her past worries about getting lost or not finding Patricia mounted. But Vicky had found Patricia, and for that, she cracked a smile.

Vicky watched her breath burst from her parted lips, but didn't feel the rigid air on her face. "You must be cold-blooded," Steve had told her before. Maybe two months ago? She couldn't remember. She couldn't even remember what it was like to be human. To eat, sleep, laugh…

She frowned.

Bitch, she thought. That's all she'd thought since she'd found out about where *it* lived and where *it* had been.

Vicky stopped and ducked by a bare brush, its autumn twigs tugged at her hoodie. She peered either way, watching the sleepy houses and thinking about the people inside. Patricia Weston blended in with the neighborhood, prowling amongst her own food. *But how?* Vicky cringed. It was *so* convincing, and for a second, Vicky thought maybe she had been interrogating the wrong person.

But then she thought better of it. It was the monster. Vicky had touched it—felt its teeth in her jugular. And Patricia knew Vicky's name.

Vicky thought the monster would change her back or kill her outright—she was fine with either outcome. But she didn't expect the monster not to do *anything.*

Vicky knew so much about it.

She'd seen Patricia kill Chad…and there was no telling what she'd done to Steve's friends, the people who found her. Vicky didn't know Barbie, but she remembered the pictures that she sent Steve. Vicky memorized the license in one of the photos:

Name: Patricia Weston, 550 Fallon Lane, DOB: 10/1/1986, Height: 5'10.

Vicky ran on, taking a left onto Houston Road, only to find more houses with cars in driveways and toys littering yards. Splashes of yellow and orange painted the ground where undisturbed leaves enjoyed a peaceful death. She stopped and threw her back against a white picket fence. Then she took off again, riding the shadows. Her muscles clenched as her weight tilted, and hunger pains jammed her in the side. She bit her bottom lip.

No, she thought, refusing to give in to the gnawing pain that she'd grown to know all too well. But she couldn't stop—she was not going to stop. She had to hide and think, and she knew just the place. She only hoped that the posting was still *in foreclosure* as it was a couple of hours ago.

People don't close real estate deals in the middle of the night, she thought. *Do they?*

The pain in her torso deepened, making her shudder as she stopped at an alleyway, just out of the glow cast by a lone streetlight. She bared teeth, letting tears flow. Vicky couldn't face another day with shaky bones and a growling, turning stomach. She couldn't bear the gory opening on her side.

The monster had done that to her. The small wrinkles around its eyes, and the fair shade of its once pale face were only a mask.

CHAPTER 3

Cover

Once she saw the house, Vicky knew she had found it. It stood two stories high with a winding walkway that split at the steps and led to the driveway, which looked freshly paved and unscathed. She couldn't say the same for the sore thumb of a house. Even in the dark, Vicky could still make out the angry blemishes outlining the wooden boards that covered the windows and the front door. Burnt bruises stained the once bright siding, turning parts of the blue house to a smoky gray. She knew someone was selling it; it was marked *Foreclosed* and *Real Estate Owned* on its Zillow profile, meaning that the lender, or bank, had taken the property back.

"Looks like someone tried to burn it down maybe," Dr. Gonzalez had said as they drove across I-96, heading west and away from Steve's property. Despite the twenty-minute drive, Vicky felt her skin crawl with the unsettling shock of a difficult escape. Dr. Gonzalez handed Vicky her phone to pull up Patricia's address after agreeing to drop her off in Lakeshore. Even in the dark, Vicky watched fear drag the doctor's tanned face. Vicky was to blame for that. But fleeing Miller was their best chance. There was no telling what else Steve's hands were capable of. The thought of his bloody fingers made her ripped torso ache, the reminder sending invisible chills up her spine.

Now at her temporary residence, Vicky stood, searching for comfort in the thought that Dr. Gonzalez and her father were safe. She instructed him to pack a couple of bags as she and Vicky headed up the road. "I'm on it," his gravelly voice sounded over the car radio, draped in a thick El Salvadoran accent.

Vicky quavered, imagining what Steve would do if he caught up with the Gonzalezes. He'd probably put Dr. Gonzalez in Vicky's place, stringing her up in the shed after deporting her father. And he'd get away with it too, so long as he stayed in Miller, where his uncle ran the sheriff's department.

So good at keeping his promises, she thought. The idea of him waiting for her in Patricia's neighborhood was a very real possibility.

The smell of charred drywall clung to the air as she ran up the side of the house, searching for an entrance, wondering if a door was accessible if the bank planned on selling the place.

She passed a side door; it was blocked off by a pale board.

Shit, she thought. Would the neighbors notice a missing board on the side of the house? *The bank sure would.* She made a note to revisit the idea because the sun hurt more than getting arrested for trespassing.

The large backyard appeared to be untouched by the house fire. The emerald grass was frosted over with no trees, which explained the absence of leaves and pinecones or those weird copper seedlings that whirled around on campus all autumn long. There was also a garage, shed, and deck. The deck was attached to the back of the house with what looked like a pool. Envy crept into Vicky's bones, as she'd always envisioned that for herself. Once she became a civil rights lawyer, she was going to buy a house in Commerce Township and build a deck with a solarium on one side and a pool on the other.

Vicky frowned, worried about the future she planned. But she shook the pessimism, knowing that she'd take her shot again and reclaim her path. *Yeah*, she assured herself. The current situation set her back a semester, but once the devil woman saw things Vicky's way, she'd be back on track in no time.

Vicky admired the garage's oak-finished door, which probably used to open for a Benz or a Range Rover. She walked along the side of the garage and found a matching smaller door. She turned the knob and found it locked.

Okay, she thought as she jogged over to the shed, and her heart hitched. The shed didn't have any windows and, unlike the garage, it looked like a family project. The wooden panels were nailed together, leaving uneven gaps and splintered wood. She was sure that the shed couldn't keep the rain out. She tapped a finger against the door, and it responded with a shallow *thunk.* A padlock rendered the shed impassable. She cradled the stainless-steel lock in her hands and pulled it down. It didn't let up.

Okay? she thought, her options dwindling.

Anxiety crept through her limbs as she ran across the yard and climbed onto the patio. The door on the other side of the pool was boarded up.

No, no, no! Sitting outside, waiting for that stubborn, hurtful sun was not a part of the plan—it couldn't happen. She trembled as the memory crept to life. The sun rays had raked her skin, tearing her open, allowing themselves inside to boil her blood and cook her flesh.

"No," she mumbled. "Not again." As if feeling the greatest star rise from the horizon and flash on her heels, she ran to the shed and glared at it.

The homemade building was made of cheap plywood—wood that was breakable, wood that no one would miss, and wood that someone would hear breaking.

She picked up the padlock again and studied it. It wasn't too old or rusty. The stainless steel glistened in the bright moon.

She was getting inside, and nothing, not even the very capable padlock, was going to stop her. She dropped the padlock, letting it hang in the loop of the hasp that it had joined. Then she slid her slim fingers between the metal loop and the splintering wood. She closed her eyes and thought about her hands. She thought about the damage they had done in the last several hours. She thought about wrapping them around Steve's ivory, slender neck. She thought about his heart throbbing, his blood racing.

With shaking fingers, she yanked the hasp, ripping the flat side from the wooden wall. The padlock and its accessories failed as the nails clattered against metal and toppled into the grass. She let herself in, the door creaking in resistance to her intrusion.

She closed the door behind her and stretched her arms out front, surprised at how quickly her eyes adjusted to the emptiness hidden beneath the shadows. But why wouldn't her eyes understand the darkness? They'd had lots of practice. She frowned. *Yeah, from study sessions* I *hadn't called for. It was for his—*

"Stop it," she said aloud. "He won't find me. And–and by the time he does, I'll be with the police and…he'll be too scared to touch me again." Her own insecurities convinced her that her hopes were flawed. If she knew anything about Steve, she knew that she was lying to herself.

Cringing, she sat on the floor and crossed her legs. She opened her bag and felt around until she felt a smooth screen. She pulled her burner phone out, offering herself some light. It was closer to 4:30, and there was no time to waste.

With the will to take another stroll around the neighborhood under the cover of night, Vicky shoved the phone back into her bag along with the padlock—she ditched the hasp. She went to push herself up, then stopped short as aches rippled through the wound that refused to age. She doubled over, cursing its creator.

Steve. "Fucking psycho," she growled.

Tears filled her eyes, smearing the darkness around her as her heart dropped to her stomach. She hoped her hiding spot was a good one. But then she realized that it didn't matter. She wasn't staying long.

C H A P T E R   4

Derelict

Darwin lay on his stomach, his small legs sprawled out as he snored softly. His silky dark hair was messy and dried tears were frozen on his tawny cheek. Trish didn't bother putting his bedtime onesie back on after changing his diaper—he was too fussy. But after what seemed like hours, he finally passed out. There in the dark, the curtains shielded them from the morning glow and the chaotic place that she'd lost all control over— they rested safely in the quiet nest.

She wondered what he was thinking about in his deep-sleep state, and she wished she could escape with him. But the closest she'd ever get was by watching him from the conscious world. She hadn't slept in a long time, and Darwin liked to remind her of that. He'd be on his back, breathing deep and steady. His little belly rising and falling as he dreamt. Sometimes he'd smile at his dreams, and other times he'd pout and stir, waking with the wrath of someone who was perpetually sad. Trish always hoped to be there when he woke from those happy and unhappy places. She'd smile or hug him, letting him know that it wasn't his reality. And he was delighted to find her there—his mom, his mommy, the only love he'd known next to Randel, who spent most of his time at work or out of town *for* work.

Software solutions can't sell themselves, she thought.

During Darwin's tirade, Randel had returned Trish's call via text:

Sorry. I was sleeping when you called me back. Maggie told me you got home late. Must've been a crazy night. Call me when you wake up.

Trish sighed, putting off her response, failing to find the energy to address his inquiry. Darwin's face crumbled, and Trish held her breath. He had just fallen asleep after screaming and crying throughout the early morning hours, his night-long tantrum beginning with small groans when Victoria arrived. Then his disgruntled groans grew into ongoing fussing right after the unwelcome guest fell into the night.

Trish spent all morning rocking him on her knee and walking him around. They'd taken trips up and down the stairs, and around the kitchen and bedrooms. But he only screamed, and as he did, Trish asked the question: *How in the hell did Victoria find us?*

Darwin had been upset before, but there was something different about that morning's shouting fit. He seemed disappointed when he looked at her with his dark, wet eyes as if it were her fault.

But of course, it was her fault: she'd broken her promise.

When she was pregnant with him, she didn't think it was real. She read about women whose bodies played tricks on them, and the ring had done just that since 1890. Aside from knowing that it made her human form gradually age, protected her from the sun, helped her hold down some types of human food, hid her fangs, stopped her claws from sprouting out her fingers, and gave her the ability to feel external temperatures, how it actually worked was lost on her. No matter how much she stuffed journals full of commentary and information, she was still early in her understanding. The ring had done many things, but it did not make her an actual human. The sun still gave her headaches if she stayed in it too long, and the smell of sulfur—even a little—made her gag. She didn't have a cycle, and she never bothered to visit the gynecologist. But one day, when she felt especially sick, Randel suggested she take a test. She did, humoring him, and found that she had been fooling herself. She buckled at the knees upon finding the positive pee stick.

From that day on, she was careful. She wore the ring for the entire nine months, forcing herself to eat food, which Darwin took most of for himself. He allowed her to eat buttery grits with honey, sweet potato fries, and chicken sandwiches. She craved blood, of course, but he made her *not need it*. He made her human again, and she loved him so much that she talked to him as if he were her daily diary, another journal to stuff with secrets and observations. He knew about her mountain town in West Virginia and what Momma looked like. He knew about the chicken coop and the eggs and Josef. Darwin even knew about the pink-eyed monster and Ally. He also knew that he was precious and that she'd protect him, even if that meant putting his life before her own. She promised, crossed her heart.

But she broke that promise, and Darwin nagged her all night because of it. He fought to break her loving embrace as his nose ran on her shirt while he shouted frustrated shrills in her ear. She couldn't make Darwin smile. He only tussled and slapped, refusing milk and music.

Trish's nostrils flared as she turned on her back. Glaring at the ceiling, she saw the face of the disturbance that pissed her boy off so deeply. Victoria was supposed to be dead, bled out in the woods or eaten by wild animals attracted to her bloody scent. Or—or—

Trish pulled her hand down her face. Victoria Scott was not supposed to be out there searching and finding Trish. She wasn't supposed to follow Trish home.

How did I miss that? Trish thought as she racked her brain, looking for something, anything that could be identified and plugged, fixed, avoided in the future.

Then she remembered what it was.

I should have drunk Victoria completely.

Trish's chest thudded and her still-full belly pulsed in response; Toby's blood nourished her, still fulfilling.

Ugh, she thought as she rolled back on her side to face her sleeping baby. *Never should have gone back to Miller*, she scolded herself.

Not only was Victoria lurking, but she had a goal: to be changed back.

Trish shook her head. If she could change someone back, she would have done it to herself, wouldn't she? Didn't Victoria think about that? And even if Trish could change Victoria back, she wouldn't, because Victoria was supposed to be *dead.* Not undead.

Trish pushed herself upright, sitting on the edge of the bed. She needed a plan before Randel came back to town—

Was that tonight?

She rolled her eyes. Sometimes, his schedule was so scattered that she couldn't keep up with it. If he wasn't calling and texting, worrying and inquiring, he was coming in and out of town. One day he's home, one day he's not. Her husband made things a little harder than necessary sometimes. *If only he could stay fucking still, I—* She rubbed her temples, huffed. *This isn't Randel's fault...*

Victoria clouded Trish's mind, scrambling her thoughts.

Trish could grab Victoria's arms and pull them from her sockets. Then, she'd take the girl's cheeks in her hands, and bury claws into Victoria's slowly decaying flesh, then snap her neck. Then, Trish would pull Victoria's head from her neck and dispose of her between two isolated lakes. She'd surely be dead then. *Dead, or permanently demobilized.*

Darwin scoffed and twisted his little body. Then he stopped, sighed, and settled again.

Deciding that her thoughts were too loud and violent for the room, Trish headed for the hallway, leaving the bedroom door ajar.

Alright, she thought, getting back on task. *Turn the girl into pieces and hide her.*

She paced slowly, conjuring up lakes and locations she'd have time to get to—ones that don't meet—ones that were deep—ones that—

Trish growled, balled her fists and turned to the wall, wanting to put a hole in it. But instead, she turned on her heels and kept her pace. Victoria looked frail and famished. She had on a bloody hoodie. She had fangs...sharp fangs. She looked dead and she rushed into Darwin's room. *Covered in dried blood, looking all feral and deranged,* Trish thought. "Probably scaring the poor kid," she reasoned.

Trish cringed. *She knows where I live.*

She paused. *How? Why last night? Why the night when...*

She bit the inside of her cheek.

Steve. Trish strained at the thought of another very real threat of a sick drug dealer who wanted to kill her on his drug-addled quest to slay a real-life monster.

But how did he find out where Trish lived?

She paused, thinking back on that night.

She saw Barbie standing over her, taking a picture. Then Barbie took Trish's license. *Did Barbie send more pictures to Steve?*

"No," Trish hissed. Barbie may have exposed Trish for killing…

Tastebud-teasing Toby…

Trish grabbed fistfuls of her own hair. *Steve knows where I live.*

Another vampire. Steve's voice again, his ivory skin pale in the deep night, his chiseled chin carrying his menacing smile.

Trish's fists shook, allowing pain to pulse through her scalp. "Damnit." An inaudible shrill. Anger jarred her vision of her home. Her safe, beautiful home. "You did this," a breathy whisper to herself.

Another… Steve's taunting, deep voice.

"This is your fault…" Trish said aloud.

Vampire.

"I—"

Change me back! Victoria's plea.

A hard knock at the door made Trish flinch. She tilted her head and sniffed, hating how dull the smells on the other side of the door were when she wore the ring. She shuddered when the knocks grew louder, more anxious. Quickened and short.

It was 7 am. No one showed up at her house on a Thursday at 7 am without letting her know ahead of time. As she approached the door, she grimaced at the obstruction. The bullet that she shot in her house had left a stain. She covered the through and through hole with black electric tape. *Get a new door*, she added to the ever-growing list of things to do before Randel got home.

Trish sniffed again. Randel was still out of town and Pita never showed up unannounced…not anymore. Not since they talked about personal space. Pita took well to the request because she, too, enjoyed space away from the PTA and her kids and her flamboyant husband every now and again. Trish was the only one who knew about Pita's *man pal* that she messed around with every Tuesday morning.

Trish tensed.

Change me back. Victoria's cry in Trish's recent memory.

Trish shook her head. Victoria wouldn't dare step out into the daytime. She didn't have the serum, the lifeline that kept Trish alive, and without it, Victoria would surely burn. But then again, Trish thought it may be Victoria. The girl lacked every bit of nuance.

"Hello!" someone said. Trish relaxed. It didn't sound like Victoria. The voice wasn't frail and light. Saddened and sweet. It was raspy and feminine. The voice of someone who should put cigarettes away for good. Trish peered through the peep hole to find Mrs. Pepper, the retiree from next door. Mrs. Pepper stood there in a silky pink nightgown; her silver hair tucked underneath a clear shower cap. A flowery robe barely covered her wrists. Her nervous glare darted left and right as she massaged the back of her veiny hand.

"Patricia?" She banged again. "Please open the door," she shouted. "Are you alright? Patricia! Patricia, open up, or I'm calling the police!"

CHAPTER 5

Accepted

Vicky settled on the floor of the shed, resting against the wall across from the door. She sniffed and found slightly charred air, stale dust, greenery, and rainwater thanks to the standing puddle on the side of the house. She used it to clean dried blood off her hands before she retreated to the shed for the second time during those early morning hours. She peered around. The light of the early dark blue sky ricocheted off the walls. Some of the dimmed scattered light rested on her ankle. It was warm but not burning. She pulled her legs into her chest anyway. The dull light would evolve into a bright, flesh-searing yellow that was unforgiving, and she vowed to never allow it to rub her skin ever again.

She rested her gaze on her bent knees and found herself yearning for a taste of daylight. She and Mom used to sit on the porch steps on Friday evenings watching cars drive by and kids ride bikes. A dark-skinned thin woman all of 4 foot 10, Mom hummed and sipped some tropical-flavored cooler. Vicky sipped on her favorite red pop. They gossiped about Mom's coworkers on the assembly line—the woman could build an entire car on her own if she wanted. After Vicky declared Mom's coworkers "messy" or "too much," they'd move on to gossiping about fast girls and ugly boys in Vicky's classes. They'd laugh for hours. Even the winter couldn't stop their tradition. Bundled up on the snowy porch, Vicky would drink hot chocolate, and Mom had a hot toddy.

Vicky missed those evenings with Mom, movie night with Daddy, and gaming sessions with Moody. She'd die if she never saw them again—her rocks, her supporters. Her family. Her chest heaved as her mind drowned in a single thought:

Will I ever see them again?

Be positive, babes, Mom used to say. Her sultry, calm voice was so clear that Vicky peered around the shed. All she found was her backpack, a tool bag, and a cardboard box set against the wall.

She closed her eyes. Her head wavered and her body relaxed as she listened to Mom, allowing her memories to take her back to a better time.

It was over a year ago when Vicky and Mom were getting dinner ready for the family, and drinks ready for a mid-spring Friday night *porch talk*. The stereo blasted house music—or dub step, as Steve had called it—as the DJ hyped up the audience by welcoming the evening commuters to the weekend.

"It's a hot April Friday in Detroit this evening! Y'all get home safe, get dressed, and then step out. We at The Whale downtown tonight where it's eighteen and up, ladies free before 11, and all drinks are half off until 2 am," he announced as one mix faded and another took over the speakers.

"Oh, girl," Mom said as Vicky headed from the living room to the kitchen. She flipped a burger, coating the raw side in sizzling grease. "Turn that shit up, babes."

Vicky turned on her heels and headed back to the stereo, turning it up. The bass shoved the walls and shook the floor and rattled the family portraits stationed on the glass end tables next to the green leather couch and love seat. The portraits never fell over, although they always threatened to. Vicky pursed her lips and swayed to the running beat and deep bass as if it were commanding her to fall into the music, body first. She thought, *I wonder if Brit's cousin is manning the door at The Whale tonight?* Underaged or not, they always got in.

"Get it, babes!" Mom shouted from the kitchen. Vicky turned to find her waving the spatula and rolling her body. Forty-five or twenty-eight, Mom was still the best dancer that Vicky had ever known. Every Friday night since Vicky could remember, Mom taught her and Moody to dance. Although Moody stopped attending *Friday Night Dance Club*—Daddy's weird name for it—around the time he turned twelve or so, Vicky and Mom clung tight to the tradition.

Mom flipped another burger, and the angry sounds of hot grease filled the room. The smoke must've irritated Mom's eyes, because she shouted, "Hey, open up the windows!"

Vicky rocked her shoulders as she headed to the window, and saw Daddy grab the mail from the mailbox, which hung next to the door. She clapped her hands and rushed for the stereo to turn it down. She'd checked the mailbox that afternoon and found it empty. At first, disappointment dragged her down, filling her with a momentary dread, but then, just as she had for the past three months, she got on with her day, knowing that she hadn't been rejected, and hope was still alive. The routine was tiresome, but worthy.

But mail had run that day; the mail lady was late.

Vicky's heart leapt as Daddy stepped inside, the top of his fade only inches from the top of the door frame. His mechanic's jumper smelled like motor oil and burned tires. The once pristine navy-blue uniform was covered in a mix of black blotches and dry liquid stains that had no hope of coming out in the wash.

"Hey, Daddy," she said.

"Hey, V. I got something here for you."

He handed her a piece of mail. It was as long as a pamphlet from the doctor's office. The sender line read:

Office of Admissions
Miller University, School of Liberal Arts
Miller, MI 49441

Her first choice. She heard the music further soften as she stared at the letter.

"Ohh, who is it from, V?" Mom asked as she wiped her hands with a dish towel. Things had gone quiet in the kitchen.

"Uh…" Vicky shuddered. "Miller." The declaration came out so soft that she could barely hear her own words. She cleared her throat. "Miller," she said again.

"Well open it," Mom said, her big toothy smile spread wide and her excited brown eyes glowing.

Vicky felt herself frown. Everything that she had worked for up until that moment rested between her clamped fingers. Miller University's Political Science and Pre-law program was her first choice—her only choice. One envelope away. Or maybe…

Mom's smile faded. "Babes, what's wrong?"

"What if I didn't get in?" Vicky asked.

Daddy put his arm around Mom's shoulders. Her petite frame was overshadowed by his tall stature and wide birth. "Come on, Vicky," he said.

Her heart fluttered. "I mean, nobody in our family had ever gone to college, and my high school sucks…and this is the best school in the state. W–what if I didn't get in?"

"It's not the end of the world," Dad said. "You're perfect. Alright? If you didn't get in there, you will get in somewhere else. You are my daughter. I know you. If you didn't get in, you'll take some time to be pissed, but you will never give up on something you want."

Mom smacked her lips and pulled away from Daddy. "If you didn't get in, it's *their* loss! You hear me? You are intelligent and talented, and your essay brought me to tears. Why wouldn't they let you in?"

"I—"

"ROTC, debate, dance… A 3.6 GPA. A bomb-ass essay. *Pssft.* Girl, go on and open that acceptance letter—Doug, get ready to go get us some champagne." Mom's smile returned.

Vicky looked at her parents and saw the optimism in their eyes. They were always so sure of her capabilities, and if she never opened it, she would never know, and neither would they. She looked at the envelope and carefully stuck her fingers underneath the small opening of the flap and tore the envelope open. She pulled the letter out:

Congratulations…

Her chest nearly caved, and tears welled up in her eyes. "I got in." Her eyes grew big. "I got in," she shrieked. "Oh my god! Mom! Daddy! I got in!"

"Yeah! I told you! I told—" Mom took Vicky in her arms and cried. "I told you! My baby goin' to college! I told you!"

Daddy took them both into one of his bear hugs, oil stained and all.

"Daddy! I got in!"

"Good job, V," he said.

"Doug, go get—"

"I'm on it," Daddy said as he pulled away from the family embrace, grabbed his keys from his pocket, and hustled for the door.

"I can't believe it," Vicky sobbed. "Mom, I can't—"

"You better believe it, V," she said, wiping her face dry. "Alright, get Moody on the phone, and tell Granny—you know she'll get her ass over here—and, you know what, go shout it out in the street. Baby, you did it!"

They shrieked again, bouncing on their haunches.

"Okay, okay, I gotta go finish cookin'. Get everybody over here. Tell em' we got burgers and I'll order pizza. Get your buddies from down the street and those kids from around the corner. Oh, oh, and call Doug and tell him to pick up a wine box—we finna have a party!"

That was only one of the best Scott parties to bless their busy neighborhood. Family and friends cancelled their plans just to go hang out with Vicky, lifting her up as she enjoyed one of the greatest heights of her life.

But now? Vicky had relived that memory because it felt like her peak. Once the monster had taken her life, things had gone surreal. As she opened her eyes, she couldn't help but glare at the door. The orange sunrays peeked through the wooden panels as the deadly star made its rise over the horizon. She only hoped her corner remained shaded for the next twelve hours.

She let out a shaken sigh. If only she could go back to that night at the frat house and stick by her original answer of "Fuck no," the last two months would not have happened. She would be in class, prepping her protest. Buses needed to be booked, and signs needed to be made. That damn refinery, which was oddly close to Patricia's house, wasn't going to close itself. After all that planning, Vicky would be smoking or laughing with her friends.

Friends, she thought, then sneered. "Thank you, Teresa," Vicky whispered with disdain tangled between her baring teeth as she cursed her roommate's name. "*Messy*-ass Teresa."

CHAPTER 6

Attention

Trish cinched her robe and narrowed her eyes at the peephole. Her neighbor, Mrs. Pepper, looked troubled as her eyes shot around, her hands visibly shaking. The night had already been a long, nasty one. The last thing Trish needed was Mrs. Pepper's nagging. Trish ran through a short list of what the woman could want.

Was the garbage can still on the curb? Nope, that was taken care of on Monday.

Are the leaves blowing over to her yard? No, Randel raked on Sunday.

Coming up empty, Trish turned the knob and opened the door. A chilly breeze filled the foyer. "Mrs. Pepper, what's—"

"Oh, thank goodness you're alright!" Mrs. Pepper put her small, wrinkled hands on her face. "I was worried sick." She frowned and her eyes glazed over. Her silk floral robe wrapped her petite frame, failing to cover up the veins riding the length of her short legs.

What the fuck is she—

"I thought something awful must've happened. I'm just so happy you are alright. Is–is the baby alright? I–is Randel alright?"

"Sure, everything's fine." Trish opened the door wider. "Is every-thing okay?" *Why are you hyperventilating and freaking out on my porch?*

There was no way Mrs. Pepper saw Victoria; she ran off a few hours prior. And no way did Mrs. Pepper hear them arguing, because she would have said something earlier. The woman was the average bored, retired, nosy neighbor. She couldn't mind her own business even if she finally found some of her own. Before Trish could step outside to look around…*like looking for the nonexistent monster underneath the hyperbolic bed*…Mrs. Pepper collected her bearings and spoke.

"I–I stepped out to get the paper this morning—damn paper boy tossed it too close to the road. Every time I call the paper company to complain, they always send the same boy who does the same—"

"Mrs. Pepper…"

The woman took a deep breath. "Anyway, when I went to get it, I noticed—well—I saw…" She looked toward her own house, which was on the other side of Trish's driveway.

Trish flippantly asked, "What?"

The woman frowned, and Trish stepped onto the porch, almost pushing past her neighbor.

"What?" Trish said, as her view of the street lengthened. The street was as it always had been, with frosty emerald grass, multiple-leveled brick houses, and baring maple and beech trees.

"Your Jeep. Something…" Mrs. Pepper's voice trailed off, as if her next words would poison the air.

Trish approached the Jeep. *Did I drop anything?* She searched the ground for bloody rags or bags from the night before. The silver doors on the passenger side, the side that faced Trish's house, were as clean as they were the night before.

"It's on the other side," Mrs. Pepper said, now leading the way. As Trish followed, she could taste the metallic tang of blood mixing with the sweet, crisp autumn air. Then her heart lurched.

Crimson smudges coated the driver's side doors and gas tank. Some streaks broke from the gory glaze and dripped onto the concrete, creating a path of blood drops. Twisted furry bodies were shoved partially under the Jeep, their severed heads haphazardly placed behind each tire.

"I didn't know what to think," Mrs. Pepper said. "I–it looks an awful lot like blood, and I got…"

A cold shiver ran down Trish's spine, her breath hitching as Mrs. Pepper's words faded into an ominous echo.

Steve, Trish thought as her blood went cold.

Trish drew closer, spotting bits of fur sticking out of the crevices between the doors. *How did I not hear this happening?* Then she remembered: Darwin's tantrum had gone on until about a couple hours ago. She scowled. No way Steve had such tact. He made himself known—too ballsy to be sneaky. *But Victoria's that quiet,* she thought. Trish hadn't even heard Victoria lurking around the house until she knocked, *wanting* to be seen and heard. She couldn't imagine how quiet the girl would be if she was intentionally sneaking around.

Victoria's shaken threat ignited in Trish's memory: *"I'll leave, but you will change me back."*

Another vampire... Steve's taunt.

Trish sniffed again, stepping closer. In her human form, she could smell blood—not as acutely as when she hunted and fed, but clearly enough. *This* blood carried notes of iron and sweet leaves. The matted fur reeked of blood and garbage juice. The carnage had come from the decapitated raccoons scattered below, and the sloppy work looked rushed. The vandalism was deliberate, timed.

She felt herself relax a little.

"...and I just wasn't sure what else to do." Mrs. Pepper's voice came back into Trish's hearing. "Patricia, what's going on? What is this? Is this real? Is someone dead? Are you in trouble? What's..." Mrs. Pepper trailed off.

Trish didn't answer. Instead, she stared at the grotesque art. She envisioned Victoria snatching the racoons off garbage cans or dark yards before killing and draining them dry on Trish's Jeep. The girl was fast and strong enough to do it in the final hours of the night. *Hm,* Trish thought.

"Patricia?"

But if Steve had committed to his game of cat and mouse, he could have been the one out there vandalizing the Jeep.

"Patricia?"

But Victoria was light on her feet— no one would hear her work.

"Patricia?"

Why didn't the alarm go off? Is Victoria easy on her hands too? Or is Steve that damn stealthy?

"Please talk to me."

Trish sighed and gave Mrs. Pepper a quick glance before leering at the mess. The sun was coming out now. No doubt others had seen the carnage or maybe even called the police. Unless they hadn't. When she glared around, she noticed that some motion sensor lights were still guarding some of her neighbor's properties, and the street stood quiet. She turned back to Mrs. Pepper, finding her face slick with tears. "What time is it?" Trish asked, almost at a whisper.

"Seven something," Mrs. Pepper said, crossing her arms over her belly. Frosty air erupted from her flaring nostrils.

Guilt tugged Trish's nerves. She wished she could wipe Mrs. Pepper's memory of the sight. But instead, she tried talk therapy. It wasn't like Mrs. Pepper didn't know Trish and Randel; they had cookouts together a few times every summer. And Trish was sure that Mrs. Pepper kept an eye on their house whether they were there or away. It was annoying at times, but trying to control a human only made things worse.

"Mrs. Pepper, thank you for bringing this to my attention," Trish started. "But I can assure you that everything is fine. It looks like some kids pulled a heartless prank. Maybe those are props." She pointed at the furry bodies. "Halloween wasn't too long ago." Trish smiled. "There's no need to worry. My family is fine, and we don't have any enemies or anything like that."

Mrs. Pepper put her hand on her chest, stepped closer, and let out a deep sigh. Nicotine and coffee stained her breath, and Trish wished she couldn't smell it, but the woman's mouthy fragrance travelled far, encompassing all. "Oh, thank God." She grabbed Trish's shoulders and pulled her in for a hug.

Trish allowed it but didn't care for being that close to Mrs. Pepper. She stank of menthol and a hint of sulfur. "I was just so worried."

"Alright, alright. Thanks for checking in on me. I really appreciate it. Now, I have to get this cleaned up, alright? No police necessary. I'll have it cleaned up before anyone can see it."

Mrs. Pepper pulled away and sniffed. "Oh, honey…" She wiped her eyes. "I already called the police. They're on their way right now."

Before Trish could ask the woman why she lied earlier, specifically stating that she was *going* to call the police, she heard the faint call of sirens roaring in the in the distance.

CHAPTER 7

Teresa

August 30, 2024

Vicky slumped her shoulders as she stomped along the sidewalk, sandals slapping the bottoms of her feet. She couldn't help but scowl at the back of her roommate's head; Teresa's platinum blonde blowout was shiny in the late summer night. Vicky waited for Teresa to slow down and explain herself, but she didn't. Instead, Vicky's list of concerns grew as they hurried up the well-lit sidewalks of Miller University's Fraternity Row. School had just started earlier that week, so every brick mini-mansion, all labelled with Greek letters, hosted a party.

After a few minutes, Teresa finally slowed down and turned to Vicky, her emerald eyes full of worry and eyebrows drawn together. She reached out a hand for Vicky as if beckoning her to hold it. Vicky searched for the words to shout at her. She knew what those puppy-dog eyes meant, just like she knew what holding hands meant.

What did you fuck up now? Vicky thought.

They'd been roommates through their first year at Miller, making this one the second. They'd smoked their first joint together, attended their first all-night party together, and they even shared their first hangover. But even with all their history, Teresa insisted on rubbing Vicky the wrong way by doing *stupid things.*

Teresa smacked her pink plump lips. "I know what you are going to say, Vicky…" she said, as she grabbed Vicky's hand and squeezed it. She used her free hand to tuck her hair behind her ear. Teresa wore the topaz studs Vicky had gotten her for her birthday before summer break.

"Oh really?" Vicky cocked her head. When they left the room, there were promises to go to the 7-Eleven for snacks and joint paper, and then a much-anticipated visit to Steve's. Vicky hadn't seen him since before summer break, and she needed him to help her alleviate the stress of having a quiz and paper due on Tuesday. She wanted to smell his cologne, smoke some of his new bud, and feel his warm body against hers. It was set to be the perfect weekend. But Teresa passed the underclassman parking lot, where her car was parked, and kept walking to Fraternity Row.

Teresa sighed, a response that was less than satisfying to Vicky, who felt her face scorch. "Why are we standing in front of the Beta house?" Vicky dropped Teresa's clammy palm and crossed her bare arms. Vicky wore her favorite pink knitted tank top and acid-washed jean shorts for Steve—not the loser-ass horn-hounds on campus. Such children. They acted worse than high school kids sometimes. Whenever they tried to flirt with her, she'd ask them if they wanted a mint or tell them that they had a stain on their shirt. *Ugh*. "I thought—"

"I know, I know," Teresa said as she winced. "But I really need to get something out of there."

"Then go get it."

"I–I can't," Teresa said, pouting.

"Oh, come on!" Vicky griped, hating what Teresa was getting at. "Really, Teresa?" she asked. "I thought we were going to the store first, not here. What the hell?"

"I know, I know. You're right." Teresa closed her eyes. "But I really need you to do me a favor." She stuck out her lower lip. "Pleeeeease, roomie, pleeeeease."

"What?" Vicky asked.

"I need you to go get my rings out of Kyle's room. They're sitting on his nightstand on—"

"No! We've only been on campus for four days, and you're already messin' around with somebody's man. No, Teresa!" Vicky shifted her hips as she glared at a group of boys who were heading to the Sigma house next door.

"Oh, come on, don't be like that. I thought you said you loved me. Just go get them, please. He said he'll pawn them if I don't pick them up right now. He doesn't want Veronica to see them lying around."

"No! *You* go get them. He's not about to catch me snooping around his room looking for jewelry. That *will not* end well."

"But you're so much faster than me."

Vicky knew that much was true. Growing up, she had done her fair share of sneaking around, but she never got caught. Moody and her cousins recruited her to steal popsicles and ice cream from the kitchen in the middle of the night simply because she was quiet and fast. But now she was grown, and she had no reason, or business, sneaking around.

Vicky grumbled. Teresa always meant well, but she was messy. The girl simply couldn't help it. Her antics were fun most of the time. She'd gotten them into the dean's retirement party and frequently charmed their way into yacht parties on the lake. But she lacked every bit of street sense; that's where Vicky came in. She frowned. "I don't like being lied to, Teresa," Vicky said. She felt her face harden as she imagined herself *accidentally* spilling water onto Teresa's laptop later.

"Come on, please, please, please?" Teresa begged. "I really need those rings."

"Why'd you take them off?"

"Cuz I didn't want to get them dirty."

"Ugh," Vicky said, wanting to laugh, but she decided she was too angry to give Teresa the satisfaction.

"Say you'll do it," Teresa said. "The longer you wait, the longer it'll take us to get to Steve's house."

"Why didn't you just call Kyle and tell him to hide your rings? Cover up the fact that he's an asshole and a cheater?"

"He told me to come get them before they get here. Veronica called him, interrupting us, so…she hasn't been in his room yet." She looked at the ground. "He took her out and said this is my only chance."

Vicky put her hand on her forehead. "Damn, you're dumb."

"Nobody can see *me* going into his room—her sorority sisters are in there, and you are much faster than I am."

"Girl…" Vicky rolled her eyes. "Dummy," she spat.

"I know. Now please help my dumb ass out." Teresa's bottom lip quavered. Although furious, Vicky hated the idea of Veronica and her friends ganging up on Teresa—it could lead to expulsion for everyone, Teresa and Vicky included. She loved herself and her stupid friend too much to allow that to happen.

Vicky put her hands on her hips. "I get to use your car for a week."

"Done."

"You have to buy me some weed too—quarter of whatever strain I want."

"Absolutely." A smile broke across Teresa's face.

"And we are *not* staying on campus or going to any of these lame-ass parties. We are going straight to Steve's."

Teresa pursed her lips, having disliked Steve since they'd met him at the 7-Eleven about a year prior. But she'd come along with Vicky for their smoke sessions anyway, more to keep an eye on him than Vicky. "I just don't trust him, Vicky," Teresa had always said. But it didn't matter how Teresa felt. She and Vicky always had different tastes in men: Teresa liked wannabes and Vicky liked confidence.

Vicky dropped her arms to her sides and surveyed the house. A loud party raged on as colorful lights speckled the windows and people stood in the yard smoking with total disregard for the rules. So long as no fights broke out, campus security was nonexistent. "Where is his room?" Vicky asked.

"Go up to the second floor and turn left. His room is at the very end of the hallway on the right. He has a single unit—it's the only one in the house. The rings are on the nightstand. You'll see them as soon as you go inside."

Well duh. Vicky huffed. "Alright. Call Steve and let him know that we're still coming over." She stepped forward then stopped. "And ask if he needs anything from the store."

***

Vicky strolled up the busy walkway, bypassing inhalers as they exhaled nicotine fog, weed puffs, and fruity vapor. No one seemed to notice as she reached the porch and pulled the screen door open. Before the crowd swallowed her whole, she peered over her shoulder to find Teresa standing on the sidewalk. She blew kisses and smiled hard at Vicky. Vicky shook her head.

She entered the loud living room. All the lights were out except a strobe globe. It stung her eyes when she stole a small glance of it, watching it roll pink, blue, and green lights around the ceiling and walls, coating the worn furniture in party colors. Fog crept across the living room, covering the makeshift dance floor. Some people were already lit, dancing and grinding to the trembling bass.

Vicky continued, finding different clusters of her peers ranging from groups of nervous freshman boys to chattering partygoers all too excited to start the year off in a drunken stupor. She stopped herself from turning her nose up at them. It had only been a year since she herself evolved from a sorority wannabe to hanging out off-campus with an actual guy with his own house, car, business, and clothes that didn't come from Walmart.

A wooden picnic table, which usually lived on the front yard in the summer, was set up against the wall, just next to the hallway. On it were two punch coolers and two foggy beer kegs.

She turned a little, shoulder leading the way through a few girls wearing bikini tops and cut-off shorts. One of them had a pale belly, its sleekness glistening in the dim light from the hallway, which was just to the left. Vicky ran the back of her hand over her dampening forehead, hot as hell. She felt her stomach turn as the smell of cheap vodka tainted the humid air, making her want to gag.

Even still, with wet bodies rubbing against her skin and loud-mouths shouting obscenities in her ears, she pushed on, squinting through the faux fog as it lapped up from the floor and clouded her vision, turning everyone into swaying, gyrating, jumping silhouettes.

"Shots!" a guy shouted. He used his navy-blue shirt to dry his sweaty face and then pulled it back down his bony frame. The green Greek letters *Beta Tau Mu* were across his chest. He went for another girl who wore a red bikini with white dots on it. Other guys dressed like him rushed for her. As they picked her up, she giggled and laughed; no hint of a protest slid past her lips. They gently laid her on a wooden table and poured what looked like a bottle of Everclear into her navel. The first guy took a shot off her belly and everyone who was paying attention cheered, including her girlfriends.

Vicky focused on her path. At least they were preoccupied and not worried about her—someone the fraternity hadn't seen in a while—making her way to the steps and up to their rooms. Rooms where they slept, studied, got dressed, and jacked off. She shivered as her skin crawled.

Damnit, Teresa, she thought.

Vicky stopped when she came to the end of what appeared to be a line that ended at the hallway entrance and started in the kitchen, which was in the back of the house. She peered ahead, seeing the staircase off to the right, and no one blocking it.

She pressed herself against the wall to get by the line and ran up the steps. She was on her toes as she always had been when an anxious heat pressed on the back of her neck, somehow forcing her to move faster. Although the errand was madly inconvenient, it wasn't all that bad. Everyone was too drunk or having too much fun to question or stop her. And she got to use the car for a week.

Maybe I'll go to the city this weekend, she thought. The city was always fun that time of year, with everyone in a good mood, and gatherings and parties going on from 8 am to 6 am. Of course, Teresa could come along if she wanted. They'd had fun the last time they went to Detroit.

When Vicky made it to the top of the steps, she smiled. Everyone was so oblivious—it was almost like she didn't even need to sneak. She felt so good that she decided that once she had the rings safely in her front pocket, she'd go back down to the party, have a shot off some girl's abs and hit a community joint before Teresa chauffeured her off to see her future man.

The thought of Steve made her go warm inside. She missed the way his deep baritone sang in her ear when she woke up next to him the morning after a stony hike around his property. She could do that every day. Move off campus and in with him. Kiss him every morning and smoke with him every night after homework was done. She couldn't wait to see him, and according to him, he was just as excited for her. The cock pictures throughout the summer suggested as much. *Get the rings*, she thought. *Get the rings and go to him.*

At the top of the steps, she looked both ways, having forgotten how big the second floor of the Beta house was.

The hallway was dark, save the sliver of light that crept from underneath some closed doors. There had to be maybe six rooms on that floor alone, and three on the floor above.

Vicky and Teresa spent a lot of their freshman nights there. Once Vicky realized that frat parties and houses were as lame as the boys who joined them, Teresa had to bribe Vicky to tag along.

Vicky went to the left of the staircase and heard people chattering behind the first door on the left. The skunky smell of kush burrowed into the hallway, making her heart sink with pleasure. She couldn't wait to smoke her own joints with Steve and Teresa. She never shared with the other people who were always in and out of Steve's house. She secretly hoped he was home alone, and that Teresa would just drop her off. Vicky needed his touch. She also felt like talking shit behind Teresa's back.

Vicky continued down the hall. Behind the door across from the smoke room, a girl cried hysterically. The bathroom's echo surrounded her cries, bouncing them around and sinking her deeper into her own sorrows.

Ugh, Vicky thought. Though she spent time there, she avoided the bathrooms. Not only were they nasty, having to pee was always a perfect excuse to leave.

"No, fuck you!" the sad girl said. "You can't…"

Her voice faded into the booming music from downstairs.

Vicky forced her way into the last room on the right. The door was unlocked, just as she expected. She closed it behind her and locked it. The space was as small as a cluttered single dorm room. There was a long twin bed, two dressers, a microwave which was set on a small refrigerator, a desk with the biggest monitor and tower that she'd ever seen, and clothes stacked high on a laundry basket. There was also a lone closet.

Vicky looked around and didn't see a nightstand. In fact, the pictures on the dresser looked a lot like Chad Reid, a student ambassador and trombone player. Vicky remembered that he was a junior and a hell of a brass player. She'd seen every jazz band concert since she'd been at Miller and actually liked watching him on stage. Still, her heart tumbled to her gut; this was the wrong room.

Gritting the backs of her teeth, she went to pull her phone out. "Air-headed ditz," Vicky mumbled. She opened her and Teresa's year-long text thread, ready to air her grievances to her sometimes-dim-witted friend.

She typed:

OMG it's

Vicky stopped. A violent chill shot through her limbs.

There were voices on the other side of the door.

CHAPTER 8

Sultry

A guy chuckled, his sensual tenor warm as he spoke. His softened voice dug deep into Vicky's gut, squeezing it. Shaking it. Someone responded to his romantic babble, sharing the same hushed tone. They spoke as if they were whispering into each other's ears, bragging about how they were going to make each other feel something orgasmic.

Vicky clenched her phone tight in her hand as the doorknob caught on the lock, stopping short of giving them entry.

"What's wrong?" the woman on the other side of the door asked.

"I—I don't remember locking this door," he said.

Oh no… Vicky thought. It had to be Chad. Who else would question the locked door? *The rightful inhabitant. That's who.*

The woman giggled. "Why wouldn't you? There are a lot of people down there." The calm in her voice made Vicky quaver. It was deep, but feminine. Mature and smooth. The woman's voice was almost enticing, relaxing Vicky's shoulders, making her dare to rest within the stranger's words. No wonder Chad wanted her alone. Vicky cocked her head slowly as she watched the back of the door, curious about the siren and hoping that the door stayed closed between them.

"Ah, I got it," Chad said, his husk almost a grumble. The chime of jingling keys shoved Vicky back into reality, diminishing the odd spell.

No, no, no! Vicky thought as she slid her phone back into her front pocket. She turned at the waist with her hands out, begging the room for a place to hide. What would Chad think if he saw her, a stranger—a band groupie—snooping around his room?

I–I can say I got lost and thought it was the bathroom. She bit her lower lip. *Stupid,* she thought. *Then he'll ask why I locked the door!*

Before she could think of another excuse, Vicky dashed for the closet, crouched inside, and closed the door enough for the latch not to catch. She couldn't afford any noise. The soft creaking of the closet door becoming ajar made her wince.

The room door flung open and allowed Chad and his guest inside. Vicky heard lips and tongues smacking as the door slammed shut behind them.

"Lock the door. I don't want any disruptions," the woman beckoned. Chad did as he was told. The bed squeaked as they giggled.

Vicky closed her eyes and covered her mouth. She didn't know what was hiding alongside her in the closet, but she was lucky to have enough space to stoop low and keep quiet. The high moon glazed the small opening of the closet as she heard pressing lips and rubbing hands. She focused on the nocturnal light.

Then a thought came crashing down: Vicky hoped her phone didn't go off. She didn't get the chance to tell Teresa that she was a moron, and the retrieval was taking much longer than it should have; her friend might have been worried and would call soon. Vicky felt her palms go clammy.

Please don't call, Teresa, Vicky begged no one. But then she remembered that she placed her phone in silent mode earlier that day when she began writing an essay for her Congress and the Presidency course. She was working on a persuasive essay explaining her stance on the filibuster in the Senate. She sighed a bit of relief, silently thanking herself for the study habit.

Chad and his friend made out for what felt like an eternity, making Vicky wish she could jump out the window just to rid herself of the sounds of sloppy wet coitus.

The smacking and rubbing sounds stopped abruptly and Chad made a muffled and deep gurgling noise. It sounded like he was straining. Alarmed, Vicky leaned forward to search the small opening. She hoped Chad was into S&M or was playing a sick game that he was in on. But her breath caught in her throat when she found them. The woman had him in a chokehold. Vicky wasn't sure how the woman ended up behind Chad on the bed, but her legs were wrapped around his middle and her free arm was wrapped around his chest. During the silent assault, Chad kicked and twisted to no avail; the woman's grip was iron clad. Her dark hair flailed as she rocked with Chad's struggle, and her pale youthful face was full of contempt as she concentrated. The scene reminded Vicky of the videos she'd seen of an anaconda squeezing the life out of a capybara in the dark green waters of the dim rain forest.

Tears blinded Vicky to the horror as she listened to Chad's guttural plea for freedom, which came out as a small squeal and stifled huffs. *Oh my God*, she thought. Vicky's mind whirled, contemplating if she was witnessing a murder, thinking she should do something, and wondering if she might be next. She breathed through her flared nostrils. *God, please,* she thought as she begged herself not to make a sound.

After a deep breath, Chad's body relaxed, and he stopped fighting. His tongue lolled out, and his eyes, wide and lifeless, reflected nothing.

After a few minutes, the woman unwrapped her arms and legs from his body and allowed him to lean over and lie on the bed. She tilted her head and glared at him, a small smile playing on her cherry lips. The woman's face was awash with pride, as if she knew his struggle was no match for her. Her flowing black hair remained unscathed, just as her dark eyeliner and mascara still neatly outlined her eyes. Her pale skin camouflaged in the moonlight, and for a second when the woman allowed bright moon rays to play on her face, her eyes looked…pink.

Vicky blinked hard. *What the hell?*

The monster sat next to Chad's lifeless body and picked up his wrist. She licked her lips.

Vicky squinted and her heart hitched into her throat.

The thing opened her mouth, exposing long, sharp fangs, and drove them into Chad's wrist. Vicky stopped breathing as she watched the woman drink. She licked and slurped his blood, not making a mess. Only taking it all in.

Vicky's stomach turned, forcing bile up her throat. She swallowed it down. *Oh no! Oh God, oh no!* Tears raced down her face as she crumbled. *Call the police*, she thought. But she shook her head. The closet was dark enough for her phone to give away her hiding spot if she illuminated the screen. And Chad was already dead. She'd be more useful afterward when she ran and screamed her head off for help *while* calling the police. She'd be able to identify the woman— *thing*—and help put her way for good.

Vicky leaned back, wanting to hide from the terror. But she couldn't look away. Instead, she blinked away fresh tears until the monster pulled her mouth away from Chad's wrist. She squeezed his arm and used her free hand to get something out of her purse: a pocketknife. She cut the space on his arm where she had been drinking, then she laid his bleeding arm on the bed and looked him over.

Vicky sat back. *I have to get out of here. I have to go. I have to...* All movement stopped, and she leaned forward again.

The monster sat still, her head tilted slightly as the room itself was silent but the sounds around them persisted. The sad girl was still yelling on her phone in the bathroom, and downstairs, people shouted for more shots. The music boomed, indiscriminately making the beat and lyrics heard.

Then the thing's pink irises morphed into something else. Evil etched her face as her red gaze landed on the closet door.

Shit, shit, shit! Vicky's breath exploded from her nose as she pressed her hand against her mouth, trapping her scream in her throat. But the monster stood and stepped slowly, narrowing its eyes. She lifted another hand, exposing claws as long and thick as boning knives. The woman, or thing's, nails had been short during the attack. *Weren't they?* Vicky thought. She considered pinching herself, begging her consciousness to pull her from the depths of her nightmare. But she knew that she was not asleep.

No, no, no! Vicky thought. She looked around the closet. Upon seeing nothing but clothes and shoes, she stood and peeled her hand from her mouth. She gulped as her knees threatened to give out, but she wasn't going to cower. Vicky balled her insecure fists, ready to fight and make noise, because unlike Chad, Vicky saw the monster coming.

The thing bolted for the door and flung it open.

Vicky pounced.

CHAPTER 9

Parade

November 7, 2024

Trish gawked at the people dressed in white plastic jump suits, face masks, and booties as they walked the perimeter of her house. A cluster of them inspected the Jeep, and others combed the grass. Uniformed cops stood on the edges of her property, securing a wall of neighbors on either side. The neighbors, some familiar and some not, craned their necks and covered their mouths as they avoided eye contact with her. She pretended not to see or think about how she'd fix things with them. She could lie or play victim, whatever came to mind at the right time. Instead, she cringed at the overprotected crime scene unit as they plucked her grass and used oversized Q-Tips to swab the driver's side window of the Jeep. One of them plucked bits of fur from the doors and another scooped up animal parts from the ground.

She peered over her shoulder at the open front door. She didn't need the police asking about the black tape that she used to cover up a gunshot, and she needed to hear her son should he wake up during the commotion. Darwin had slept through the sirens and the constant comings and goings of random police officers and nosy neighbors. He even slept through the incessant buzzing of her phone when Randel called eight times. Each call was followed up with a text:

Trish, is everything alright?

Trish, Pepper told me someone covered the Jeep in blood. Tell me that isn't true.

Trish, answer the phone. We really need to talk.

Trish? Trish, Pepper said you wouldn't take her phone when I called for you.

I am worried as fuck over here. Answer the phone!

You always shut me out!

I'm so tired of your sneaky shit! This is exactly what I'm talking about when I call you standoffish and cold! It's like you don't even care!

I'm coming home.

With no time to craft a convincing lie, she slid on jeans and a drab heather-gray sweater and finally responded after the police arrived: *We are fine, honey. Pepper is overexaggerating everything. I will tell you all about it after I talk to the police. I don't want to talk on the phone with Pepper around, so please…I can handle this. Will be in touch soon.*

She wasn't sure if her text landed the way she wanted, calming him down. She doubted it because his answer was:

I'm going into a meeting. Call me as soon as they leave.

Her gut fluttered, amused at Randel's obsession with work, and concerned about the time she needed to concoct a convincing story for her sometime emotional, overbearing husband.

Refusing to stray, Trish stood like a statue at the foot of the porch steps, assessing the unfamiliar situation.

Neighbors chattered and pointed fingers and phones at her bloodied car from where they huddled on the curb two houses down on either side of the police perimeter. The neighbors on the left side of the house slowly migrated over to the right side so that they could get a better view of the damage done on the driver's side. Some people wore work clothes while their cars heated in their driveways, while others wore robes and sipped strong coffee or herbal teas.

A silver flash erupted in Trish's peripheral, pulling her attention back to the inconveniently placed crime scene. One of the crime scene people took pictures of the grass while another bent at the waist and walked slowly, as if trying to find something. A couple officers surveyed the space on the ground around the car. "Well, she didn't drive this home like this. The splatter is stagnant," she heard one of them say as he pointed a gloved finger at the driveway where bloody drops painted the once ashy gray concrete.

I hope the sun burns Victoria a new asshole, Trish thought, envisioning Victoria's beige skin boil and split as she roasted alive. Trish smiled. Maybe nature would do the girl in before Trish could find her.

This could also be Steve's doing, she thought. Her muscles tensed as his threat hung in the air around her "But I will find you. And when I do, I will kill you," he had said last night in the woods.

"I was horrified!" Mrs. Pepper's scrappy voice carried up the street as she retold the new neighbors, Pete and Cecilia, about her early morning discovery. Pepper had changed out of her shower cap and nightgown, and opted for a pink puffer coat, jeans, and short gray curls. "I was like, Patricia, what the hell is going on over there?! And you want to know what she said to me?"

Ugh, Trish thought.

"She said it was a prank! *A prank?*" Mrs. Pepper said, becoming more animated with each retelling. Trish knew better than to correct her—if anyone truly cared about the details, they'd ask Trish or the police directly. She let the idiot neighbor dramatize and exaggerate all she wanted, as long as the rumor stayed on their street. No news trucks meant a win in Trish's book.

"Ma'am," a man said on approach. His tanned khakis and wool peacoat told her that he wasn't a police officer. But the silver badge around his neck told her that he was a detective. He put out a hand. "I'm Detective Anthony Woodward from the Lakeshore PD, and I'm here to speak with you about what happened to your vehicle last night. Do you mind if I ask you some questions, Ms…?"

"Patricia Weston," she said. She straightened her back and met his gaze. "Yes. I'll answer any questions you have." She matched his tight grip as she shook his hand.

His tanned nose blushed from the chilly air and his deep brown eyes rested in her currently dark ones. "Thank you," he said as he pulled a pen and notebook from his coat pocket. He cleared his throat. "Is there anyone else in the house?"

She gave him a stiff nod. "My baby…my son."

"Oh really? How old?"

"He just turned one. He's sleeping and I don't want him to see this. It's best that he stays where he is."

Detective Woodward wrote something down and said, "I understand. I have a couple myself. Can you walk me through yesterday up until this morning? What did you do? Where did you go?"

Keeping a still expression, she said, "I work from home, so I watched Darwin while I wrote an instruction manual for a pressure washer. Then around 6, I left him with the babysitter, went to yoga, and had a few drinks."

"Where did you go?"

"Uh, Yogi's Studio and Drake's Bar in Grand Rapids." The lie slid off her tongue with an expected ease. Both places were popular holes-in-the-wall that didn't keep records of drop-ins, didn't bother paying for cameras, and stayed packed with people from all over West Michigan. She'd been to both places a few weeks ago, so it was likely that the staff would be fuzzy about the exact time of her presence. She also only paid cash.

"And you drove…" He eyed the Jeep.

"Yes." She nodded. "It didn't look like that when I got home last night."

He continued writing. "Alright. What time did you get back here?"

"Around 2 or 3. It was a long night. I just needed a break, ya know?" She offered a faint smile.

"Hm," he said.

Trish watched him write. His face was made of stone as he focused on her words, no doubt looking for holes. To her dismay, the man was hard to read, like most cops that she had the displeasure of running across.

"What did you do when you got back?"

"I sent the babysitter on her way and went to bed."

"What's the sitter's name?" He fired off questions as if they were stuck in a convoluted game of answer as truthful and as fast as you can.

"Magdalena Poloski."

"Hm," he said. "Does the babysitter invite people over in your absence?"

"No. I hope not." She felt her face ball up in disgust. Trish wouldn't put it past Maggie to commit such a violation of the house rules. The girl was laxed and unphased, luck seamlessly falling in her lap no matter how little she worked or cared. But Randel seemed to like her so… *Relax.*

"Does anyone other than you have access to the home?"

"Yeah. My husband, Randel Weston, is out of town on business. Other than him and me, no one else has access to my house," she said, wanting to be offended. Clearly, Detective Woodward suspected that she knew the person who'd do something so vile. He was right, but he didn't need to know that.

"Okay." He looked at her. "Tell me about your morning. What did you do and what were you doing when you found your car like this?"

"I–I was pacing the hallway, thinking about the things I had to do today, when Mrs. Pepper knocked on the door. She told me about my car and said that she had called the police."

"Yeah. She told us that you didn't want to call us," he said matter-of-factly.

Yeah, of course she said that.

When Trish didn't comment, he went on. "Do you know anyone who would want to hurt you? I mean, anyone who would threaten you?"

She frowned. "No. I don't. I stay to myself for the most part. My son and husband are my only friends, really."

"What about your husband? Does he have any enemies?"

"No. Not that I know of."

"Alright. Can I have a contact number? Once we run the samples, I'll give you a call and let you know what we found."

After she gave him her cell phone number, he closed his notebook and placed it and his pen back into his pocket. He reached inside his coat and handed her a card. "If you have any questions, please call me. From what I've seen so far, it looks like a rotten prank.

Someone gutted a couple raccoons and rung them out onto one side of your car—the side that neighbors would see before you did, maybe."

She sighed. "That— Yeah, that sucks. I'm sorry that I can't be more helpful."

"Yeah, well."

The police broke the yellow *Do Not Cross* tape away from the mouth of the driveway, making way for a tow truck to back up.

"What's this?" she asked. She took a few steps toward the crew, who began clearing the way for the tow truck operator.

"Well, we have to take the car into the lab and run the samples to determine who or what the blood came from. Initial testing shows that that *is* blood smeared all over your car, if you couldn't tell. We assume that all the blood belongs to the poor critters that crossed paths with the suspect, but we have to be sure."

It is animal blood. All *animal blood,* she thought.

"We might be able to get some kind of trace information on the perpetrator as well," he said.

Good luck, she thought. If Victoria had done this, they would not pick up her DNA if she was like Trish. Humans could never identify it or decode it. It was probably overlooked or a great mystery that they studied in a secret lab underneath DC. She'd left her fair share of blood and hair at crime scenes, but trace evidence never landed the authorities at her doorstep.

But if it was Steve's… *Good riddance.*

"We're also checking with surrounding counties about any similar incidents. This pattern of animal mutilation sometime escalates."

She swallowed the lump in her throat; her many victims wrapped her in a sickening nostalgia. Some of their attacks could be classified as such "That's horrible," she said.

"Yeah, well," he said.

"How long will it take for me to get the Jeep back?" she asked, perplexed about getting she and Darwin around.

"Don't know," he said. "We can try to get back to you as soon as possible though. If all the blood is animal blood, you'll get it back in about a week. If it's not, we'd have something bigger to worry about."

Great. She added buying a used car to her list of things to do right before she got rid of Victoria and Steve.

She nodded. "I understand. Take as long as you need. I work here, so there's no rush. I'll keep an eye out for anyone strange or if I think of anyone who would do this."

"Make sure you call me if you do," he said.

"Thank you," she said as she secretly cursed his unwanted presence. She didn't want him poking around in her life or solving the crime, because even though he seemed to be on her side, he'd find out about the blood that soaked her own hands. If Detective Woodward learned that he'd shaken the hand of a real-life Boogeyman, Trish would have to take care of him too.

PART 2

Care Plan

CHAPTER 10

The Burning Twilight

Vicky winced as fiery claws sunk into her ankle, killing her meditation. The brazen reminder of the sun's existence pushed her to yelp, but she held the squeal in her throat. She snatched her leg away from the golden disturbance and watched sunrays peak through penny-sized openings in the shed's weathered ceiling. She pulled her knees into her chest and looked at her leg. Enraged blackened welts stretched across her right ankle; the aches pulsed underneath her broiled skin. She pulled her pant leg down, shading her soon to be new bruise.

Vicky wished she and the sun could go back to the pleasantries that they'd held. Pain nicked her ankle, and she struggled to remember what it felt like to walk and ride bikes in the summer, chill on the Riverwalk, or gallivant up the sidewalk on Saturday afternoons. Memories of her past relationship with the sun fell away with every new encounter. *The sun even wants me dead*, she thought.

The glowing spots on the floor pretentiously exposed the weak spots of the shed. A migraine rolled around her head as the taunting discovery mocked her. But not for long. Her chest bloomed with animosity. Patricia was going to turn Vicky back to a human, and the sun wasn't going to take her shelter.

Scowling, she peered around for the first time, taking in her surroundings under natural light. Her eyes quickly fell onto the red tool bag that sat opposite her shady corner. The bag leaned against a box. The box's edges were withered and stained with splotches of old dampness on the two sides that she could see. The objects sunbathed in the corner, shining in the yellow light on all sides. Vicky looked up. The panels on the opposite corner of the ceiling just barely shielded her from the vengeful rays.

She pulled her bag from her side where she placed it between her thigh and the wall and retrieved her phone. It was 8:37, and the battery was at 4%. Her breath hitched as her stomach roared. She peered at the ceiling again. It was only 8 in the morning. As the day went on, the sun would go higher. Her darkened corner would only be dark for so long. And even though she didn't plan on lying low in the shed forever, she needed the space to be livable.

Or whatever the hell... she thought as she looked herself over and cut her eyes. Her body did not function as a living thing any longer. The list of symptoms that she had in her backpack said as much.

Carefully, and with small movements, she pulled her hoodie over her head. She looked down at her side and allowed a small smile. Her once light blue hoodie was stiff and brown on the right side of her torso where an untreated gaping wound had been. The bleeding had officially stopped, and the gash had turned into a penny-sized scar. The lines that stretched from the hole had faded into scars.

Fast healer, she thought.

She wrapped the hoodie around her left wrist and pulled the bulk of it over her arm. Once her arm and hand were protected, she stopped and studied the bloodstain. She could smell everything and everyone else, but she couldn't smell her own blood. It was a lot like being away from home for the semester and then returning to notice that the house smelled of shea butter and cherry blossoms: Mom's favorite things.

Vicky wondered if she smelled like that.

She shook the thought and tucked her legs underneath her, leaning forward to reach for the tool bag. Dust danced in the sun beams, beckoning her to come closer. The hot rays pricked her cheek, threatening to eat through the outer layer of her skin, but her covered hand tugged at the end of the tool bag. She grabbed the strap tight and snatched it, safely pulling it to her corner. With the tool bag won, she moved her attention to the lonely box.

"Don't worry," she told it. "You're next." She sat down on the floor, crossed her legs, and placed the tool bag in front of her. Inside, she found a hammer, mix-matched double A and triple A batteries, duct tape, measuring tape, a screwdriver, and a mallet. She shoved everything inside her backpack except the duct tape. She set her bag aside, held onto the duct tape, and gazed at the box.

Vicky took deep breaths, then got to her feet, standing in the shade, keeping her hoodie wrapped around the length of her arm. She tore a piece of duct tape free, reached for the arm's length ceiling, and pressed the duct tape tight against the small sunspot that had yanked her from her stupor. It fought, stinging her touch. Then she moved over to the right, and covered eight other small holes, forming a shady path to the sunny box. Snug against the edge of the sunbeams, she used her coated arm to pull the box into the newly formed shade.

She unfastened the flaps and found what looked like garden tools caked with hard gray dirt. Digging through cables, an old filter, a rusty hand rake and shovel, she discovered a small dusty cloth case containing binoculars. She separated her bounty into two piles: useless and useful. Once the box was empty, she tore it into long shreds and taped them over the three dark stains on the floor—stains that would become a problem if left untended, especially the large one near where the box had been.

She shifted her attention to the two piles on the floor. The useful pile consisted of the hand rake, cable, and binoculars. The other pile, the undesirables, was kicked against the wall, taking up the corner where the shredded box once sat.

Vicky crossed the shed and picked up her backpack, shoving the new tools inside before setting it in the center of the floor. Exhaustion weighed on her head and shoulders as the searing aches in her ankle faded to pins and needles. She pulled her hoodie from her arm and spread it across the floor as a makeshift bed, positioning her bag beside it as a pillow. Then she lay down, resting her head against the backpack. Her breath deepened, and the smells of stale dust, mold, still water and old wood lingered around her. Her muscles jolted and then relaxed as she drifted into rest—a deep stasis—whatever the hell she'd been doing during the day that kept her aware of the noises and smells around her as she stored energy for the evening. But when she closed her eyes, she didn't sleep. She remembered. She relived.

The night she was bitten flickered in and out of her memory like a dying lightbulb as she drifted into restful wakefulness. Thick, sharp teeth drove deep into her neck, disrupting circulation. Lukewarm breath pressed against her skin until warm blood drowned the wound. Her arms, feet, and legs went numb, resisting her fight to push away, to *get away*. In that moment, Vicky was sure she was dead, as reality withered and faded into nothingness. Her eyelids were too heavy— the blackened fog consumed her.

No, her last thought before the ball of blackness ate her alive. And she let it—anything for the parasite to stop eating. Darkness wrapped her, filled her with certainty and comfort. Welcomed her with love and assurance.

Then, thuds all around her as the blackness released her, shoving her back, forcing her chest out. Its once loving embrace turned cold, letting her fall through gray nothingness. She whirled around as coldness kissed her in the mouth, caressing her teeth and gums.

"Again!" an urgent, unfamiliar voice.

"Again! Stay with us!" another unfamiliar voice.

Vicky's eyes flickered, white light blinding her, its brilliance almost blasphemous as her chest caved in shocked cramps.

"She's with us!" a shout.

Her body tensed, full of hurt, as a tortured scream begged to rush up her throat and fall past her lips. But the sirens—the sirens, they were too loud. And the tires ground against the concrete too damn harshly, and the electric pulses shooting through her limbs were so *fucking* numbing. She seized, giving in to the noise and pain. Her tongue and face tingled with aches.

"Up the morphine, *now*!"

"Hang in there with us, Victoria!"

The voices. She didn't know the voices. And the smell…

Fresh. Meaty. Crimson. Thick... her mind whispered, penetrating the chaos.

Her cheeks tingled, and her gums grumbled with shreds of pain. *Savory. Sweet. Nurture. Life.*

Her chest tightened, and her stomach convulsed. She had no control. For the first time, she was at the mercy of—

Blood. Blood. Blood!

Lucid Crimson Waters

September 1, 2024

Blood waited on the other side of the darkness.

Lucid red liquid trapped Vicky within its bleak thick wetness, forcing her to swim. She became a part of the mass, living in a bloody slab of fresh, juicy, warm embrace. Her mouth leaked, drowning her tongue in a watery nectar. The sweetness of her mouth's fluid motivated her to part her lips, succumbing to her craving's desire to drink the sticky crimson lake. Her throat ached for it to swirl around her tonsils, and her heart needed the lake's blood to pump through her.

She smiled, contemplating a joyous laugh as she argued with herself.

This is wrong.
This is peace.
This is death.
This is devotion.
This is blood.

At that thought—at that moment—her lungs burned as the flow of air abruptly stopped, disallowing the will to breathe.

The insides of her cheeks prickled, and small claws scraped and poked at her left arm. As the pinching sensation escalated into something noticeable, Vicky flailed. Her skin screamed as her body ignited in ravaging pangs like fire catching wood. Something abrasive had joined the bloody lake, and she was swimming in it.

She swam and swam, looking to get away, but roiling burns dug deep and grappled her bones, seizing her arms.

No, she thought as her arms went limp, refusing to fight the heavy blood. Instead, they floated aimlessly. She kicked hard, propelling herself up, trying for the surface, not caring about what awaited on the other side. She kicked and thrusted, slightly crunching her abs and then straightening her back, driving her body upward. But spasms tightened her calves, and her thighs tensed and froze, crippling her legs with an unforgivable pain that assaulted them, killing them.

She felt her heartbeat in her skull as her throat tightened. Flashes erupted around her, staining the red pool with shades of white and pink. She shook her head, feeling her face crumble as she sank. She closed her eyes, allowing God, the Devil, or nonexistence to carry her away.

But she didn't see the light they talked about at church. She couldn't find the Devil wagging the red finger of dismay, and she didn't fall into the pure blackness of nothing.

Raven hair, stocky claws, pale skin.

Vicky shook her head and shivered. She fell deeper into the reddened waters and suffocation crushed her lungs.

Cherry lips, magenta eyes. Blackened pupils as wide as the pits of space.

Vicky's shaking seized as she opened her eyes and threw her head back.

Long, sharp fangs.

She remembered feeling them plunge into her neck, and she felt her blood flow backward as the monster withdrew before Vicky felt nothing, saw nothing—*was* nothing.

Then *they* showed up. They told her to stay alive. They shocked her heart into beating. They wrapped something around her neck. She could hear them, feel their hands on her as they moved her from one place to another. She could smell them, engrossed in their scents: musk, skin, sweat, muscle, gas, blood, blood, blood!

When their warm hands lifted her, she fought the urge to grab an arm or face, a leg or a neck, and sink her teeth into it. She could rip a head from its neck and lick the bloody stump.

On some zombie shit, she thought. Her mind lulled while she sank through redness.

She recalled wanting to run, but her limbs had been paralyzed, ignoring her dire need to flee. Instead, her body had wanted to embrace the pain and bask in the new smells—craving blood as the price of freedom. It was as if her body, mind, and soul hissed obscenities and reprimanded *her* for resisting. But then, and now, she was still in control—yes, she was still the owner of her limbs and heart and mind…and she could destroy them if she wanted. As the bloody lake pulled her deeper into its depths, Vicky opened her mouth and inhaled.

***

She cracked her eyelids and winced as a white light pierced her face. She scowled as the smell of the hospital room invaded her nose and crept across her tongue. The place smelled like a pathogen cocktail, swarming with viruses and bacteria; a sickly aroma of the inside of a dirty mouth wafted around her nose.

Vicky's arms and legs crackled with pain. Her stomach turned as her own blood pumped through her veins, carrying agony that stifled her thoughts. She winced as twisted aches crawled up her left arm and invaded her chest. She let out a raspy groan as she balled her fists, willing the agony to stop spreading, to stop falling down her middle and cramping her pelvis. But it fell down her right arm and crept down her fingers. It wrapped her body, stiffened her neck, and gripped her breath.

What the fuck…? She turned her head, glaring at the disturbance in the back of her left hand. An IV needle purged her system with fluid. Her legs stiffened, and her middle clenched underneath the grasp of pain. She watched the veins in her hand and arm pulse, pressing against the underside of her skin, aggravated and suffering as shimmering salt crystals clustered around the top of the gauze. She felt the flow course through the opening in her hand, feeding liquid hurt to her veins.

"Ahhhhh!" she shrieked as she reached for the IV and snatched it out. Blood splashed the IV bag and the silver stand that had been holding it. The gaping wound sputtered, pouring out onto the white sheets.

"Ahhh!" Vicky screamed as the monitor shouted alerts, ringing in her ears.

The door flew open, and people dressed in scrubs rushed inside. She swung her arms and squealed, spraying the hospital staff with blood. "Fuck!" she shouted as she turned to her side, trying to get out of bed, trying to get away from the hands that held her down. There were four, five of them. She couldn't tell because she watched one of them, a doctor in an oversized white coat, rush around the restraining group and raise a needle; its intended use made Vicky's eyes bulge. She thrashed and kicked, struggling against strong arms and hands. But they held tight, not saying a word. Two nurses held Vicky's right arm still, and the needle tip sank into it. She shrieked as the doctor injected the needle's contents into her blood stream. The hospital staff's arms remained tight on her legs, arms, and waist as her screams petered out to small moans.

"It's okay, Miss Scott." The soft-spoken trembling voice of the doctor. "It's okay," she assured Vicky. Within seconds, Vicky's limbs loosened, and the faces of the nurses and the doctor fell behind a black wall.

Vicky fell, but she didn't hit the floor. She belly-flopped into the bloody lake. The initial impact was soft and forgiving as it embraced her. The micro monsters that had bitten and pinched her skin were gone. She smiled as the lake's warmth hugged her tight, pulling her deeper inside.

C H A P T E R   1 2

Conscious

Vicky woke with the smell of blood dousing her senses in iron and a hint of a new earthy spice. Her mouth watered, beckoning her to fall back into the soft currents of the heavy mass of fluids trapped in her mind, soaking her thoughts in gore. Instead, she sneered at the incessant beeping that sounded off in her dreams, day and night. The monitor went on and on, uninterrupted as it read her vitals, undeterred by her true need for silence.

Damn thing is more like a dreary soundtrack to my acid trips, she thought. Then her face crumpled as she drew her head back, having taken note of the date on the screen. *September 2, 2024,* the neon green letters on the monitor taunted. She furrowed her brow. As she went to sit up, she stalled, finding her left arm wrapped in gauze from her forearm down to her knuckles. The sight brought back an unwelcome memory full of stabbing liquids that invaded her body and the IV needle that she ripped from her vein. Instead of an IV bag pumping saline, she only found patches plastered to her chest. The patches fed information to the monitor on the left side of the bed.

"September 2nd," she whispered. She glared off into the distance, fighting to remember recent words from familiar faces. But the last thing she remembered was Teresa's begging pleas as she bribed Vicky. That was days ago.

Friday, the 30th, Vicky thought. *Now help my dumb ass out,* Teresa had said, her emerald eyes begging for a palatable response.

It'd been three days since that happened, and there was no Teresa, Mom, Daddy, or Moody, nobody there to tell Vicky that everything was fine. She felt herself quake, and her head throbbed intensely with sickening awareness. No one was there to tell Vicky that a crazy woman had attacked and bitten her. No one was there to tell Vicky that the injuries were minor, and that she'd be back on campus in no time. And at the very least, no one was there to tell Vicky that the police needed to question her about a murder. Chad's murder. The monster strangled Chad and sucked his blood. Vicky's throat tightened. Yes. If no one else wanted her awake, she was sure the police would. They should be hungry for a statement, an identity…something.

Did they catch her?

"Maybe," Vicky said through the lump in her throat. But it didn't matter. Caught or not, Vicky was still in the hospital under observation. *Why?* she thought. *Why am I still here? What's wrong with me?* She'd never been in the hospital for longer than a couple days. There was the time she had her tonsils removed, but she only stayed overnight after that. But three days? Vicky wished she could call someone and ask, but there was no use; she could not speak to the people that came around while she swam in her red, messy, dense lake. It was as though her mind prohibited such an act, speaking to people—asking for help. Vicky turned on her side and pulled her knees up to her chest. There were so many signs and symptoms that she could not explain.

Even in her dazed, dreamlike stupor, she felt people move around the sanctum of her reality, oblivious to the bloody inner workings of her slumber. There was the person who breathed heavily as they stood over her before swapping the plates of food that she didn't eat. And then there were the women who moved her around, changed her bed pan, and washed her skin. Vicky was sure the pan was empty; she hadn't eaten or drunk anything that she knew of.

Vicky smelled musky sweat, flowery perfume, morning breath, and cleaning supplies whenever the bloody lake allowed her brief contact with the world outside of her consciousness. There'd been the hint of musty armpits, powdery skin, and suffocating citrus cologne riding the currents only for a moment before blood filled her nostrils and she sank back in.

Regardless of the people's clinging odors, Vicky knew they were all bewildered by her. Some people stopped and watched—poked and prodded. And she let them, too helpless to do anything but swim, look, drift, peer, and sink.

In the ever-changing mood of the world encompassing her body, she recognized a couple of visitors from the times that she made it just beneath the lake's surface. When they used their gloved fingers to open Vicky's eyelids, she could see their confused faces waver behind the thin red film of her safe place. Dr. Polson, a tall, thin, olive-toned man with dark hair who had to be in his early forties, and Nurse Cammy, a short black lady with curly hair, watched over Vicky like hawks. She watched their lips move, felt them breathe on her skin, and heard their faraway voices. Most of the time, she was too careless to make out their words; they only made concerned muffled sounds. But she did make out their names from their name tags. They'd flash small lights in her eyes, and instead of small black spots that she used to find after such an exam, the red film thickened, blinding her. All the while, as if stuck in a timed sleep paralysis, Vicky could not move, and she dared not wake.

On the days when they did not help her see, she'd smell Dr. Polson's fresh woody musk and Nurse Cammy's dainty sweet skin when they swabbed Vicky's mouth, scraped small patches off her skin, or pulled blood from her veins. Their presence oozed into her dreams or—or…

Meditative state?

While the doctor and nurse glowered, Vicky lingered within the warm red pool. It felt good on her legs and breasts—in her hair and on her lips. The warm nest hidden within her heart was safe and filling. Familiar and cozy.

Now fully awake, she pulled the blanket from her face and clenched her jaw, then quickly opened her mouth. Her gums tingled at the disturbance—sore and raw, as if she'd had her wisdom teeth pulled again. Vicky swallowed hard and allowed the tears to pour from her eyes, scattering the dim light shining overhead into strange angles that blurred the sky-blue ceiling.

Sickened with confusion and stuck in a well of human ailments, she buried her face deep into her pillow to mute her disillusioned howls and to clog her nose from the smells that were so strong that they didn't make sense. Bile and piss. Illness and blood. Sweet, warm, eternal blood. She pulled the thick white blanket over her head, hiding from the world, wondering who else had been in her room as she swam in her own mind. Who did the other smells belong to? Did her family know where she was? If they did, would the lake release her long enough to see them? Doubt tugged at her gut, and she let out a staggered sigh, knowing the truth.

No. Probably not.

She cried that night for her new self. She prayed for Jesus—no, God—no, Mom and Daddy and Moody to save her. Should she even talk to them? She didn't want them to worry, because the first thing Mom would say was, "Nope, bring yo ass home. Macomb University is also a great school, and it's much closer."

Vicky wiped her tears, smiling at the thought of her family running to her rescue. They always did, like that time she rammed her bike into the oak tree on the corner, splitting her elbow and lips. She screeched loud as blood coated her teeth, and they all came running. And there was that time she and Moody were tossing the football, and he caught her in the nose, busting it, but not breaking it. He stopped the bleeding and bought her a chocolate ice cream cone from the Mr. Frosty Ice Cream truck for a week. They were excited and scared to send her off on her own, knowing that she'd need them. So, no. Vicky wasn't going to worry because she didn't want *them* to worry.

"Everything is okay," she said. "Everything is gonna be fine."

CHAPTER 13

Notes

The next night, Vicky swung her legs over the left side of the bed and placed her feet, covered in evergreen hospital socks, onto a hard linoleum floor. Her stomach turned at the smell of garlic and burnt sugar that reverberated from the buttered toast, mashed potatoes, and chocolate pudding. The platter sat on the counter across from the bed.

She peered at the monitors that recorded her vitals and reported the date and time: *September 3, 2024, 1:49 am.* "Hm," she grumbled. The night seemed to be her body's preferred time.

Vicky grabbed the monitor's stand and pulled it along with her, not wanting to alert the staff of her movements as she took the room in for the first time. The back of her gown was open, making her only a little self-conscious as her bare ass hung out. She shrugged, admittingly enjoying the brisk air from behind.

Just as the night before, the long baby-blue curtains were drawn, and both doors—one that led to the hallway, and another that led to what Vicky assumed was the bathroom—were closed. Aside from the hospital bed, there was a navy sleeper chair and a long counter. Over the counter was a mounted flat screen the size of Moody's gaming monitor. There were four bottles of water and a white plastic bag sitting on the counter.

As Vicky approached the counter, which was parallel to the bed, she knew what she'd find: there was her dead phone, gold necklace and pinky ring, and a black ink pen—*This isn't mine*. Her clothes and wallet were gone.

She peered around, hoping that they'd moved the wallet somewhere else. She pulled the drawers open and searched the cupboards in the counter. There were gauzes, bandages, extra blood pressure cuffs, and no wallet. She distinctly remembered putting her wallet in her shorts pocket because she hated carrying purses when it was hot out.

"But my phone's here," she said to no one. She thought back to Chad's closet. Did she drop the wallet? *Fuck,* she thought. A flustered sigh. *I don't...* She put up a finger. "I slid it in my pocket!" she proclaimed. "So... Shit," she said, more perplexed than she was before. Her license, school ID, debit card, credit card, four hundred dollars... She patted her hips to find that she was wearing a hospital gown. "Duh," she whispered. "Where the hell is my wallet?" Only then did she notice the two notes on the counter. They appeared handwritten and were addressed to her. Vicky picked up the first one.

Hi Ms. Scott. My name is Dr. Polson, and you are my patient. We are trying to find out how to treat your condition. We can only observe at this time. Please reply if you can. Your vitals show that you were awake last night, so I hope this letter finds you well. We are doing everything we can to treat your condition. Thank you so much for your patience.

Dr. P

Next to his note, Cammy left a simple one saying:

Victoria, it's an honor to take care of you. We will get you right. Dr. P's the best. Cammy

There was a staff picture underneath Cammy's note. Black inky circles rounded her and the doctor's smiling faces amongst the sea of colorful scrubs and white coats. *Here to help you,* the red cursive letters scrolled across the first row's shoes had said. Just over the back row was the hospital's name in large, cursive font: *Saint Bernard's General Hospital.*

Vicky narrowed her eyes, feeling them water as she glared holes into the photo. The notes didn't tell her where her wallet and clothes had gone. The notes hadn't told her where her family was. The notes hadn't told her *anything*. Vicky knew she was still under observation—that the monitor had snitched on her. She knew what their stupid faces looked like—what they smelled like and what their names were, and surely when she watched them observe her they didn't look as confident or competent as they did in that goofy-ass photo. Whenever she'd seen them, they looked miserable and puzzled.

She scowled. All those qualified, smart, capable individuals stood with their chins up and wide smiles. Some of the doctors even had a hand or two haphazardly shoved into their white coat pockets. But none of them—*not one asshole*—could tell her why she had the nose of a bloodhound, why blood seeped through the crevices of her dreams, or why she wanted to eat the blood—drink the blood—be the blood or…or…why her gums were suddenly burning!

Vicky's sinuses opened, allowing the room's garlicky smell to dig deeper into her nostrils. Her gums tingled intensely as her teeth embedded themselves into her lower lip. Her sweetened saliva mixed with her bitter blood.

Vicky dropped the photo on the counter and rushed for the bathroom. In her hurry, the sticky patches from the monitor's probes tugged at her, impeding her rush as if to remind her to pull the damned thing along. She ripped the patches from her chest and hurried for the bathroom, snatched the door open, flipped the light on, and positioned herself in front of the mirror. She ignored her unkempt hair, which was hanging onto small, matted crinkles, and opened her mouth. She lifted her upper lip. Sharp teeth, the third one from the center on either side, protruded from her gums. She shook her head as her heart slammed into her chest. Her core trembled, trying to knock her off her weakening knees.

"Wh—" Her jaw trembled, eating up any questions—any words—that dared slip past her lips.

She gasped, holding back a scream. "I— That's…"

When her knees finally gave, Vicky slid herself into a sitting position onto the toilet. She bent at the waist and retched, not caring about turning around and throwing up in the toilet as she had been taught as a child. But nothing came out; her belly was empty.

She felt silly as she battled her brain's irrational rationalities:
Vampires don't exist.

Fangs.

There are stories and movies about them, like Salem's Lot *and* Dracula; *me and Daddy watch those movies every October.*

Pale skin.

She looked at her arms. They didn't appear to be a different shade of brown. Or were they?

Pink eyes.

She shot up again and glared at the all-knowing mirror. She looked into her eyes, then shuddered. They were darker than their normal hazel.

It was then that she noticed the shrilling monitor. She rushed back into the main room to find her incoherent vitals screaming *Error, Error, Error!* The prolonged warning beep burrowed deep into her ears. She pressed—smashed—buttons and screamed, "Shut up! Shut up! Shut up!" She grabbed the stand with one hand and slapped the screen with her other until it went black, but the noise persisted. Vicky pushed the nuisance onto the floor and kicked it, stomped it until cracks bit into the glass surface. Only then did it go quiet.

Her heaving chest swelled and fell as she pushed air through her clenched teeth. "This can't be real!" she grunted. She marched over to the counter and snatched up the notes and picture of her useless healthcare team. She shrieked as she ripped them into small pieces and scattered them over the dead monitor.

Vicky eyed the plate on the other end of the counter. "I can eat, I can… I'm not…" she declared as she grabbed the buttery toast and shoved it into her mouth. The unpleasant clumpy mess turned into mush as she slowly chewed. Too much saliva moistened her mouth as the rancid butter assaulted her taste buds. But she forced herself to swallow. The lump travelled down her throat and dropped into her stomach. Her gut turned in response, and nausea made her cheeks tingle. Vicky doubled over and gagged before vomiting, throwing the curdled bile onto the floor.

"No!" she growled. "I wanna go home!" she cried. She needed to see her family. She needed to talk to Teresa; maybe she had her wallet? And she wanted her own doctor back in the city, not those middle-of-nowhere, know-nothing assholes.

Clothes or not, Vicky was getting out of there and getting actual help. She pulled the white blanket from the hospital bed and put it over her shoulders. Then she headed back to the counter, shoved her things back into the plastic bag, and tucked it under her arm. She rolled her eyes—*Bet you'll carry a purse from now on*—and headed for the door.

Vicky turned the knob and stopped short; the door was locked. She released the knob and glared at it. There was no latch or button or any means of locking the door on her side of it. *They locked me in here…from the outside.*

Surely she could leave whenever she wanted. Right?

No—no, they can't. Can they? She'd seen videos and read about people leaving the hospital against the doctor's orders. Sure, they had to sign something stating that they were leaving on their own accord, but they could walk out the front door unless they were being released to the police. Vicky hadn't done anything wrong; *she* was the victim. She had witnessed a murder. She saw Chad die.

Is that why the door was locked? Because there was a cop on the other side watching her—guarding her from the monster?

But Vicky didn't need the police—she needed Mom and Daddy. She even needed Teresa—who was probably feeling really guilty and confused, lost without knowing what happened to Vicky.

What did the doctors actually know?

Enough to have me locked in this room. Enough to keep me from my family and friends. Enough to keep my clothes and wallet.

She could still see the monster plunge its fangs into Chad's wrists, its greedy slurping just barely audible over the booming speakers from the party. It hungrily swallowed the thick, syrupy, sticky red liquid, filling up on him as he died.

Vicky wondered what his blood tasted like. Was it as warm as the blood from her dream lake? Or was it better? Was it savory and filling like a filet mignon? Or was it sweet and sour like a caramel-covered green apple? Her mouth watered with sweetened saliva as her stomach growled. Chad's blood must have been delicious. So tasty that the monster risked exposure to have it. They were in a house full of strangers, after all. Vicky closed her eyes. Staging Chad's suicide may have worked too.

Vicky blinked frantically as her heart dropped to the pit of her stomach.

No, that's fucking disgusting, she reprimanded herself. *What are you, a cannibal now?* She froze. *What if the doctors and police think that too?* She put her hand over her mouth, recounting the many movies and shared conspiracy theories. *If I have a dangerously contagious disease or...* Tears fell from her eyes.

"What do I do? What do I do?" she asked through hurried breaths. *Slam on the door,* her thoughts raged. *Kick it in, scream, demand to be let out.* But instead, she stepped back, afraid and somehow knowing that if she'd done that, the would-be police officer on the other side of the door would shoot her.

Instead, Vicky cleaned up her vomit using a cheap brown paper towel that she found in the bathroom and threw the rest of the food in the garbage. Then she sat on the bed, thinking of the body that she no longer recognized. She contemplated the mild cramps that started to tear through her stomach and ran her tongue over her sharp teeth.

C H A P T E R   1 4

Elephants

On the third night of full consciousness, the new monitor—which was almost identical to the one that she smashed the night before—read *September 4, 2024, 2:04 am.* Vicky lay on her back and glared at the ceiling, contemplating another difference: it wasn't light blue; the ceiling was white. Then something dawned on her. She sat up and peered at the monitor again. The monitor was on the right side of the bed, not the left. Her chest clenched as she looked around. She smelled Dr. P's woody cologne and Cammy's sweet perfume, sure. But the room was different. The sound of circulating air beat her ears and the rails on her bed were silver and in the up position. There wasn't a TV or a counter.

White walls surrounded her with no windows, and an oversized humidifier-like machine hummed in the corner. A lone black desk chair sat beside a small table with only two drawers.

Vicky got up and headed for the door while pulling the monitor along. She peered out the face-sized window and into the bright hallway. There was no one out there—nothing in sight. There were only white walls and a white-tiled floor. She dared to twist the knob of what was her new sterile box, and just like in her last room, the door was locked on the outside.

She backed away and started for the gray door to her right. She opened it. *Bathroom,* she thought, noting that it had a similar layout to the bathroom in her room prior to this one.

Did they move me because of the monitor? she thought as she paced in circles around the new space.

"I was the one attacked," she proclaimed. "I didn't kill Chad," she went on. "Why am I in—" *Prison...* she thought, too afraid of what speaking it out loud would mean—what it might do.

Shaken, she marched over to the table. "Please be here," she whispered as she pulled the top drawer open. She moved some medical supplies around, and slammed the drawer shut, not finding what she needed.

"Please, please, please be here," she growled as she searched the second drawer.

And there it was, sitting neatly atop a stack of notes was Dr. P's perfect script:

We had to move you. Please call me. It is VERY urgent. 555-889-2235. Press 9 to dial out. Dr. P.

Vicky looked up, noticing the corded phone attached to the wall over the nightstand. She hadn't used a phone that looked like that in a long time—Granny had one that she only used for bill collectors. Vicky wondered if there was one in the last room, but she didn't remember seeing one. She snatched up the phone receiver from the wall mount. She pressed 9 and listened as the dial tone pierced her ear. Instead of dialing Dr. P's number, she dialed one of the two numbers she knew by heart besides her own.

She listened as the numbers sang in her ear as she dialed them.

The number you have dialed...

"Ugh," she groaned. She hung up and dialed the other number.

The number you have dialed cannot be completed. Please...

She sniffled and sobbed. "Fuck!" she spat through clenched teeth.

Vicky felt her world descend into a living nightmare, as if she were trying to call for help but couldn't get the numbers right. But she knew that she'd dialed her parents' numbers correctly. When Vicky was five, her parents made her sit at the kitchen table and write their numbers and home address hundreds of times until she was able to recite them without fail. The repetitive exercise took weeks, but it engrained her lifelines into her head. And her parents hadn't changed their numbers since then.

She slammed the phone down, swallowed her frustrations, then picked it up again. She dialed Dr. P's number. He answered on the third ring.

Key Takeaways

Dr. P's deep husk rasped on the line. "Hello?"

"Dr.—" Vicky cleared her shaking throat. "Dr. Polson?"

"Yes," he said. His voice perked up, knocking all signs of sleepiness away. "Victoria? Victoria Scott?"

She didn't speak. Tears welled in her eyes as the sound of her name thrusted at her gut.

"Ms. Scott, are you there?"

"H-how long have I been out?" she asked, knowing the answer, but struggling to grasp it.

"Two days before your vitals showed that you were active at night," he said. "You've been in my care for five days now."

She didn't speak. She continued wondering about her family and friends. Did they know what had happened to her?

"How are you feeling?" he asked.

"Uh—" She ran her tongue over her teeth. She winced. Although her fangs were retracted, her teeth were tender to the touch. "What–what's wrong with me?" she asked, failing to keep her sobbing a secret.

"We don't know." He let out a defeated huff. "I can't tell you what's wrong, but I can tell you what I have observed." When she didn't respond, he went on. "You are suffering from rapid weight loss, which plateaued yesterday, keeping you at 90 pounds. You've developed retractable and unnaturally sharp canine teeth. You have a saline allergy which caused you to go into toxic shock the first night you were admitted. The IV almost burned the veins out of your body. But after a day in a coma—"

"A coma?" she asked, her lips shuddering at the laundry list of symptoms.

"Yes—your arm healed very quickly after we removed the IV, but we are keeping it wrapped until the wound is fully healed. Do you feel any pain in your arm?"

"No."

"Okay. Do you drink water at all? We leave bottles of water, but you don't drink them. You haven't urinated in the bed pan, but you don't seem to be dehydrated when we pull blood. Do you drink tap water and urinate at night?"

"No," she said.

"Well, that's problematic."

"Why?" she asked, not sure if her question addressed her lack of dehydration or her new state entirely.

"It's problematic because it's been over four days, and you haven't had any fluids." He paused. "And even without proper medical intervention, the injuries that you sustained on the first night—when you ripped the IV needle from your arm—have healed substantially. The scarred tissue underneath your skin developed in a matter of hours. So did the lacerations on your neck. It's baffling that you haven't drank or eaten anything. We–we tried to feed you with a tube while you were comatose, but you aspirated instantly and your body…" He paused again. "Your body rejected it."

As they listened to each other's breathing, she rubbed her neck and found the familiar clump of gauze. She relived the feeling of hot sticky blood pooling on her neck, and the creature's slimy tongue maneuvering around the punctured openings. Vicky remembered going limp and seeing specks of blue and red and pink as the shape of Chad's lifeless body blurred and smeared, his essence falling in with the dark blanket on his bed, the oak of his dresser, and the small blinking lights of his computer monitor. The shadows of his room, the space that knew everything about him, fell into each other and darkened, crowding her vision as she listened to the grotesque pull of her blood as the monster robbed her soul.

"Your teeth came in two days ago." Dr. P paused as if knowing she'd have questions. But when she said nothing, he went on. "While under sedation, your body tensed—every muscle locked, and the monitors alerted the nurses that you were not breathing. When the nurses ran in to check on you, they thought you were choking. Your nose was bleeding, and your lips held blood in your mouth like a trapped door. In order to clear your throat, they needed to open your mouth; Nurse Rob had to pry your mouth open in order to save your life. After trying for about five minutes, your jaw finally loosened, and you stopped choking. Nurse Rob grabbed his penlight to see if the obstruction in your airway had cleared but, as he drew close, you opened your eyes. It was the first time, and only time, that you've been awake during the day. He said he was startled. The other two nurses in the room drew back, but he held his stance. He said your name, but you didn't answer. You only peered at him. He said your eyes were pink."

Pink eyes.

"Then you sat up." He paused.

She held her breath and searched her mind for the event, but there was nothing. There were only the dark depths of the red lake.

"It didn't make sense because the dose of anesthetic that we gave you was too high for you to be awake, especially with your weight… there was no way," he reasoned. "Your body starting spasming and your muscles flinched, restlessly. But you were awake, shaking and staring." She heard fear creep through the receiver as he went on. "You raised your hand—and your nails… They–they had grown into claws. White, long, pointy claws. They were longer than any bear or sloth—any animal that we know about. It's–it's just that…the ends were not curled. They were straight."

She looked at her hands. They were pale, but her nails looked normal, bitten down to the quick. *Claws like boning knives.* They felt cold against her cheeks when the monster held Vicky's face.

"You grabbed him by the throat." Vicky heard his voice shake. "Your claws sliced the sides of his neck, leaving bloody slits. You pulled him toward you, your body rocking with dyskinesia. Then you opened your mouth and pulled him toward the sharpest teeth they'd ever seen. Rob tried to shake you off, but he said your grip was impenetrable. Your body was unstable as your muscles jerked and your limbs trembled, but your iron grip didn't let up. He screamed and yelled, as did the nurses calling for help while they pulled at your wrist and hand. But his blood soaked your fingers, and you were unfazed. Luckily, Dr. Madison came into the room and injected you with a higher dose of benzo. Then you dropped Nurse Rob, and you went unconscious."

Vicky cupped her mouth, then drew her hand back as an intense pain shot through her gums. She could not remember hurting anyone. And she didn't remember *growing teeth*. She only remembered waking up the night before and finding them there when she thought about blood. "Oh my God," she whispered.

"Insomnia—" he said.

"What? I sleep all day."

"Yes. But it isn't very restful."

Because I swim all day, going with the red currents.

He went on. "Skin discoloration."

Vicky frowned. Her brown skin looked beige in the dim light; there was no doubt about it anymore.

"UV allergies, lack of appetite, lack of..."

Overwhelmed by the list of clinical signs, she stopped listening, engrossed in shame. *That poor nurse,* she thought. He was only doing his job, and she scarred him for life, almost killed him. And after all that, the hospital still didn't know what was wrong with her. Flustered with that final fact, Vicky dropped her shoulders, wanting to cry in Mom's arms. But all she could say was, "I'm sorry. I am so sorry. I—"

"Victoria, I—"

"My parents..." she said. "Were they here? Can they get me? Did you talk to them?" She rattled off the questions in quick succession.

Dr. P sighed. "They came, yes, of course. Your family cares a lot about you. In fact, they've been to the hospital every day since you've been admitted. Some of your friends came by as well."

Vicky's throat tightened as she allowed a smile. She imagined Mom standing at the front desk demanding to see her daughter, lobbying for Vicky's release.

"But I could not allow them to see you," he said. His words made Vicky's chest deflate, knocking the wind out of her.

"Why?" she growled as she tightened her free hand into a fist. "What gives you the right to turn my people away?!"

"The police showed up too," he said, disregarding her gripe.

Her heart leapt as she blinked back tears. "The police?" *So, they are interested in my side of the story*, she thought.

"Yes. Victoria, you were attacked at a party." His calm, steady tone almost drove her up a wall. It was like he was carefully choosing his words. "The volume of blood loss should have killed you, but the paramedics, emergency doctors, and nurses were able to keep your heart beating. It was a miracle, really. They saved your life."

"So?!" Vicky shouted. Why was he praising them? She was still there in the hospital with no clue what her issue was. "Did the police find her?"

"Her? The person who attacked you was a woman?"

"Yes," she spat.

"I don't know. But I don't think you should talk to them."

Vicky paused. "W–why?"

He sighed. "Victoria—"

"Vicky."

He cleared his throat. "Vicky, after the incident with the nurse, the monitor that we found crushed in your room, and your rapidly progressing symptoms, I had no choice but to contact the CDC. Neither me nor the hospital have seen symptoms of this sort...*ever*. But for the safety of the staff and to minimize the potential of an outbreak, I was instructed to move you to the quarantine unit."

"W–what? I—watched her kill Chad. I— She almost killed me. She–she bit me in the neck—"

"She bit you?" he asked.

"Yes! I'm not the monster. *She* is."

Silence.

"I have to tell the police, don't I?" she asked.

In a hushed voice, he said, "We've been instructed to keep you quarantined until the CDC sends someone to come and pick you up in a few hours."

Her heart throbbed. "Pick me up and take me where?"

Silence.

"Pick me up and take me where?" she shrieked.

"I don't know," he said. "But I don't think it'll be good for you or your family or friends."

"What does that even mean? I didn't do anything. *I swear.*"

"Vicky—"

"What did she do to me?" She pressed her back to the wall and slid down until she sat on the floor. Her body quavered as she sobbed. "I wanna go home," she said.

"I don't want to see them take you either. You're my patient, and I want to learn more about your ailment. I want to treat you." She pictured him placing a hand over his heart as he made his declaration. "I don't know what they have planned, but I do know that this may not end well. Especially because the local police suddenly stopped calling to see if you were conscious. It's as if their relentless need to question you dried up after my initial contact with the CDC." He sighed. "Are you sure you never had these symptoms before?" She heard papers flipping. "Your mother sent your medical records and…I didn't find anything that—"

"No. Who has?" she asked.

He went on. "There's nothing about your symptoms in the research. There's nothing about it in hospital files. I've even contacted some of my medical school friends, and no one has heard of this. I've called around to different states, searched Clinicaltrials.gov… I reached out to some colleagues in India and China. I've looked everywhere. I—"

"So?" she shouted, wanting him to shut up or get to the point. "Now what? What are they going to do to me?"

"I want to get you out of there."

She blinked, surprised. She was sure he was ready to give up. But no. "How?"

"Listen…" he said as urgency crept into his words. "I don't know what the government's plans are, but I have an alternative and I promise that I will keep you safe."

"No. No—you already can't figure things out now. Why should I trust you?"

"Do you have any other ideas?"

She ran her free hand through her crinkled hair. "Yeah. Let me talk to the person who is coming in tomorrow."

"I doubt they'll listen," he said. "The agencies are instructed on what to do with certain cases. They will not risk public health for a single patient."

"Then why can't I leave now?" As the question left her mouth, she found the answer. "Wait… Do you think I'm dangerous?" She narrowed her eyes, pulling pieces together out loud. "You've been trying to talk to me for days, and you knew I was up at night. Why don't you come see me at night?"

He breathed into the phone.

She nodded, having made up her mind. "Where are the rest of my things?"

"Everything that is in your bag is all we have. The police took the rest. But I wouldn't be surprised if they lost possession of the evidence."

"How are you going to help me if you are too afraid to be in the same room as me?"

"The agent wasn't too keen on sharing what they knew about your illness, and I fear for your safety. I can't allow them to take you without trying harder on my end first. I'll get over my… I want to help you, but I can't do it in the hospital."

She wanted to push more. Ask him what he thought had happened to her. What he thought the government was going to do. But if she ran out, the agency might have people waiting in the hallway or at the front door. They could very well be listening in on their call. She looked around. There wasn't a camera that she could see. She couldn't call anyone other than Dr. P, and he was the first person she'd contacted in days. With little choice, she sighed.

"Victoria, listen to me very carefully," he said. "Because if you get caught—"

"I know," she said.

He talked, and she listened.

CHAPTER 16

Mr. FBI

Vicky breathed slowly and deep, fully conscious during the day for the first time.

I'll give you just a little Adderall. Enough to keep you awake, but not enough to make you flinch, Dr. P had told her the night before. Remaining still and pretending to be unaware wasn't as hard as she'd thought, but parts of her yearned to swim in the bloody depths of the healing pool deep in her mind. She centered herself, feeling as if she floated over the bed and wasn't lying on it. Her limbs felt numb as her body relaxed. It reminded her of what it felt like to drift off into a deep sleep.

Still, her nerves played tricks on her, daring her to jerk her thighs or twitch her fingers. But she stayed perfectly still, just as Dr. P had instructed. Even with her eyes closed, she could still see the whiteness of the sterile quarantine unit. If she were unaware of her location, she would be convinced that she was in the psych ward, restrained by an invisible straitjacket.

When the door opened, the anticipated intrusion was as loud as glass shattering in an empty church. Vicky held her breath but relaxed when she smelled Dr. P's woody cologne. *Breathe, dummy,* she thought, as she allowed a soft breath. Then she smelled something new. *Mint?* Convinced that the smell belonged to a stranger who had entered her realm of the hospital, she decided that it had to be the federal agent.

Body heat radiated from Dr. P and the Fed on either side of her bed, playing games with both of her arms, tugging the climate from warm to hot, too cold, to warm again as she adjusted to their presence.

"Have you spoken to any of her friends or family since she's been admitted?" the minty Fed asked. She imagined some man, any man, dressed in a black two-piece suit with a black tie and sunglasses, even though he was indoors.

"Yes. They've been by every day since she's been in our care," Dr. P said.

"You didn't let them see her, did you?" the Fed asked, his serious cadence remaining the same. "The last thing we need is for the press to pick this up."

What? Vicky shouted in her head. Mom and Daddy were *amazing* at keeping secrets. Like that time when they found out that Vicky clogged the sink in the church's only bathroom. Service had been boring that day, so she decided to see how thin the cheap toilet paper was. She placed one sheet over the drain as the water spewed from the faucet. Then she stacked another sheet over the drain, then another, then another… Fifteen minutes later, she was out of tissue and her shoes were so soaked that her dress socks had gotten wet. Her parents were *pissed*, but they anonymously paid for the repairs in full and hosted a food drive for the community which fed everyone who needed it for a few months. Her parents were good people; they never would have told anyone about Vicky. In fact, they probably would be more effective at keeping her safe than the hospital.

"I can't explain *this* to her parents, let alone the press," Dr. P said. "Due to the nature of her condition, the hospital administration instructed us to keep her isolated from other patients and guests. It wasn't until I talked to you yesterday that we had to remove her from the general ICU and into the quarantine unit."

"Did you talk to them this morning?"

"Uh, yes. They called to see if anything happened overnight. They plan on coming this afternoon. I didn't tell them that she was leaving. I'll give them a call after you all leave."

"You told them what I told you to say, right?" the spearmint, or double mint, man said, sounding pushy. She wanted to yell at the man because she felt Dr. P's nervousness and, for some reason, she cared about him. He could have turned her over days ago—washed his hands and said, "Forget it, I have other patients to deal with." But no, he didn't. He kept trying. In that moment and in her state, Dr. P and Nurse Cammy were Vicky's closest friends, and the agent could go walk into traffic.

"Yes—yeah. I told them that we discovered that she had picked up a new virus that was incredibly contagious, and that the hospital staff was required to wear specialized PPE before *we* even came into contact with her. I told them that we were awaiting word from the CDC on how to proceed."

"Hm," the Fed said. "Run through the symptoms for me again." She heard what sounded like flapping notebook paper.

"Let's see," Dr. P started.

Can't eat food, she thought, running through her own list as they discussed it last night.

"Rapid weight loss."

Teeth are sharp.

"She has fangs. She didn't have fangs when she first came in through emergency. She..." Dr. P sounded as though he had trailed off.

IVs sting like a bitch.

"We had to remove her IV because she had a bad reaction. She hasn't had anything to drink since she's been admitted, but she is not dehydrated."

"Hmm," the agent said, inquisitively.

"She developed claws..." The room went silent as Dr. P trailed off again.

"Polson?" the agent asked, way too comfortable by referring to Dr. P as simply "Polson." Vicky imagined herself rolling her eyes.

"Sorry. Um, we had to keep her away from any windows because she sustained first-degree burns when she came into contact with sunrays."

Disregarding the last bit of information, the Fed asked, "What did you try to feed her?"

"We've tried everything. Bread, pudding—"

"Raw meat?"

"Uh. N–no. What?" Dr. P sounded perplexed.

"Hm," the agent said.

"Agent Morgan, can I ask what's going on? She is my patient, and even though she is conscious, it's not like I can ask her what's going on. She isn't responsive. And even if she was, I'm sure she is as confused and scared as the rest of us."

"Doctors get scared?" Agent Morgan almost sounded as if he had a smile playing on his lips.

Dr. P scoffed, in more disbelief than Vicky. "I've never seen anything like this—never studied anything like this. I wish I could ask my colleagues about it—"

"If you tell anyone about this, you will go to federal prison," Agent Morgan barked.

"No, no, I know. I didn't ask anyone but, excuse my language, but you only see shit like this in horror movies and fantasy books. I can't make sense of it."

Ignoring Dr. P's sentiment, Agent Morgan said, "Let's go and get the paperwork done. Once we remove her, we'll scour this room and any other room she's been in—"

"What? We cleaned the other room already—there's a patient in there!"

"Move them. We need that room. I hope there isn't a prob-lem." Agent Morgan's tone sounded threatening. When Dr. P didn't respond, Agent Morgan said, "You've done a great job, Polson, and the FBI thanks you for watching over her, but we'll take it from here."

Dr. Polson hesitated. "I–I don't think she should leave… She's not *well.*"

Ah, Vicky thought. *That old college try that Dr. P said he'd put forth.* She imagined that Dr. P was as scared as she was; breaking the law for someone that you barely knew was never ideal. So, it didn't surprise her when Dr. P proposed a simple solution: asking the government if Vicky could stay in the hospital longer. She had her doubts when he pitched it over the phone, and she doubted that it would work now.

"It's like her disease makes her *not human*," Dr. P went on, his words making her heart shudder. "We ran her blood, and her numbers make no sense. We can't detect DNA, and her potassium levels are almost nonexistent." He swallowed so hard that Vicky heard his throat click. "Her iron levels are below anything that I have ever seen—there isn't enough to get a red blood cell count. Her white blood cell count is tenfold higher than any patient with an auto-immune disease. She–she should be dead." He paused, probably remembering that his rant was news to Vicky. He hadn't said any-thing about it over the phone. Although she wanted to grit her teeth at the unwanted and seemingly embarrassing surprise, she remained still. "Her body should have rejected her heartbeat long before it rejected food," Dr. P said near a whisper.

"Which is why we told you *not* to run blood tests," Agent Morgan hissed.

"I already had some samples sent down to the lab before I met you yesterday."

"And you didn't mention anything then…"

As if to change the subject, Dr. P said, "What am I supposed to tell her family after you take her away?"

"Tell them that she died and that you had to burn her body to stop the virus from spreading."

"What?" Dr. P's question was riddled with disdain, and Vicky felt herself flinch at the brash explanation. *He can't be serious*, she thought as she fought to hold back tears. *I don't wanna die…* she declared to herself. Her heart raced. *I—* The words dissolved in the sounds around her: the men's breathing and the monitors' beeping. The HVAC's humming and the PA system's muffled demands that were meant for the rest of the hospital to hear. Not Vicky. She was stuck listening to the plans that would lead to her doom. "This isn't a movie, Agent—"

"That's a good point," Agent Morgan said. Then he sucked in a quick breath. "*Or* you can say that her body was turned over to the CDC after she died from the rare disease caused by whatever virus you told them about." He sounded so sure of himself. Vicky knew her family, and she knew that they would not sleep until they found her. Government facility or no.

"That's ridiculous," Dr. P challenged. "If this were my—"

"It isn't, and if it were, I'd tell you the same thing. It is *too late* for her. She is no longer a living patient who requires a doctor or a hospital or blood tests. She is dangerous to society for reasons that you will never comprehend. You're lucky that I haven't shot her in the head yet."

"Why don't you?" Dr. P asked, as if willing Vicky to get up and attack him and the agent.

Don't taunt him, asshole, she thought, secretly hoping that his affront was part of the plan. She hoped Dr. P was bluffing, because if he was, she'd give him permission to drop the doctor job and become a professional poker player.

The men stood in silence for what felt like a decade.

"Because..." Agent Morgan finally said, "...we can learn more about her if the brain remains intact. Relax, Polson, you don't have to do the hard work of putting her down. All I need you to do is sign her over to us, and we will provide you with a script that will tell you exactly what to say."

Bullshit, Vicky thought. Why the subtle change of heart? One minute, the man tells Dr. P to lie about her death; next, he's telling Dr. P that the FBI will give him a script. *What the hell is this man?* she thought. He was nothing like the agents on the *X-Files*. They seemed nice and helpful. This one seemed sneaky and malevolent.

As if sensing the same thing, Dr. P moved the exam along. "Would you like to see her eyes?"

Vicky felt the doctor's gloved fingers on her eyelids, as he promised. His gloves seemed to adjust to her body temperature. It was strange, because Vicky always remembered every doctor's exam being led by cold hands.

She heard the agent step back; the clicks of his dress shoes were so quick that she thought he leapt away to catch something that was falling to the floor. "No," he said. "I don't want her to see me."

Dr. P scoffed. "She's sleeping."

"They don't sleep."

"Look." Dr. P must have been motioning at the monitor, or at least that's what Vicky imagined him doing. "She's clearly sleeping."

"She isn't human, Polson," Agent Morgan said. "Her heart rate is slower than a sleeping person's, and when I touch her skin—" Vicky felt hands on her skin again. This time, they gripped her arm tight. She wanted to flinch, but she held back and allowed the man to make his point. "It warms. Look," he said, probably also motioning for the monitor. "Her body temperature spikes to match mine. She is awake because they never sleep. They fall into a restless meditative state during the day."

"How do you know all of this? Have you seen this before?" Dr. P asked as if he were one step away from asking Agent Morgan on a beer date so that he could pick his brain.

A pause.

"No," Agent Morgan said, clearly lying. "Is there anything else that you observed about her? Like here. Can you remove the gauze?"

She felt Dr. P remove the gauze from her left arm.

"Hm," Agent Morgan said. "IV incident?"

"Yes, her veins swelled and pushed the liquid out. Then she healed in a matter of days. The open wounds turned into dim scars."

"And?" Agent Morgan said. Vicky guessed he was pointing at something else on her body.

She felt the surgical tape pull her skin as Dr. P removed her neck dressing.

"Ah," Agent Morgan said.

"Yeah. The lacerations also healed. Two parallel cuts that stop right here and…" The doctor didn't finish his thought.

"Hm," the agent said. She heard a camera snapping photos. "Cover it back up, please."

Dr. P did as he was told, then asked, "So?"

"We're going to go to your office, you will sign some paper-work, and we will take her off your hands."

"Should I shut the hospital down? Is she really contagious?" Vicky understood Dr. P's panic; anyone would. But if she was con-tagious, they would have shut the place down already. There would be more urgency in Agent Morgan's voice. But he was calm, speaking steadily.

"Has she bitten anyone?" Agent Morgan asked.

"Excuse me?"

"Has she bitten anyone?" Agent Morgan asked again.

"N–No."

"Before that? Are you absolutely sure that she didn't have fangs when she first came to the hospital that night?"

"Yeah. Her canines elongated and sharpened a few days ago. We had to give her a sedative—we thought she was having a seizure because she was writhing in pain as they were coming in."

Vicky didn't remember that. She only remembered waking up with sore gums and that uncomfortable feeling of her teeth protruding when she thought about blood. *Not now*, she warned.

"Good. Then the definitive answer to your question about an outbreak is no—the hospital has nothing to worry about."

Vicky noticed that Dr. P didn't mention the incident with the nurse. *Ugh*, she thought. It was hard to imagine herself trying to take a chunk out of a man's arm, let alone a man who tried to help her. Still, she wondered why Dr. P hadn't mentioned it. Maybe he really was trying to protect her.

"So why the CDC? Why not take her to a hospital that specializes in rare diseases? Why take her away from her family and friends? From her life?"

"Don't worry yourself with that. Just know that she won't harm herself or anyone else."

"That's not—"

"Let's go. I need you to sign some paperwork and we'll transfer her over."

"Who is this 'we' that you keep referring to? Other doctors? Scientists?" Dr. P asked sternly, thoroughly flustered. He was definitely the type of person who hated to be left in the dark. Vicky wondered if he had taken any time to watch TV, because he would have learned that the government keeps their secrets close, and that there is a department within a department for everything under the sun. *Including monster hunters,* she thought.

"Again," Agent Morgan said, "something that you don't have to worry about."

CHAPTER 17

Flight

Once Dr. P ushered Agent Morgan out of the room, Vicky sprang into action. She removed the probes and patches from her chest and peered at the monitor. The screen was black. Dr. P flipped the switch right before he'd left the room, just as they'd planned.

Vicky left the bed, and, on her toes, she sprinted to the door and peered out the window. She watched the men leave her field of vision as they headed up the hallway. She could barely make out the white coats that they were wearing. No black and white suit in sight. She looked at the doorknob and turned it. Dr. P had locked it from the outside.

Good, she thought. Everything was going according to plan.

Vicky went back to the bed, looked underneath, and found the familiar plastic hospital bag that had her jewelry and phone inside. There was a black backpack next to it. She picked it up and opened it, knowing what she'd find inside: a set of baby-blue scrubs and a white coat. There was also a surgical cap with red and white hearts on it, a blue surgical mask, and a pair of nonslip rubber slide-on shoes. Everything looked clean and new, creased and wrinkle-free. There was also a red spiral notebook. She opened it and found a note from Dr. P. With no time to read it, she put the notebook back into the bag, took off the hospital gown, and slid on the surgeon's uniform. She cursed when her narrow feet slid around in the big shoes; her thick hospital socks didn't provide a snug fit. What if she had to run?

Dismayed, Vicky picked up the weighted plastic bag, then paused and looked at it. It was heavier than it had been the other night. She looked inside. Her jewelry was there; the gold ring and necklace glinted in the overhead lights. Her phone was there, the screen blacker than the abyss. There was also a new charger and a block phone wrapped in their original boxes. She accepted the gift with a silent appreciation. At the bottom of the bag was an unfamiliar black hoodie, sweatpants, and a pair of off-brand tennis shoes. Dr. P hadn't mentioned those, but she also didn't take the time to read the letter as she was instructed to do. She shoved the loaded plastic bag into the backpack and pulled the straps over her shoulders.

Her heart dropped when she heard a metallic *click,* and the door opened. But her fluttering gut eased when she found Nurse Cammy standing in the doorway. Her hair was stuffed in a hairnet; it looked like a lop-sided cloud on her head. Cammy's shoes were covered with plastic booties, her scrubs hid underneath a white coat. She also wore an N95 mask, hiding her expression. Cammy tilted her chin up and then darted off, a gesture meaning *Follow me.*

Vicky went for the door and entered the hallway. The brightness of the corridor matched that of the room, and the air cleansed her senses, smelling of rubbing alcohol, making her want to hide her nose from sanitization. She itched to put a hand over her face but stopped when she saw the light blue mask playing at the bottom of her periphery. Her heart reeled and a heavy heat wore on her back as she fought to keep up with Nurse Cammy's brisk pace. The damned shoes weren't helping; they slid off the backs of her feet, threatening to trip her in her haste.

Vicky gained on Cammy, who was slowing down and looking to her left.

She shouted, "I'll be right back, Monica! Dr. P needs me in the ICU for a few."

"Okay," Monica shouted. "I know I have some down here somewhere," she said. "I'm sure I'll find it by the time you get back."

Cammy sped up and waved Vicky along, as if telling her to hurry. They raced by a vacant nurses' station. The room just off the nurses' station was packed with racks of supplies. The person inside, also dressed in a white coat, had her back to them as she searched around for something.

Vicky quickened her steps, finally catching up to Cammy as she made a quick right and entered a room. The white room was small and didn't have any windows. The silver shelves along one wall were stocked with clean white coats and white hairnets, booties, and surgical masks. There was a door adjacent to the one that they used to enter the room, and the room hummed as air circulated. The space reminded Vicky of decontamination rooms that she'd seen in sci-fi movies.

Cammy leaned against the wall, took off her booties, mask, and hairnet, and shoved them into the silver garbage can next to the door. Only then did Vicky realize that she didn't have any booties herself.

When Cammy was back in her normal scrubs, she said, "Come on," then exited the room. The hallway didn't smell like alcohol anymore, it reeked of lemon floor cleaner, much like the one Mom used to deep clean the house at the start of every season. The elevator banks were to the left, and a stairwell was on the right. Vicky followed Cammy into the stairwell where they stopped on the landing, a big black *6* plastered on the wall next to the door.

"Take this stairwell all the way down to the first floor," Cammy said, her low voice bouncing off the walls, surrounding them in her commands. "Do not go out of the emergency exit; the alarm will go off. When you leave the stairwell on the first floor, you'll be facing the pharmacy. Turn right and go through the glass doors. Do not go through the second set of doors. Go to the left, and you'll see the door that leads outside. If you keep your head down and keep moving, you should get out just fine. But be careful; there are Feds everywhere. Once you get outside, go over to the McDonald's on the other side of the professional building. You know where that is?"

Vicky nodded, knowing that there were only three McDonald's in Miller, and the one by the hospital was farthest away from campus.

"Good. Go in the bathroom, change into the black outfit, and follow the instructions in the notebook. Okay? I'll see you later— don't get caught," she said pointedly. "Come on."

As they raced down the steps, their footfalls deafened Vicky to any surprises, but Cammy seemed to jog down the steps with confidence, so Vicky did too, keeping the pace and marking the big black numbers on the walls.

Once they reached the fourth floor, Cammy exited, and Vicky continued. Third floor, second floor…

She froze when a door from the first floor flew open, and a chattering man entered.

"…nurse went to check, and she wasn't there," he said.

A staticky voice replied, "I'm taking the elevator up. Keep your eyes open. See you on the sixth floor."

"Copy that," he said, before he proceeded to run up the steps, headed straight for her.

Vicky pivoted and went onto the second floor.

The scene on the second floor was far more animated than that of the sixth floor. It was teaming with nurses and doctors, patients of all ages in different states of hurt. The smell of blood and vomit was pungent in the air, pushing Vicky's mouth to water and her stomach to turn all at once. She headed up the hallway, ignoring the dinging sounds coming from the elevator bank to her right. She moved with the urgency of a doctor heading into an emergency surgery. She passed by rushing nurses and chatty patients as she frantically searched for an alternative route.

There has to be another way… she thought. She looked up, hoping that the red exit signs were leading her to another stairwell.

As she approached an adjacent hallway, she heard an authoritative tone cut through the urgent chatter of the hospital staff and patients. "We're looking around now. She can't be far."

She heard him, but didn't see him. She dipped into a room on the left, attempting to use it as cover should the man go by within the next few minutes. A little boy, maybe about ten years old, was sitting up on a hospital bed. He held a blood-soaked rag to his lips and peered at Vicky with red-rimmed eyes. His eyelids sank as he struggled to stare and not blink. She breathed in rich, sweet, fresh blood as it oozed onto the rag. Her heart leapt as her fangs slid from her gums, beckoning her to ease her hunger by indulging. She wanted to snatch the bloody rag and lick it. She groaned and squeezed her eyes closed, willing her teeth and the annoying cravings to crawl back into the bloody puddles of her mind.

"I'm heading up now," she heard the man say as he jogged past, his black sport coat flailing behind him as he moved toward the elevators. He wasn't hospital staff dressed like that…he was there for Vicky.

Vicky stuck her head out into the hallway and watched him go left at the end of the corridor, disappearing.

She looked over her shoulder and said, "I hope you feel better soon."

"Huh?" the little boy asked, his voice gritty and tired.

But she didn't reply. Vicky left the room and followed the blaring exit signs as they directed her to turn right at the end of the hallway. Even though she left the business of that corridor behind her, bile and blood were entangled in her sinuses. She put the back of her hand over her mask and stopped when she came to the end of the new hallway. She peered right and saw part of the elevator bank; the doors of Elevator E were closing. Then she looked left and saw the stairwell. She headed for the door to the steps but paused when she caught a glimpse of someone racing past the narrow window.

Vicky backpedaled, opting for the double doors on her right. She shoved them in, and found a long hallway, drenched in sun. The glassy bridge extended, linking the two towers that made up the bulk of the hospital. It was vacant, empty of staff and patients. She figured that the opposite tower was quieter compared to the bustle of the emergency department that she had just left. Still, she was nervous, unaware of what was waiting. She wasn't sure how it would feel on her skin, but she remembered UV allergy being part of the long list of symptoms that Dr. P had reported to her. She remembered the curtains being drawn when she woke up at night. How bad could it really be?

Bad, if he classified it as an allergy, just like he called the IV incident an allergy. An invisible stinging sensation climbed up her arm. She cringed. There was no time to gauge what the sun-bleached skywalk might do, so she did what she always did when she wanted to get things done and over with.

Vicky sucked in a deep breath and ran. The sun nipped and tugged at her skin, burrowing its way through her thin scrubs. She growled, watching the double doors at the end of the bridge as they drew close. The cars below bounced bright blemishes around, which stung her cheeks and hands and forced the reflected sunrays to seep into her clothes and eat her skin. She buried her hands into the pockets of the coat, still feeling small pinches and large pangs as they crept up her fingers. Vicky didn't think to grab gloves while she and Cammy stood in the clean room, but she wished she had.

Once she made it to the other side, she slammed her aching hands into the bar, forcing her way in, and keeping the burning sun demon out. She kept going, heading for another double door and allowed herself in.

The tower wasn't as busy as the emergency room. In fact, it smelled more like sweet perfume, stale sweat, and a cacophony of body washes spanning from Irish Spring to Old Spice. It smelled like people who weren't in dire need of medical attention. She read the sign hanging from the ceiling: *Cardiology* with an arrow pointing to the left, *Neurology* with an arrow pointing upward, *Pulmonology* with an arrow pointing to the right, and *Elevator Bank* with an arrow pointing to the right. Vicky went right and headed toward the stairwell which was undoubtedly next to the elevators.

***

When Vicky stepped outside, she regretted it. Her body flushed, taking in the subtle temperature spike in the hot September sun before she felt nothing at all. The covered valet entrance did nothing to protect her from the sun. Her exposed skin prickled and stung, and for a second, she thought it was sizzling. Head down, she rushed through the steady movement of drop-offs and pickups as the valet pulled cars in and drove some off. Once she made it to the parking lot, she jogged, watching the single-story professional building grow in the distance; it could have been miles away. She crisscrossed the parking lot, running by empty cars, and slowing to correct her sliding feet. She scrunched her nose at the smell of fried food and car exhaust.

There was a sign at the narrow road near the professional building that directed hospital traffic to the main road or through the hospital campus. Vicky knew the road at the stop light. It was the only main road in Miller that led to a low-key rural area that she and Teresa took often. Vicky continued as her cheeks cramped and twitched. She pulled her mask up, further exposing her neck to the sun. She ran faster, burning as she went straight for the single-floor brick building, which also had a full parking lot. The sign at the entrance to the parking lot listed the departments: *Professional Services: Ophthalmology, Orthopedics and Gerontology, Behavioral Sciences, Otolaryngology,* and *Sports Medicine.*

On the opposite side of the building, Vicky veered into the McDonald's parking lot, suddenly feeling ridiculous in her doctor's garb. She walked through the gap in the drive-through line which wrapped around the busy restaurant and ended at the entrance from the road. Upon entering, she relaxed. The customers were predominantly hospital staff based on their scrub bottoms and rubber shoes. They were either waiting in line or sitting at the many tables. Vicky slowed her pace as she headed into the bathroom.

She hung the backpack on the hook behind the stall door and softly touched her cheeks and winced at the pangs that shot through her face. She looked at her hands. Small boils rode up the length of her fingers, and her knuckles looked seared. She pulled her phone from her bag and used the black screen as a mirror. The same burns persisted on either side of her eyes and cheeks. Her skin felt tight on her face and hands, hindering movement.

She huffed as she switched outfits. She let out a gratifying hum once she slid the hoodie and sweatpants on; they were thicker and may do the trick against the sun. The pant legs were a bit long, but not too long to trip on as she ran. And the tennis shoes were a perfect fit so long as she kept on the hospital socks. She pulled the hoodie over her head and frowned: it wasn't enough to protect her face. She glared at the open bag where she'd packed the scrubs and coat. Then she dug out the white lab coat, put it over her head, and wrapped the arms around her mouth and cheeks. She touched her face, noting exposed skin, and decided that it would have to do. She looked over-dressed for the weather, but if anyone asked, which they wouldn't—people were pretty good at minding their own business—she'd ignore them.

Vicky pulled out the notebook and read the note.

Victoria,

Please meet me at this address. I—

Vicky shook her head and closed the notebook. Dr. P may have saved her life, but he was no closer to fixing her. And if a doctor as smart as Dr. P could not figure out how to fix Vicky, then no one could. The night before, Dr. P had asked Vicky for more time. More time to observe her. More time to try out new things. More time to not know how to help her. She didn't want to grant any more time to strangers. In fact, Vicky needed time to herself. She had a better shot at figuring things out. She did see the monster. She knew what the monster looked like and what it had done. Vicky was aware of her cravings. Not Dr. P or Agent Morgan or Nurse Cammy—she hadn't told them about blood.

Vicky needed space to think, to fix things. Then, and only then, would she call her parents and tell them that she was all right. That she only had the flu and… She stopped and sighed. They couldn't see her as she was…a monster.

She needed a few days with someone who could help her. Someone who had the space and the will to keep her secrets. Someone who had a lot of land, so much so that she and Teresa had gotten lost a couple times when they walked to the 7-Eleven on high nights.

Vicky stuffed the notebook back into the backpack and went for a run.

PART 3

Gone Mad

Worry

Randel was silent on the phone, which Trish had pinned to one ear as she walked Darwin in circles, his head resting on her opposite shoulder. She stopped at the office window and glared at the empty driveway. The police had already towed the Jeep away. She hoped their search would remain limited to the exterior. Though she'd cleaned thoroughly—bleach, vinegar, the works—DNA had a way of persisting. She shook her head, choosing not to worry about that now. Her husband, who hadn't spoken since she'd explained what happened, needed her attention. Randel responded to her story with heavy breathing. Was he furious or worried? Both emotions looked the same on him.

"Are you in the office?" she finally asked.

"I was," he said. "I'm in my room now, looking for the next flight back."

Trish sighed and shifted Darwin over to her other hip and moved the phone to the opposite ear. "No— Hun, you don't have to come back. I know how important this project is to you, and I don't think this is something to worry about."

Silence.

"Randel?"

"I'm here, and I'm coming home tonight, Trish. You— How could you say that there is nothing to worry about? Do you hear yourself? Someone smeared animal carcasses all over the Jeep! And we don't know who it is or what they want. I—"

"Randel, it was just some kids fuc—" She looked at Darwin, who could start picking up foul language at any point. Curse words were so fun to say, but their invisible power tainted the room— "…kids…"

She shook her head and set Darwin on the floor. He pushed himself up on his knees and crawled over to his playpen. He pointed at the toy dog that he liked throwing around, aiming at the vases and picture frames every time. Trish pulled out his child-sized toy train instead.

Randel sighed. "That's not the way Mrs. Pepper described it. And the local news over there made it seem bigger than just a few kids messing around—the police are launching an entire investigation, for Christ's sake! They've never dealt with anything like this."

Fucking Pepper, Trish thought as she felt her face flush. Randel caught Trish in a half-truth and skimmed over it. Trish mentioned that the police took the car to ensure that the blood was indeed from an animal. She also mentioned that the incident had happened before on the other side of the neighborhood—they were going to get the kids who'd done it. But no. Randel knew it was all a lie—the roving band of carcass-smearing kids was a myth. The news vans didn't make matters any better. They pulled up a few minutes after Detective Woodward took Trish's statements. The camera loved Mrs. Pepper's retelling as she so convincingly played the disgruntled and terrified neighbor.

Trish should have known Randel didn't buy the story because of his sheer silence.

When Trish said nothing, he went on. "I'm surprised Mrs. Pepper didn't have her security system hooked up or didn't see anything—the woman lives in between her damn blinds."

Trish snickered to herself. *Nothing a lighter and a pair of pliers couldn't handle.*

"God, what the hell is going on around there, Trish? Why would someone do that to your car? It's senseless," Randel said. "I thought our neighborhood was safe. I thought…" He paused. "And you rarely go out. Do you even talk to the neighbors? No one's upset with you, are they? They shouldn't be—Is Pita upset with you?"

"No," she said. Pita was Trish's best friend, and none of the neighbors got close enough to say anything more than a *hi* or *hello*. But there were two people who were out to destroy Trish, and neither Randel nor the neighbors had a clue about them. She envisioned Victoria or Steve wrapping fingers—hers bony, his thick—around a struggling raccoon's neck. The bones crackling before snapping. "And if Pita were upset with me," Trish went on, "she wouldn't do anything like that."

Silence. Then Randel let out one of his exasperated sighs, filling the receiver with his grievance. His ferocity poured through the phone, his lukewarm patience running out. Trish wondered if she should tear open an old wound just to throw the argument onto something else for both of their sakes because a worried or suspicious human could quickly turn into a sneaky, meddling human. She loved Darwin too much to consider disappearing his father and she loved Randel too much for him to suffer the same fate as the husbands before him.

"Is there something you want to say?" Trish asked, deciding to rip the bandage off the reoccurring gash of an argument.

"Yeah. I have to say, I don't like getting calls from the neighbors before I get a call from you! Pepper was beside herself. And then I called you eight times, and you didn't bother answering!"

Trish narrowed her eyes. "I didn't say anything to you about it because I didn't think it was a big deal." *Take the bait,* she thought, beckoning him to be more upset about her communication issues than the substance of what Pepper had said.

"Trish, what do you think the neighbors are saying?"

"Who cares about what they say?" She bared her teeth, knowing that they were saying plenty.

"Pretend you don't care all you want, but I don't want people thinking terrible things about us, and I also don't want them to think that we're not on the same page. You know, it *killed* me to pretend that I knew what Pepper was yammering on about when she called. I was so embarrassed! I can't believe that—"

"Randel, it doesn't matter. Alright? It's not a big deal. People probably already forgot all about it. And you know how Mrs. Pepper gets. She has nothing else going on. Her own damn husband couldn't stand being around her," she said matter-of-factly, wishing she too could escape to Europe and avoid Steve, Victoria, and Randel all together. But Darwin would probably hate her for that.

A sarcastic chuckle. "Oh yeah, sure. People totally forgot that one of their neighbors' Jeeps was covered in blood and smudged up guts."

"It's animal blood," she said. "There was fur on the doors."

"It doesn't matter! Either way, it was an extremely targeted attack! The police do not have *anything* like that on record. People are talking, and that makes me uneasy. What do they think of us?"

She threw her head back, hating that he was right. For the first time in a long time, it was hard to *not* care about what they might say. Invisible conversations plagued Trish's mind:

It was human blood. I just know it, the new neighbors across the street might say.

Mrs. Weston is always so secretive, and her husband is never home. There's no telling what that lady does when he isn't around and no one is watching, Mrs. Pepper would gossip.

Trish ran a hand through her silky hair. It didn't help that Randel was a neighborhood friend. Whenever he was in town for long stints of time, he played grill master at block parties and helped people cut their yards and plow snow. He even salted Pepper's driveway after icy nights. Darwin's teacher even preferred Randel over Trish.

I wouldn't be surprised if she was a serial killer. So quiet and to herself, the real estate agent down the street might say.

Someone wanted revenge. The kids in this neighborhood would never do that, the cops would declare.

Trish swallowed the lump forming in her throat. The spectacle wasn't what everyone assumed. It wasn't human blood, and the mob wasn't sending a seemingly well-to-do middle-class family a gory message. She and Randel didn't have black-market loans to settle. They weren't the target of some sick-ass neighborhood kids. No. It was all animal blood, placed there by a bitter bitch or an insane drug dealer. Nothing more. Trish would handle it the same way she made all her problems disappear. No…big…deal. But she could not tell anyone that. Especially Randel.

When she didn't say anything, he went on. "Trish, I–I don't— Should I stop travelling?"

"What?" she said, heart throbbing. "No. No, you have to. Don't you?"

"I mean, yeah, but I can move over to billing or logistics. That way, I can stay close to home and help you out. I guess I've been missing a lot with that damned commute and all the pop-up visits. Mom mentioned that I should find a way to work from home just to spend more time with you and Darwin, and I told her that I would think about it." His voice was full of guilt.

"Of course," she said. Mrs. Weston always butted in at the worst times, which was oddly just as rare as she and Mr. Weston's visits. She, a short, deeply tanned woman with flowing salt and pepper hair, and he, a big balding man with blotchy skin, would sit on the couch and fling passive aggressive comments the entire visit. Trish could hear the nasally woman's many complaints:

Oh, Randel, Darwin should be in day care with all the other kids.

Oh, Randel, you should take your family to church more.

Oh, Randel, isn't it Trish's job to make sure you have a hot meal every night? It isn't fair that you work all day and then have to come home and cook.

Oh—

Trish winced, banishing the woman's nagging. Trish didn't need Randel blaming himself for travelling or driving to and from the office. He never liked working from home. He was the charismatic one that made her look normal. Besides, life would become a disaster if he switched to working from home. How would she dispose of clothes and bloody rags? Evidence? He would only get in the way.

"You worked too hard to be where you are," she said. "Nothing as stupid as this should slow you down. I can take care of the"— she almost said problem—"house. I'll keep communicating with the police to help them catch the assholes."

"You don't even know. After this, I can't trust that you guys are okay at home alone. You need me there to—"

"I don't need you here to protect us!" she snarled. *I'm stronger than you and any fucking human on this planet,* she thought, but said, "If you want to ruin your career over something this stupid and small, go ahead."

"Hm, okay…answer me this, would you have told me about this at all if Mrs. Pepper hadn't called me? And I mean like *ever*. Even if it wasn't until I got home and noticed that the Jeep was missing. Or would you have lied? Be honest."

"What?" She gasped. "Of course I would have. I was going to call you when everything died down. If you just gave me a minute!"

His discouraging chuckle shot a chill up her spine. "Give you a minute? I don't think you would have called me, Trish. I don't think you tell me *a lot* of things."

"What are you talking about?" Trish said, holding her tongue. "I tell you everything."

"Yeah? You didn't tell me that you stayed out until 3 in the morning last night. Maggie told me when I called to make sure she got home alright. And to my surprise, she was still at our house. She texted me when she finally got home at 3 am!" he growled, his tone laced in simmering rage.

"I called you," Trish protested.

"Yeah, late as hell. You could've texted me *something*."

"Randel—"

"You're so nonchalant," he said, his words wrapped in disgust and his annoyance so present that he could have been sitting next to her. "You better hope it's not *human* blood," he started. "And, alright, let's say that it's animal blood. I'm sure it's your fault that they sought you out. They sought *us* out. So, tell me, who did you piss off?"

"Why do you keep saying that?" Trish asked. "What have I ever done—"

"Darwin's teacher doesn't like to call you, you turn your nose up at the neighbors, and even Maggie—"

"She's a self-entitled brat who's always getting high—"

"You alienate everyone, Trish. I'm surprised Pita even talks to you."

Trish furrowed her brow. "Pita is my friend, and I don't care about what people think about me and what I do, unlike you," she said. "Everything is all about being friends with *this* person and shaking hands with *that* person. Maybe I don't care about dealing with people. I'm not like you!" Frowning, she pulled her phone from her face, rubbed the smudgy screen against her pant leg, and put it on speaker. She set the phone on the leather loveseat arm. She sat down and glared at the dark screen.

He tsked, filling the office with angst. "Yeah, well, good luck with that. So, back to my original question, who's out to get you?"

Cheeks burning, Trish shouted, "What if someone is out to get you? Maybe they only saw my car out in the driveway and used it to send *you* a message."

"Don't try to make this about me. It's you. You don't know how to get along with people."

"There's no one out to get me—to get us!"

"Okay, well, I don't trust what you're telling me so, I'm getting a security system installed within the next couple days since you don't *need* me there and since you are subtly so worried about my career."

What? she screamed in her head as she picked up the phone and squeezed it, trying not to break it. "I guess, sure," she spat through gritting teeth.

"Look, you might not care about Darwin or your own safety, but I do."

"I said go ahead, Randel," she said, her gut clenching at all the torment and lies she'd have to cover up with Big Brother hanging in every corner of her house.

"And you're right, I shouldn't have to sacrifice all of my hard work and be rushed home from business because my house isn't protected while I'm gone," he said.

"*I* protect the house!"

"Uh huh. Sure Trish. I'm getting surveillance, and that's the end of it."

Whatever. Sounds like you made up your mind." She rolled her eyes. "Suddenly, you get the *final say*."

"Catch an Uber to the day care center. Be there at four." The line went dead.

CHAPTER 19

Feelings

The last thing Trish wanted was to be surveilled.

Trish texted Pita: *Can you take Darwin for the day tomorrow?*

Pita instantly texted back: *Yes!*

Then Pita followed up with: *Is everything alright? I saw what happened on the news. I called and you didn't pick up.*

Too busy watching cops poking around, Trish thought.

Pita shot off more texts: *Is someone after you? Do you need me there to keep you company? I know a good security company. They did my cousin's system and it's so sensitive that her cat can't even piss in the yard without triggering that damned thing.*

Ignoring the barrage of questions, Trish responded: *Thanks, I'll text you tomorrow. He should be ready around 1.*

Pita: *Okay.*

Ugh, Trish thought as she imagined Pita frowning, shut out by her mysterious friend. She only wanted to help, and Trish shot Pita down time and time again, opting to keep her feelings about almost anything to herself. They worked as friends because Trish didn't mind being Pita's diary, something that she could talk to and not feel judged. But as Trish read their text thread back, she realized that Pita had fallen into what Trish called the Rule of Two: *If two humans close to you notice a negative trait, change it.*

Trish scoffed. *Great*, she thought, berating herself for failing at something so basic, and annoyed by that subtle Déjà vu. Every husband and friend discovered her aloofness and took offense as if it were about them. She took a deep breath and picked up her phone.

She texted: *Yeah, some kids have been tagging cars in the neighborhood and the police are close to finding out who they are. I guess they left a clue in the yard or something. But I am alright. Randel is putting up cameras.*

Trish ended her message with a red heart emoji.

Pita replied: *Good to hear! I was so worried, but I figured you'd call me back and tell me when you were ready. Anyway, on this garbage Zoom lunch call with my brother's bride-to-be. She wants trout and fettuccine Alfredo on the menu for the reception. Not salmon and prime rib like I suggested. I mean, what planet is she from? Anyway, I'll give you a shout tomorrow. Love you!*

Trish replied: *Love you too.*

Darwin began crying as he sat on the floor near the office toy bin, having pulled all his toys out and scattered them on the floor. He rubbed his eyes, still groggy from the night before.

"You must be hungry," she said as she approached him. He reached up for her, and she carried him to his highchair.

"Are you excited about going to Pita's tomorrow?" she asked him as she opened the refrigerator and grabbed his bottle of whole milk. Then she pulled the box of Honey Grain Oh's from the top of the pantry. She set the milk down and placed a handful of cereal on his tabletop. He didn't move to grab anything. He only stared at the table. Trish cocked her head as she watched her son. His eyelids dragged and his lips remained parted.

"What's wrong, baby?" Trish asked. Darwin looked at her. Her chest clenched as she read the boy's eyes. They were dark like Randel's. They pouted, as if haunted by a memory. Then, slowly, his lips and eyes curled into a smile. He reached for his bottle with one hand, and waved the other playfully, snapping out of his stupor.

Trish rubbed his soft hair as he carried on. He set his bottle down and shoved cereal in his mouth. "Ready to go see your teacher today?"

No response.

Trish opened the refrigerator and grabbed the carton of blueberries. She poured them into a bowl and rinsed them. She pulled the chair out and sat next to her son, who moved on to blowing raspberries and moving his cereal around his personal table.

Trish ate a blueberry and felt her mouth water as she chewed and swallowed the juicy fibrous fruit. In her true form, she couldn't stomach the things. She couldn't stomach human food at all. But with the serum pumping fluid through her fingers and into her blood stream, she'd only eat berries and oatmeal, flaxseed, spinach and romaine-based salads, and small portions of turkey, anything to keep her urinary and digestive system purged of sulfur.

Finding a proper diet while wearing the ring wasn't easy. It wasn't like the serum came with a manual. It was Albert who showed her the way, explaining her diet around the time he put two and two together, right before declaring her an abomination.

Albert had also taught her the risks of a clingy man. A lot of women grew weary of a husband who worked out of town, especially the needy, insecure ones. Trish scoffed as she popped another berry in her mouth, thinking about many conversations she and Pita had as they sat at a window table at their favorite cafe on the lake. Its brown and gold rustic décor reminded Trish of the cabin that she'd grown up in.

"I don't see how you do it," Pita would sneak in between bites of some God-awful sweet chocolaty tart. "I mean, when do you guys have sex?" She'd wash her sweets down with a rich sugary caffeinated monstrosity, and wipe the whipped cream from her tanned face and cherry red lips.

Trish stared at her, annoyed at Pita's nosiness, and frustrated at the lie that Trish was forced to regurgitate life after life, place after place, and time after time: "It isn't so bad once you get used to it." Or, with a wry smile, she'd say, "We really enjoy our space, so it works out perfectly."

Trish had assumed lies would get easier over time, but instead they corroded her tongue. Being a wife felt unsustainable, and sometimes she wondered why she even bothered. But then rationality dragged her back to *her reality:* husbands made her appear normal

and offered the best alibis. They also fed into the illusion of togetherness, the strongest remedy for loneliness.

It was too bad that Albert had the displeasure of knowing Trish;
he had the potential to be one of the greatest scholars of all time.
Still, even though it was painful to see him go, he held a solid piece
of her heart, forever alive and standing out in her many histories as
Dr. Albert M. Harron, Trish's first husband.

CHAPTER 20

1924

Boston, 1924

"I knew you were following me, ya creepy bitch." Bobby Tyler Bush exclaimed, his ivory skin reddened with rage. His flannel jacket hung open, and his blue chambray button-up was undone at his neck. He stood at the bottom platform of the dank stairwell. Trish expected the apartment to be empty, or at the very least, one of the many gambling dens that Bobby frequented every night. His mysterious eyes darkened underneath the shade of his flat cap. "I saw you at Mona's and on the streetcar. You've been following me for weeks!"

"I—" lost in his eyes, mouth full of nectar and ready to bite, Trish watched him from the top of the stairwell. She pressed her hands against the sides of her house dress, the flattened ruffles playing between her fingers. Line 2 was always busy, carrying Bostonians from Cambridge to downtown every day. For the last three weeks, Bobby hadn't shared eye contact with her on their route from the Boston Commons to the North End. He hustled along the sidewalks anxiously bypassing people who clogged the busy streets of a city that only knew bustle. Trish didn't see their meeting ending in a brick apartment off Market Street, in the heart of the underground gambling and drinking scene.

"Did Ryan send you?" Bobby quipped.

"No." She cleared her throat, venom drowning her tongue, fangs ready to feast. "I don't know a Ryan."

"Liar!" His northeastern accent came out so deep, the word came out as "ly-ah." "I'm not paying that rat fucker a dime! You hear me!" His fearful words slurred as he took a step up, inching closer.

"I don't know who Ryan is," Trish assured, her words soothing against the excited backdrop of the night. Cars beeped at the people clogging the street. Jazz blurted from Mona's Speakeasy. Sweet cigar smoke wafted from Jacob's Lounge, and loud chatter echoed from the line that stretched for a block out front of the Olympus Theater. Then there was her meal—radical and aware, glaring up at her. She stepped down, prepared to drop her purse, rush him and sink her fangs into his throbbing jugular. She'd feast the way she had day-dreamed while watching him cross the narrow streets.

"Then why are you following me?" Bobby said.

"Because you—"

Bobby pulled his jacket back and reached for the pistol holstered by his high-waisted trousers. He aimed, and a white spark ignited the air around the tip of the barrel, ripping into her chest.

Pain shredded her ribs, knocking her off her feet. She tumbled, body smacking each step as she rolled to the bottom floor, landing at Bobby's feet.

Good shot, she thought as his face faded in and out of her cloudy vision until he disappeared, the door slamming behind him.

Blood surged up her throat as she coughed.

Ryan? Who's Ryan? She'd followed Bobby for a while, and there was never a Ryan. There were only backdoor gambling rooms, speakeasies, bars, the docks, and his studio apartment. *Work, gamble, sleep. The prey only…works…gambles…* Trish's thought wavered as a cramp split through her middle.

She laughed, then grunted as her heart slowed. She missed the gun…*but why wouldn't he have one…?* She choked, suffocating on the cascade of blood that left her chest, escaping the wound however it could. Her body refused to turn on her side to clear her air-way. So she lay on her back, staring at the dim ceiling. *Four floors,* she thought. *I was going to search four floors for him…* Her stomach grumbled and flipped. *But he found me first.*

She was sure her face was flushed, but there was no heat without the ring. She closed her eyes. No more hunting, no more blood, no more—

A quick wind washed over her body as the door slammed. Bobby was back to finish the job.

No, she thought. Bobby smelled like seawater and sweat. *But this person, this man, this—*

"Patricia!" he called out. Albert always called her Patricia, never Trish, because nicknames were rude to parents.

"Patricia." Albert crouched over her and put his hands on her chest.

"Ugh!" she shouted as pain plunged into her nerves.

Albert's face contorted. "No. No. No!" he cried. "What are you doing in here? What—"

He sobbed uncontrollably. The man who ate toast and scrambled eggs with his black morning blend before grabbing his suitcase and heading out into the Boston morning was breaking apart. "Stay with me, my love," he mumbled through tears. He shouted, "Why were you—Why?"

Albert dreamed of waterfalls and the deep green shades of ancient woods, of sharing tea with ocean creatures and people from distant cultures. But he always stopped himself from pursuing these dreams—planes crashed, ships sank, cars broke down on remote highways. Safety was his religion, adventure his forbidden fruit. He had no business falling in love with a woman full of secrets.

"Hel—" he stopped mid-shout. She knew why. He was looking at her parted lips. It hurt too much to press them closed. His signature perplexed scowl marked his face—the same expression he wore when an experiment failed, or results disagreed with his hypothesis.

"Uh." He put his bloody fist to his mouth.

"D–d–don't take me t–to—" She tried to speak, but the words stuck to her tongue, buried in blood. As the color left Albert's face, the *why* and *how* fell into place. He had been following her. She didn't understand how she missed his aftershave and his morning blend. Accepting her multi-level failure, Trish used her dwindling strength for a more meaningful message: "Ring. Ring. P–please." She lifted her weak arm and pointed to the purse, which sat on one of the steps. "G–get. P–put. I n–need–it."

***

Trish may have died, but when she awoke, she felt better. She was on the dining room table, a makeshift hospital bed. There were layers of comforters underneath her, and a pillow propping her head.

The sheer curtains fluttered with the breeze of a sunny day that didn't burn her skin, and her chest was painless, her heartbeat effortlessly. She lifted her hand, finding her wedding ring in place, and the serum doing its job.

Albert cleared his throat. He had been sitting in one of the dining seats.

"Albert," her voice docile and raspy As she basked in uncharted territory, willing herself to find some explanation, any explanation, to give her first husband, nothing came. She held his wet eyes in hers, and lifted a hand, beckoning him to hold it. His face had gone pale, not fair and confident as she'd grown to know.

He didn't move. "What–what are you?" he asked, shuddering over his usually well-picked words.

"I—" Trish went to speak, but her throat was dry, and her chest tightened, reminding her of recent trauma. Then her stomach growled, still empty. "What happened?" she asked, having remembered everything. From hunting, to being shot, she knew what had happened. But she wanted to hear Albert tell her.

"You were shot in the heart. As you laid there dying, I saw fangs…like a snake has fangs. Like a wild animal that uses their fangs to inject venom into its prey. You had fangs…you looked younger… you lost your color. You looked thin, decrepit, like you hadn't eaten in a while. You didn't look like you."

He sniffed and turned away, facing the window. "You looked like something out of a thriller novel. A monster. A mythological beast that storytellers conjured up to scare children into eating their

120

vegetables or something." He turned back to face her. "As you were dying, you asked for your ring after asking not to be taken *somewhere*. I put your ring on you and we brought you back here. No hospital would know what to do. I planned on turning you over if you *actually* died. But you didn't. You never did. You lived. You healed in a matter of minutes. Your heart spit that bullet out, and I watched it roll onto the floor. The fragments came out too, burrowing through your flesh, desperate to escape your inner workings. I sent Gil off to leave me to ponder this, to wonder about you. I looked you over as you slept like a sleeping queen in her crypt ready to rise again. You didn't wake, but you lived. You lived."

Eyes full of intrigue and disillusion, he walked over to her make-shift bed. "You are everything that I don't know about, and it terrifies me." Frantically, he shook his head. "I didn't know what to do. Be confused? Perplexed? Or cry? Cry over your death. The fact that you were gone. The fact that my young wife was dead, killed by a lover that she'd taken behind my back. But when I saw your fangs, there was a new question to consider: Should I cower in the corner at the unmasking of a monster? Oh, my love. You aren't what I thought you were. You are something greater than science could ever explain. A stain, an imperfection on humanity, and I'm aching to learn more. I *need* to know more." His eyes bulged. "Please. Please, can I?"

"Albert," Trish said, after clearing the dried blood from her throat. "I don't know what you thought you saw, but it's not—"

"Please, don't take this away from me. Please. Let me study. It's all I can do to keep this secret. To keep myself from going to the nearest church and washing myself, absolving myself for ever marrying something like you. For christening my eternal love to a demon forever before the eyes of my family, my students, my colleagues…" He wept, his wet breath stumbling over horrid cries. "Before the eyes of God!"

She wanted to be offended, but he was right. She wasn't a normal, pure-blooded human. She was a killer who'd lost count.

"Please? Please, let me figure you out. Learn your species. Let me help myself understand what and why!"

Trish sighed. If she were normal, she would be well past child-bearing age. She would be working Momma's farm and married to Josef. She'd still be in West Virginia, living the same life as many others had. But she wasn't normal. She fed on blood and stayed out of the sun if not for the serum pumping through her veins. She could stand to learn more about herself. And she was in the perfect place to make that happen.

CHAPTER 21

Zoom

Darwin squirmed and strained, desperate to escape the car seat. It was as if he knew that they were not in the Jeep, but in a Toyota, something that didn't belong to his parents. Trish didn't know whether to curse Victoria and Steve for vandalizing her car, or Ms. Carol, who insisted on having the ridiculous meeting. It was already turning out to be a time-suck. Trish should have been at home, planning. Not discussing Darwin's behavior, which was typical for a toddler of his age.

The classroom was bright, celebrating art and sloppy scribbled letters by one-year-olds. Toys lined the yellow wall, books lined the orange wall, and short desks the size of Darwin's toddler table took up half of the floor space. A colorful rug, speckled with every color of the rainbow and outlined with the alphabet, took up the other half.

There were pictures of babies and toddlers on the walls. Their names were scribbled over a neat etching of the actual letters. A few of them had dogs and cats. One stood in front of an aquarium and gawked at a great white shark. A few of them wore their Sunday's best, which included frilly dresses and mini three-piece suits. Some smiled at the camera, obeying whomever the photographer was, and others wore smiles that seemed genuine, as if they were saying, "Thank you for such a beautiful day." Then there was Darwin, who remained straight-faced. He was sitting in a sandbox, the sun blazing down on him as he gaped at Randel, who had caught him off guard, asking for a picture. Darwin seemed more annoyed that his father was interrupting him from using a red scooper to pick up and dump sand. Trish wondered why Randel submitted that photo to Ms. Carol when there were plenty to choose from. Especially the variety of pictures with Darwin smiling.

Darwin kicked his legs and groaned.

"You want out?" Trish asked.

He smiled and clasped his hands together.

"Can you say 'yes'?"

"Mamamama," he said instead, her smile reflecting in his dark eyes.

"Alright, alright," she said. She unbuckled him from his car seat, and he sprang into action, crawling for the toys. "Little booger," she said through a smile. He was demanding, always knowing what he wanted, a lot like Momma had been. Darwin picked up a small plastic tote and poured the blocks out, scattering them on the carpet.

Without warning, Ms. Carol entered the classroom and headed straight for him. She looked the same every time Trish saw her: light jeans and a plaid flannel shirt that billowed around her thin frame. Her red locks were tight and long as usual. She was carrying a silver laptop that she set on top of the toy chest and crouched.

"Hey, beautiful boy. We sure do miss you. Can I have a hug?" she asked.

Darwin obliged and laughed, and Trish felt herself die inside. She hated that her son loved someone who bitched about him so often. He was like Randel: a people person. A lover. He would probably grow up to be a salesman like his dad, or a doctor or teacher.

Ms. Carol stood and faced Trish. "Hello, Mrs. Weston. Sorry I'm a little late," she said as she picked up the laptop. "Had to go grab my laptop from the office. I prefer not to have it out once the kids wake up from their naps."

"That's totally fine," Trish said.

Ms. Carol headed for the area full of small desks. "Please," Ms. Carol said, motioning for Trish to have a seat.

Trish looked at Darwin, who had moved on to a stack of Magnetic Tiles. The colorful magnetic blocks clung to each other as he used them to make a small wall.

"He's fine. It's not only my classroom; it's his too," Ms. Carol said.

As Trish pondered for a short second on how this meeting was going to work with no adult-size desk in sight, the teacher approached a small table and pulled out the pint-sized chair. She sat in it and opened the laptop. She moved her finger around on the mousepad and then peered up at Trish.

Even though she felt her face fall, Trish sat across from Ms. Carol, thankful that her legs, albeit with thicker bone density and greater muscle mass, were unbothered by the obnoxiously short desk.

Ms. Carol went back to her computer and sweat formed on her brow. Her foot fidgeted as she typed, probably wishing Randel was there.

Did he have to bribe you to have this meeting? Trish thought as she crossed her arms.

"So, what is all this about?" Trish asked.

"Hang on," Ms. Carol said, the telltale noise of a Zoom call filling the room.

"Hi there," a familiar voice, much more chipper than it had been earlier that day.

"Hello, Mr. Weston," Ms. Carol said.

Trish scowled at the screen as Ms. Carol turned it at an angle to where they could both see Randel. He was handsome and clean shaven. His honeyed skin looked sun-kissed and his jaw looked strong. He had on a headset, meaning that it was a shared space. His background was blurred.

"How's it going?" Randel asked, his smile bright.

"Just fine. I was happy to hear that you could attend. It's really important that we all discuss Darwin's behavior and work as a team to find a remedy. The kids and I really miss having him here."

"We're happy to help any way we can," he said.

"Excellent."

They both looked at Trish. She gave a stiff nod and lifted a one-sided smile.

"Well," Ms. Carol began, her ivory face blanching. "A teaching assistant said Darwin was playing with Samantha, a child who he plays well with often. They were stacking the Magne-blocks together, making a tower. Once Darwin ran out of his blocks, he went to take some of the blocks from her pile. She told him no and he stood over her, staring down at her…"

Bullshit, Trish thought. Darwin stood on wobbly legs for all of one minute before he sat down and crawled to his destination. She could not imagine him standing over anyone.

"Then she said no again and…" Ms. Carol cleared her throat, "he pushed her down, pinned her shoulders to the floor, and bit her on the neck."

"Hm," Randel said. "And you've never seen that before?"

Trish felt the floor fall away as unease writhed through her. Not her child. She couldn't imagine him attacking anyone, let alone a child that was his friend.

"No. I haven't. And when the assistant pulled him off Samantha, he didn't fight. He only watched her cry while she held her neck. Now, he didn't draw blood, but he did leave a small bruise that had gone quickly. About ten minutes later, after she calmed down, he tried to give her a hug, but she ran from him and hid behind the teaching assistant."

"Wow," Randel said.

Trish bounced her knee without hitting the underside of the toddler table. "why didn't you tell me this when I picked him up?"

Ms. Carol sighed. "Because the teaching assistant did not tell me about it until that evening after all the kids left. She wasn't aware that we had to call all parents as soon as the incident occurred."

Trish rolled her eyes. *Incompetent—*

"Now, as soon as she told me, I called Samantha's parents, and I called Mr. Weston," Ms. Carol said.

"And not me…" Trish said.

"I'm sorry I didn't answer," Randel said.

"Now, we have been working on Darwin's behavior since the toy truck throwing incident, and I thought he was getting better. But then this happened, and for the safety of the other children, that behavior cannot be tolerated. I cannot allow him back without some sort of interventional methods."

She paused, then swallowed. "I was wondering if you were open to some more suggestions on how to help him with his anger problems."

"We are all ears," Randel said.

Trish said nothing, because if she did, she would scream. How does a one-year-old boy have anger problems?

"Now, Darwin is such a sweet kid. He is attentive to all of his little friends, and he's always very helpful when it's time to clean up the toys. He even calms the kids who cry when their parents leave them here in the mornings—he is very advanced for his age." She put her hand over her heart.

Randel lifted his brow. "Wow, that's–that's good to know."

"But—"

"Ah, right…but," Randel said.

"Yes, Mr. Weston. *But*, Darwin has been a little different the last few times he came in. I want to say it began a few weeks ago? He's quieter. Sometimes, he sits in the corner and watches, standoffish and lethargic. It's like I'm watching him devolve into a loner. I'm not sure what to make of it. And then, he bit Samantha."

"Ms. Carol, I'm sure this is all being blown out of proportion. Darwin's a great kid. He's just growing up, that's all," Randel said. "Maybe just a little moody."

"I understand why you might think that, but I assure you, Darwin may need help that I cannot provide. Maybe a psychologist?" She spoke with a level of confidence that made her words seem like the law of the land.

"He's a baby doing baby things," Trish snapped, proud to reiterate her stance. It was ridiculous for this woman to expect Darwin to change when he didn't know what *change* meant.

Ms. Carol sighed. "With all due respect, he is a growing child, a toddler. He is no longer a small baby. I am only reporting that I have observed his behavior getting worse."

"So what do you suggest we do then? Huh?" Trish could tell that she sounded combative. But she didn't care. "Put him on drugs? Is that it? You want us to commit a one-year-old?"

"Trish…" Randel said.

"I have a number to a child psychiatrist," Ms. Carol rattled off, her anxiety evident as she dropped all eye contact. "He's one of the best in the field. He can evaluate Darwin and suggest the best course of action."

Trish scoffed. "Are you serious? You want to send my baby to a doctor so they can give him 'sit down' pills? No, absolutely not!"

Randel huffed. "Calm down, Trish."

"You can't agree with this, Randel," Trish complained.

"I never said I did, I just— Please calm down. You're overreacting," he said.

Trish sighed and tucked her lower lip.

"Ms. Carol," Randel said. "We would hate to pull Darwin out of school because of behavioral issues. I mean, his teeth are growing in and he's—you know. He's growing. He's cranky. Do you know of any more books we can read? Or family programs we can get into?"

"Well, the books that I already told you about would suggest the same thing: professional help. I've never seen a child flip on a dime like Darwin has. I mean, there have been glimpses in the past, but he seems to be getting worse. And I have a class of thirty small children. I'm afraid that I cannot offer him the attention that he needs. If you don't do anything about his behavior, then I will have to expel him."

"You can't do that! You can't just kick him out of school," Trish said.

"I'm afraid I can. I *care* about all the children's safety, including Darwin's. And I'm afraid I don't have the resources that he needs."

"That's bullshit!"

"Trish! Leave. Now!" Randel said sharply, a look of deep seriousness on his face. Trish kept her eyes on the woman, imagining what satisfaction she'd feel while tearing that teacher's jugular clean from her neck. But she did none of that. She gathered her son, strapped him in his car seat.

"I'm sorry, Ms. Carol." Randel said. "Sometimes, my wife doesn't know how to mind herself. She forgets how to talk to people."

***

As Trish and Darwin stood in the doorway waiting on the Uber, her phone rang.

Randel sighed into the receiver.

"I know," she said. "I already know what you—"

"Was that necessary?" An echo bounced around him. He had gone to the bathroom for privacy. "Now we have to find him another day care, because I have a feeling that no matter what we do, she is not going to want to deal with us or our kid again."

A shaken sigh. *Dammit.*

"Trish, baby, I don't know what's going on with you."

"Our son is fine," she spat as she watched the Uber pull in. It was the same car they had taken over to the school, a blue Toyota Rav4. He was probably the only driver in town.

Randel chuckled.

"What?" she said as she walked up to the car.

"This is the shit!" he shouted. "You shut down as if you want to stay upset. As if you are hiding something from me! First, you stay out all night, then someone vandalizes your car. Now, you just verbally *abused* the teacher. You are falling apart. What aren't you telling me?"

Trish buckled Darwin into the back seat. He babbled and watched her. "Whatever," she said. "I was just annoyed that she wants some stranger to mess with our kid's head when he isn't doing anything wrong." She closed the door and headed around the back of the car to get in on her side. "He's just a baby doing baby—" She froze and frowned at the white car sitting in the parking lot. A familiar face watched her back.

"Trish," Randel said. "She's not saying that there's anything wrong with him, she's..."

Trish didn't hear anything after that. She watched the face, making it out. Placing it in a recent time. In a recent place. His red hair looked slick through the windshield. His gray eyes still evident with the distance between them. He waved a pale hand as the driver, a big burly man, started the engine.

"Trish," Randel said.

How long had Steve been in the parking lot?

"Trish?" Randel again.

How long had he been in town?

"Trish!"

Did he know where she lived?

The line went dead, and the white sedan pulled out of its spot and onto the street.

PART 4

Steve's

C H A P T E R   2 2

Crush

September 4, 2024

The run from the hospital to the dusty rural road was agony. The sweatpants, hoodie, and lab coat wrapped around Vicky's face provided no relief. She didn't sweat, but her cheeks stung, and her eyes burned as the unhinged sun dug its fiery claws into her raw flesh. She pressed the sides of her hoodie down, praying for the pain to cease, but quickly shoved her hands back into her pockets to save them from the searing heat.

She silently rejoiced at the sight of the two-story farmhouse sitting about 250 feet from the gravel road. Its steel-green roof served as a beacon against the flat expanse of farmland stretching for miles. A yellow tractor sat in front of the garage—or barn, Vicky was never sure which. Steve's inherited land lacked width, but it was oblong, stretching back for about a mile.

Vicky took off running again, pumping her arms and chanting: *Almost there, almost there.*

She banged on the door, shaking and jittery, her breath beating at the air.

"Who is it?" Steve asked, his baritone calm but curious.

"It's me," she shouted back.

"Oh shit! Is that my Vicky?" Steve asked as he opened the door, his pale face smiling hard and his ruby hair glistened in the killer sun.

His dimples dove deep into his cheeks, and he looked fit in his red tank and dark jeans. "I was wondering when you—"

"Can I please come in?" she blurted. Her exposed skin prickled as if someone were sticking needles in her hands and cheeks.

Steve frowned and his chest seemed to broaden as every bit of elation drained from his face. "Oh shit, yeah, come in." He put his big hands on her shoulders and gently guided her into the foyer. Vicky had never taken the time to study the area between the front door and the basement. The brick wall of the foyer was covered in picture frames. She didn't recognize the faces. She heard men's voices somewhere off to the right, but she only saw a brown sectional sofa and a wooden end table. From where she was standing, the house looked clean and orderly, but it smelled like sweat, weed, and cleaning supplies.

"Follow me," Steve said.

She nodded, sure that parts of her face were boiling and that he'd seen the damage. She hadn't seen anything other than the blisters on her reddened hands.

Vicky's heart rattled in her chest as he pulled her by the hand up a narrow hallway. When they passed the living room, Steve squeezed in beside her, shielding her from the people in the dining room. The men carried on talking and laughing. The sweet smell of Steve's cologne barely shielded her from the men's musk. They also smelled like something else, other than weed. Her mouth watered, releasing a sweet nectar that coated her tongue and forced her teeth to extend. Her face crumpled. Her new venom made her jaw tingle. She ran her tongue around the inside of her mouth.

He opened a door and led her down the steps and into the basement. In the main room, there was a TV and Xbox in a glass entertainment center, along with a black couch, loveseat, and recliner. The glass center table was covered in magazines—celebrities and new strains of marijuana plants adorning the covers—and the room reeked of skunky weed with a hint of a chemical stench. There was also a deep freezer against the wall near the door to one of the two basement bedrooms.

They went to the bedroom where they usually lay together when she spent the night.

He closed the door behind him and turned the light on.

She put the backpack on the bed, leaned against the counter of the private kitchenette, and pulled the rubber shoes off.

"So, where you been? I been—" His brow rose once she pulled the hoodie off, exposing her face. "Shit. What happened, V?"

"I don't know."

He drew his head back a little. "What's wrong with your teeth?"

"I–I don't know," she said, heading for the body mirror attached to the back of the private bathroom door. She rushed past Steve and took off her hoodie and pants, standing naked. She ignored the fact that her skin was lighter, as if she'd been hiding in a basement for years. Fleshy burns stripped away the golden-brown from her face, and the exposed skin beneath turned an unhealthy pale pink. Her cheeks had lost their small plumpness, and her mouth had fangs. Her lips were plump and pink, and her eyes were dark.

"You look a little pale," Steve said softly.

She surveyed her body. Her slim waist started with a large bust and ended with thick thighs, and her ribs barely pressed against her skin. Gauze was still on her neck and arm, but she was too afraid to remove them. And her gut still ached; the smell of weed and cologne was sickening. But the smell of warm blood, Steve's blood, was inviting. She gasped, realizing that the mirror in the hospital had told the truth. She bared her fangs; the vile things protruded, sharp and pointed, ready to impale.

"Where'd you come from, Vicky?" he asked, drawing closer.

She turned to face him, meeting his eyes. "I–I was in the hospital."

"Did they—"

"I left because the FBI was... Shit got weird, and I needed to figure things out. I needed space and freedom to think, you know? I'm so sorry for coming over here like this. I–I didn't know where else to go."

"I'm always here for you."

"Thank you." She frowned. "Thank you so much." Her head throbbed, and she didn't feel hot or cold. Her muscles tightened, almost shriveling.

"Can I touch them?" He pointed at his own mouth.

"What?"

"Can I touch them? You can say no. I just—"

She shook her head, her mouth watering at what his finger might taste like—what his blood might taste like. Savory, thick, red… "You shouldn't. I don't even want to." She narrowed her eyes, baffled at his curiosity. "I–I'm happy you're not running the other way. I mean, the damn doctor was scared of me. But why would you want to touch them? I mean, who wants to touch someone's teeth unless you're being paid or—"

"No–no, you're right. I only wanted to touch them because I wasn't sure if they were real," he said unapologetically.

She blinked. "Oh… Wait. You think I'd run around and burn in the sun for fun?" She smacked her lips. "Man, get the fuck outta here! I'm not crazy. Something attacked me—something *did* this to me. I'm not faking," she growled. What the hell was wrong with Steve? Didn't he know her well enough to know that she wouldn't fake being at the hospital or fake burns? How desperate did he think she was? *You are desperate*, she thought. *Just not in the way he thinks you are.*

He nodded. "You're right. You're totally right. I know you're not crazy and that's not what I was getting at. I just wanted to know if they felt like normal teeth. That's all. And you said you were attacked?"

She gave a stiff nod.

"By who?"

"You mean by *what?* I don't know." Vicky threw her hands up. "I don't know what she was. I don't know anything!"

"She?"

"My face and body really hurt. Can you—"

He put a palm to his face. "Ah, shit. What am I thinking? I'll be right back."

Five minutes later, Steve returned with some burn ointment and a few ice packs.

He helped her rub the ointment on her face and hands and said, "You can stay as long as you want. We're going to figure this out. I promise."

"Thank you."

"Anytime, V."

"Can you plug in my phone while I—"

"Do you think that's a good idea? The phone, I mean."

She pulled back and looked at him. "I need to call my—"

"How much you wanna bet the Feds are listening and tracking your parents right now? If I were you, I wouldn't talk to anyone until we get you back to normal."

His words seemed to pull all the air out of the room, making her feel alone in a vacuum. There was no doubt that her parents were worried and searching alongside the FBI for her, inadvertently risking her freedom. Mom, Daddy, and Moody would never put Vicky in harm's way, but it would be easy to trick them into doing so, as long as they thought they were helping or feeding into the false promise of her safe return. But that wasn't going to happen. The Feds were going to send her away and tell everyone that she was dead.

She tightened her hold on Steve's waist and cried into his chest.

"It's okay, baby," he whispered. "I'll do everything I can to help you get back to normal, alright?"

"I don't even know if I can be normal again," she said.

"Well, you're breathing. That's a good start. You're walking and talking. Those are also pluses. I'd say you have a strong chance of getting back to normal." He smiled and pressed his soft lips against hers. Then he used his tongue to part her lips and ran it along her sharp teeth.

CHAPTER 23

Lists

Can't feel the temperature, Vicky added to the ever-growing list of symptoms. It had been a little over two days since she'd left the hospital, and Steve suggested that she jot some things down to better help them understand her new physiology. They'd spent the last hour in bed, going over what they knew and drawing out theories.

"You may be cold-blooded," Steve said as he pulled his black t-shirt back on. "You know, like a snake?"

"Oh, ha ha," she mocked.

He raised his hand, holding his jeans in the other. "Wasn't making a pun about your fangs, just observing." He smiled.

Vicky knitted her brow, her stomach starting to ache again. She remembered learning about warm- and cold-blooded animals in school. Warm-blooded animals were always just that, warm. Cold-blooded animals adjusted to the temperature of their environment, so they didn't feel the change in temperature for too long. Their bodies always acclimated, just as hers had whenever Steve held her or when he left her in the basement alone. The heat from his body released her, leaving her to the coolness of her new room. But snakes didn't live anywhere that was too cold; they'd freeze. "For real? You think so?"

He nodded as he buckled his belt. "What does it feel like to take a shower?"

"I get hot, then I don't feel anything anymore." A lump caught in her throat as anxiety settled in her chest. Even though the revelation wasn't new, she tried to push it down. She could not remember what a hot shower *felt* like, but she remembered liking them a lot. None of what she had written down, from the sun allergy to the IV shock, made any sense. She wished Dr. Polson was there to explain it or draw some real conclusions. All the information felt like pieces to a jigsaw puzzle of a blank sheet of paper. "What am I going to do?" She frowned as Steve sat on the bed next to her. "Do you think this would be easier if we looked some of this stuff up?"

"You sure you're ready for that?"

She sighed. The urge to call Mom, Daddy, and Moody was stronger than her gut led her to believe. She even wanted to call Teresa and Britt, but Steve was always there to remind her that the police or Feds would track her and take her away. They thought it was better to give Steve her phone and the burner phone that she'd gotten from Dr. P to keep her away from social media, just in case.

When she said nothing, he said, "Be honest, V."

She bit the inside of her cheek, wanting to tell him that she'd control herself. Tell him that the internet was for research only, nothing else. But she couldn't lie to him.

"I'll get you a laptop when you are sure that you won't feel the need to contact anyone. We have to get you better first. The Feds will leave you alone when there is nothing to chase. I promise." He put his hand on her heart. "And I really don't need them to come here." He walked over to her side of the bed and sat down. He leaned over her, beckoning her to sit up and press her naked body against him. The spike in her body temperature wasn't as abrupt, but it happened, then the feeling disappeared. He wrapped his arms around her and held her.

Not caring to rehash the same debate, Vicky asked, "Cold-blooded though?"

"Well…maybe not exactly. It sounds like you acclimate. Cold-blooded animals can feel the heat. It seems like you adjust and stay there."

She thought about those nights that she stepped outside for fresh air. Or those hot summer afternoons when she drank ice water, cooling herself from the blazing sun. Only then did she truly appreciate and yearn for those times. Steve had lots of theories about her and captured everything that she'd told him. But there were some things that he didn't know, like how her mouth watered around him and how she dreamt about licking his blood off her fingers. But when she woke up next to him, she was met with the smell of his overwhelming cologne, very little like coppery, savory blood. Even as she hugged him, the overwhelming sweet chemical smell made her throat sore. She didn't remember him wearing that much. She cringed as a cramp dug into her gut.

"We will figure everything out. Do you trust me?" he asked as he pulled away and looked down at her. His deep gray eyes looked like moonstones in the dull yellow light of the lamp on the nightstand.

"Yeah."

"Try to eat something, will you? Don't think I didn't notice that you didn't eat anything." He nodded at the kitchenette, which had a microwave and a small refrigerator on the counter. The private basement suite reminded Vicky of a private solo dorm room. "There are pizza rolls and pot pies in there. Help yourself."

"Okay," she said, thinking of the last time she tried to eat. Her body rejected buttered toast, pushing it back out onto the hospital floor. Since she'd been at Steve's, she drank water when her mouth felt dry. It didn't make her feel sick, but she did feel hungrier.

Steve leaned in and kissed her on the cheek and stood up. "I'll grab a thermometer too."

She nodded and watched him leave. She lay back on the bed, wishing he was still there trying to cradle her to sleep. But he always fell asleep first, leaving her to think about how much she loved having him around. He was kind and understanding, just as he always had been on those days when she'd visit him after class. Sometimes, he'd pick her up from campus, and others, Teresa would be her chauffeur. They'd end up in the basement, smoking, talking, watching movies, or in that very bed. She'd vibed with Steve like that for eight months, and she missed him over the summer. And now, she finally had him all to herself.

CHAPTER 24

New Aches

After weeks of Vicky bringing up her newfound respect for privacy and her depleted urge to reach out to people she knew, Steve surprised her with a small travelling laptop along with a Malaysian VPN. He'd also bought her a block phone and instructed her to contact him for emergencies only. The phone did not have internet, only minutes and text. He'd given her the code name Tori, and his was Man Man.

He helped her set it up, then went on about his day, leaving her alone to exit her cocoon and softly re-enter the world. Instinctively, she went to Google and began typing: *Twi...* Then she stopped, second-guessing her potential sign in attempt. What if the FBI tracked her? Even with the VPN, they would know that she was on her account. Were they monitoring that too?

"No cure, no family," she said, repeating the loneliest mantra she'd ever thought up. She wasn't nearly ready to step out of the shadows of Steve's basement. Not only had she not spoken to her family or friends, but she also hadn't seen or spoken to the many people who had been in and out of Steve's house. They all smelled different, with scents so loud that she knew the regulars by their odors. There was King Must Pit, Kush Face, Vodka Tony, and Chemmy Stan. Vicky laughed to herself, as she knew what they were discussing, and what Steve did for work on his inherited farmland. *A drug dealer and a law student fall in love...*

Instead of harping and making up corny tag lines for romance novels she would never read or write, Vicky did what she'd promised Steve when he finally got her a gateway to the world and researched symptoms. She started with the most domineering symptom, barring the huge bloody elephant in the room, and typed in *severe sun allergy*. The photos under the xeroderma pigmentosum search looked a lot like hers had, but unlike the people that were afflicted with the disease, Vicky didn't lose brain activity, and her skin had fully healed in a matter of days. The exposed pink flesh on her cheek bones became scaly and then scabbed over, only to become smooth skin after a week of being in the basement and applying burn ointment.

She repeated her search with other symptoms on the list only to find diseases that half-matched her own, but nothing fully. She even looked up vampirism and laughed because the myth only applied to her *sometimes*.

When she had fallen bored with her searching, she watched politicians argue on the house floor and deliver half-assed press conferences. She poked holes in policy proposals and dissected bills. She even compared what she found in bills and what the news reported on. She rolled her eyes, realizing that a small portion of the one-thousand-page bill was shared with the public.

"Half-assed indeed," she'd say, chuckling to herself.

There was one news story that kept her intrigued. It wasn't much of a news story, but more of a press release that she replayed for days: the grand opening of yet another refinery near Lake Michigan. It wasn't enough that the refinery was going to taint the air that they breathed, but they would pollute one of the freshest lakes in the country for profit. She snarled at the picture of the CEO of Bigman's Refinery and wondered if the Conservation Initiative was still going through with the protest that she had planned.

She typed in *Bigman's Refinery protest*, and there she was. Her smiling face crossed the Google search page. The first several pictures were the same: she was wearing the knitted tank top and jean shorts that the police or FBI had taken. Teresa took that picture while Vicky was sitting on the bed sipping a tropical cooler as she waited for Teresa to get them over to Steve's.

The page was flooded with stories about the mysterious disappearance of Victoria Scott, a hopeful co-ed from Miller University. Headlines sprawled across the search results: *Local Nineteen-year-old Miller University Student, Victoria Scott, Missing.* The video had been released two days after she left the hospital—two days since only Steve knew where she was.

She clicked the headline and was taken to a local news site. A video sat beneath the title, frozen at the beginning. Her parents and brother stood behind a podium, terror-stricken. Vicky's heart lurched. She'd known people would be looking for her, but seeing the hurt and distress etched on their faces stunned her.

Didn't her parents have faith in her ability to look out for herself for a little while? But then it hit her—why would they think she was alright? She hadn't cleared her bank accounts, which they had access for transfers and tuition payments. She hadn't taken anything from her dorm. From their perspective, she had simply vanished.

"Don't search your name," Steve had told her. "It'll only be a distraction."

But there she was, hovering over the play button to what was no doubt a plea from her family.

Vicky clicked.

A fair-skinned man with a balding head and bushy mustache—*Sheriff Bolton*, the ticker at the bottom of the screen announced—stood behind the podium with Vicky's family to his left. The crowd consisted of hungry journalists eager to report back to their station with a newsworthy update from…

Wait. Vicky paused the video and narrowed her eyes at the man on the screen. *Sheriff Bolton?* She thought the FBI was interested in her. The police were no longer in charge of her case. Confused at the peculiar change of the agency in charge of her whereabouts, she continued the video.

"I am only going to release what we know at this time," Sheriff Bolton started. Vicky wasn't sure who he was angry with, but his reddening face and aggressive tone showed every bit of his angst. "On August 30th, Victoria Scott was seriously injured at a party that was being held on Miller University's campus. It was the party where

Miller University student, Chad Reid, was found dead in his bed. We fully intended on questioning Victoria about Chad's murder, but while receiving care at the hospital for the wounds she sustained during the attack, she left without checking out. Her family, parents, and the Miller community are hoping she is safe, and will not stop looking until we find her. If anyone has seen her…" Moody held up a picture of Victoria. It was the same one that Teresa had taken of her that night. "Please call 911. She is a gravely injured witness to a murder."

Journalists fired off questions; each one seemed to add a pound of lead to Vicky's gut.

"Do you have information about the attacker?"

"Do you know what caused Chad Reid's murder?"

"Is Victoria Scott a suspect in Chad Reid's murder?"

"What did the doctors say about Victoria's condition?"

Sheriff Bolton raised his hands and patted the air as if telling them to pipe down. "We are not taking questions at this time, but the family has a few words." He stepped aside and allowed Mom to step forward. Daddy was on her left, and Moody was on her right, still holding up a poster of Vicky. Mom wore all black while Daddy and Moody wore white t-shirts and jeans. Her parents' eyes looked swollen and red, while Moody had dark rings around his. He looked the way he had when he worked five twelve-hour shifts in a row.

Mom looked into the camera and said, "Victoria, if you are out there listening, please come home. We need to know that you are alright. Okay? We love you so much, babes. Please come home. And if anyone has seen her, please, please call in and let us know. We are offering everything we have—$70,000, for her safe return. And if you don't want to call the police, contact us on Facebook. We set up a page. It's called…" Mom's voice cracked, and Daddy and Moody grasped either shoulder, feeding her strength. "It's called Find Victoria Scott." Mom looked up at the sky. "Please, God, protect my baby." Tears fell down her face, prompting Daddy and Moody to help her move away from the podium.

The reporters continued with their questions.

"Is Victoria a suspect?"

"What was her condition when she left the hospital?"

"Did you see your daughter in the hospital before she left?"

Vicky hadn't noticed when she started to sob. She missed them so much that she was willing to trick herself into thinking that her new self was a side effect of some coma or a sick joke her brain was playing on her as she lay in her bed back in Detroit, dreaming of the upcoming semester at Miller. But it wasn't a joke. It wasn't a dream. That thing had bitten her and turned her into a…

People deserved to know. Her family needed to know that she was fine, she was breathing. She wasn't the monster. The thing that had bitten her was the monster, the real threat, and she was going to help the FBI find it.

Vicky typed *Facebook.com*. The homepage asked for her login credentials.

Her fingers hovered over the keys, itching to release her information, but hesitant to reveal her location. The police weren't in charge anymore. The FBI was. So why the secret? None of the reporters asked about the FBI agents who had been in the hospital. None of them seemed to know anything about what happened there. So why would the FBI turn the case back over to the police? Doubt dragged her brow. Agent Morgan didn't seem like the type to turn his apparently super-secret mission back over to the local police. No. Never—he would not do that. Agent Morgan was eager to send Vicky off without her family even knowing.

"CDC my ass," she said.

Something didn't smell right. Her family may have been hurt, but she could not risk coming out of hiding just for something horrible to happen and her never seeing them again. Signing into her email or any account, including her bank account, would expose her to the outside world, a place she wasn't ready to face just yet. Not until she understood what she was. Not until she fixed what she had become.

She drew a tear, having to embrace another change in her. She picked up her notebook from the nightstand next to her burner phone and added *antisocial* to the list.

Hungry?

October 18, 2024

Steve let himself into the basement suite holding the paper handles of a bag that was covered in graphics. Vicky recognized the bag from one of the many stores that she was sure to visit at the mall. She missed hanging out there with Teresa and whoever else wanted to come along. They would take shots of the most expensive vodka that they could afford and hit a joint in Teresa's car before they headed inside. By the time they walked around and bought something from Bath & Body Works and Victoria's Secret, they'd head to the food court to get boba tea and over-filled Styrofoam takeout containers of fried rice and honey chicken.

Vicky smiled at Steve as he pointlessly closed the door behind him. It wasn't like there was anyone in the house at that late hour besides the two of them. Vicky knew. It wasn't because his friends and "employees" were always abhorrent and overexcited, but it was their smells and the way they talked about barrels, smoking, snorting, rolling, sliding, hiding, and moving. That's all they ever talked about, all six or seven men who frequented the dining room, and the one or two women who hung around for God knows what. But the girls talked more about going out to eat or getting food. Vicky listened to Steve laugh along with the men as they teased the women before they announced that they were getting ready to go get something to eat.

Sitting in the basement for over a month made it easy to dissect the inner workings of Steve and his friends. It was like they spent all afternoon working in the dining room, making plans and bagging weed or crystal. Or going to get burgers, chicken, fries, and pizza. Nothing that Vicky craved.

Before speaking to her, Steve stopped at the foot of the bed and glared at the glass bowl on the counter in the kitchenette. It was empty, save for the broth that dried up, leaving its remnants to cling to the sides. "Still not hungry?" he asked.

"What do you mean? I ate it," she lied. Earlier that afternoon, as she showered, Steve made her a bowl of soup and made her promise to eat it. But one whiff of it made her stomach turn. When he left for the day, she poured it in the toilet, and watched the chunks of carrot, potato, and chicken swirl around the porcelain bowl before the pipes took it away. Vicky drank a cup of water, and went back to the laptop, looking up new music and laughing at goofy videos.

"What, did you drink it?" Steve picked up the glass bowl and turned the opposite side toward her. The dried broth's pour pattern was too wide to fit into her mouth. "Or did you pour it down the drain?"

She sighed. "You monitoring me now?"

He glowered at her, not laughing at her self-interested quips as he usually did.

"I'm not hungry," she reminded him.

"You haven't eaten since you've been here," he said. "You can't starve yourself to death, Vicky."

Vicky. He only called her Vicky when he was being factual, ready to lecture her. "I'm not hungry," she growled.

"Did you at least try to eat today? Like at all?"

"I—" She dropped her eyes to her keyboard as the laptop's fan whirred, compensating for the incoming heat from her thighs.

He shook his head. "You promised you would try to eat something."

She huffed. Food made her nauseous and crampy. It was like having the stomach flu with no way to pass the virus. She'd tried many times, as Steve kept the mini refrigerator packed with all types of frozen processed foods and fresh fruit. She hated all of it. "We tried food, and it never went well. Remember? Hot Pockets, taquitos, apples… I just…I drink water," she said.

Silence passed between them as he focused on the ceiling. Then he sighed and said, "You're right." He looked at her and offered a faint smile. His chiseled jaw looked strong in the yellow lamp light. It made her body ease when she didn't know that she was tense. "So, let's try something else." He set the bag at the foot of the bed and pulled a cigarette carton from his jean pocket. He opened it and pulled a pre-rolled joint loose. Vicky could smell the skunky green filling the room. "Smoke with me."

"I don't think I can," she said, almost choking on the thought of the skunky smoke suffocating her sinuses and lungs, tainting her empty gut. She'd hated the way Steve sometimes smelled when he came back to the room after a long day of scheming and doing whatever it was that he did. She covered it up by asking if he'd take a shower with her, forcing him to hold her as the water washed the stink away. Then he'd douse himself in cologne that she wanted to toss in the trash.

"You used to smoke," Steve pointed out.

"I know," she said. "I just don't think I can anymore."

"Bullshitter," he called her.

"Shut up," she said under her breath.

"Alright, look, you should smoke because it'll help you eat. People do it all the time, especially sick people. Smoke with me like we used to every weekend, and I'll take you to get something to eat—whatever sounds good to you. You gotta try."

She stared at the black screen of her laptop, trying to think of another way to tell him no. Smoking wouldn't work; it would make her sick. She could feel it in her bones. She wouldn't want to eat; she would want to vomit. She detested the smell; why would she want to eat the smoke? "I don't want anyone to see me like this."

"You don't have to worry about anyone seeing you. Look." He lifted the bag that he set on the edge of the bed and handed it to her.

"What's this?" she asked, as she opened it and looked inside.

"A present," he said with a half-smile.

Inside the bag, she found a small pink glass bottle; a flowery sweet smell wafted from it. There was also a light blue hoodie, a pair of dark gray sweatpants, and a pair of black combat boots. Vicky pulled the hoodie over her head and down her torso. It fit perfectly, hugging her thin frame. She cocked her head when she saw the last thing in the bag. It was a black ski mask. "Are we robbing a store?"

Steve chuckled as he lit the joint, filling the room with the rancid aroma. "I would never put you in that type of situation," he said. "Here. I'm ready to chill."

She glared at the lit end of the joint glowing red as it spewed out darkened smoke. She thought of the many foods she'd tried and failed to keep down. She even thought about what it was like to be high: floating and unapologetic about feeding into cravings. She once ate an entire medium pepperoni and olive pizza on her own because her stomach growled, and her teeth seemed to gnash at the thought of feeling cheesy sauce and buttery bread between them. But now, her mind went hazy as the smoke played in the air, forcing her to breathe it in. Her mouth watered as her eyes rode up the length of the papery joint and landed on Steve's long fingers, then his thin wrist. His blood flowed through the blue tunnels that rode parallel up the wrist and into his hand. She wondered if the red waters of life tasted like pot or the food he ate. Or did it taste sweet like caramel apples, or savory like bacon?

"Here," he said, shaking the joint, beckoning her to take it.

"I don't want to be high while I'm like this. It'll probably get weird," she blurted, fighting to snap herself from a trance that she hadn't asked for. Or did she? *I might take a bite out of you*, she thought.

"Hit this, and I promise I'll get you something to eat. And if you get weird on me, I'll just tie you up." He chuckled.

"But—"

"Vicky. We tried everything. I really want you to smoke and see if it helps your appetite. And don't worry about getting weird. I know you. You're not like that, alright?"

***

Vicky was high, and nothing was good. She threw up the quarter pounder, no onions, and the small fries. Her body shook as if she were malnourished, her ribs showing through her skin. As she vomited and complained, Steve stayed silent after a while, finishing his chicken nuggets and watching videos on his phone as he sat on the edge of his side of the bed. He didn't seem to notice her bristling as she lay down. In fact, he slowly turned the volume up. The sounds of cursing and smacking skin while people cheered filled the suite.

"Look," he said, finally acknowledging her.

Before she could protest, he turned the screen toward her. There were two women fighting in the middle of a residential street. One was whaling on the other; her fist slammed into the other woman's cheek, splitting it. The other woman stood her ground even though her nose was twisted and her eyes looked purple. Her face bled profusely while the main assaulter only had a bruise on one of her cheeks. People stood around, cheering and recording.

"I don't want to see that shit, Steve," Vicky said, her voice lazy and body too lethargic to give an accurate response. He knew that she didn't care to watch two people beating on one another. It never sparked a thrill in her chest like it had for some of her friends in high school. She thought it was tacky, immature, and a one-way ticket to a bruised-up face and an assault and battery charge.

"Come on, just look and tell me how it makes you feel."

"What? No! I said I don't wanna see that."

"Vicky, come on. If you look and answer my question, I'll leave you alone."

She turned on her side and tucked her knees into her chest with her back to him. Pangs beat at her stomach, wanting her to do what she didn't want to do. She did not want to give in to that urge, that new craving. She inhaled deep. The blood pooling from the woman's face made her fangs leak. She wanted it. She was *so* hungry. And a quick sip lay nearby, begging her. Pushing her.

"Man, come on. Look," he said. He reached around, shoving the screen in front of her face. The harsh glow from his phone stung her eyes, which seemed to hate the light more and more as the days went on. She would have thrown his phone if she could. But she only shielded her face and barely waved him off.

"Do you like that?" There was something sick about his tone. It was low and cynical. Dry and daring. "It doesn't make you curious?"

"No! I don't want to see that." She slapped his hand; he drew it back.

"Why are you acting like that?"

"I said no!"

"Is it because you're worried about me? Don't worry about me. You love me too much to hurt me."

"Steve, just please stop it." She cradled herself.

"What if I showed you some pictures instead?" He showed her photos of a car accident. Mangled bodies hung in between gnarled metal and busted glass. Ripped skin gave way to bloody wounds.

"Stop it," she blurted.

"You have to eat. If this is what you want, I can get it."

"No," she shrilled.

"You ain't eaten shit since you been here! I can feel you shaking! Your stomach is growling. You need to eat something, Vicky, and it ain't normal food," he said, his voice booming.

Her heart dropped. She wasn't sure if she'd heard him right. "What?" She hopped out of bed.

He slowly got up and rounded the bed, his expression dry and unmoved. His eyes were glazed and eyelids low. Standing toe to toe with his phone still in hand, he said, "You heard me." He lifted the phone again: a gunshot victim was sitting in a lawn chair, bald head split open with pink brain matter leaking. Blood stained the collar of the victim's white tank top. "You like that, don't you? Is that what you want?"

"No!" She batted at the phone, hiding away from the disgusting image.

"Be for real, Vicky: you want that. You want blood. Look at your teeth. Look at your appetite. And you're afraid of hurting me. Why? It's cuz you want warm blood from an animal...or a person."

"No, I—"

"Just look! You'll understand where I'm coming from if you—"

"No, get it away from me!" she shouted, shoving him in the chest. He stumbled back, losing his footing and landing on the bed. He lost the grip on his phone, and it hit the floor, screen down.

He gawked at her, his eyes no wider or concerned. But his silence said otherwise. She wasn't sure if he was mad or afraid; his high state effectively covered his true feelings, shielding her from what he was really thinking. Finally, he rubbed his chin and licked his lips, making them wet. "Alright." He righted himself, standing up from the bed and retrieving his phone. He slid it in his pocket and left the room, closing the door behind him.

Breathing heavily as if she'd been holding her breath the entire time, she stared at her hands. "What did I do?" she asked between tears. She didn't mean to push him. But how did he know about blood? *Your teeth…he's not stupid.* "So, kill someone or something? *That's* what he wants me to understand? What the fuck?" she said aloud.

Vicky shook her head as remnants from her high played in the back her mind, communicating cravings that she had yet to fulfill. She wanted something savory. Forbidden. Blood. Her fangs ached as the photos and video stained her memory. She bet they tasted sweet but savory, thick but lucid, as their blood flowed down her throat, filling her gut.

She didn't banish the thought this time. She basked in it.

C H A P T E R   2 6

Night Walk

October 30, 2024

Steve's nighttime visits became scarce, beginning with him coming down every other night for a few days. Their time together went from blissful shower times and cuddling to nothing. She yearned for him running his hands along her body, for him to press his lips against her neck before falling asleep with her in his embrace. But the loving massages and discussions of the list turned into Steve barely speaking to her. He'd stroll into the suite, remove everything except his boxers, and lay in bed with his back to her. When she'd go to touch him, he'd pull away. Then he stopped showing up, leaving her alone to battle her hunger pains for what felt like ages.

His neglect was left to be desired by someone who was up to play petty games. Vicky certainly wasn't in the mood for it. She'd told him as much through texts that he ignored. She'd even hear him upstairs with his friends or employees. They'd laugh and joke about nonsense, all while she texted him, telling him that she was sorry, that she didn't mean to push him. But he'd ignore her, leaving her in the basement alone. Vicky had lost count of the text messages that she'd sent. Her longing morphed into loneliness, changing the tune of her messages. They became less *I miss you*, and more *maybe I should leave*. She'd fare better if she were out and about, maybe taking Dr. P up on his offer instead of risking becoming homicidal, because

153

no matter how much Steve ignored her, she was still hungry and she was still a monster.

Two weeks into the silent treatment, Vicky had gathered her things and cleaned the suite. She texted Steve:

I'm leaving.

As she slid the phone in her pocket, it buzzed. Her heart leapt as Man Man, or Steve, finally replied:

I'm coming down to say bye. Give me a minute.

She gave him three hours. She was in the middle of studying the map to Dr. P's house, or the address he wrote in the notebook he'd given her. He lived on the outskirts of Grand Rapids, so it was going to be a long night—five hours of walking in the dark to an appointment that she was almost two months late for.

Better late than never, she thought, wishing she had gone over to Dr. P's sooner. Maybe she'd be closer to a cure. Sitting in Steve's basement did nothing but make her hungrier and agitated—and made her like her dream guy less and less.

When Steve finally knocked on the door, she peered at the time on her laptop, having not noticed how late it was. 11:36 pm. She looked at the door as if it were a nuisance. Why was he knocking at all? Steve usually walked right in.

"Come in," she said. Her heart rushed, reminding her of how much she truly missed him. Even though she was done playing house, she thought up scenarios that would make her stay. Five hours was a long walk, after all.

Steve wore a smile that she hadn't seen since before she shoved him. She felt rewarded with his unspoken forgiveness. Still, she felt shameful for having attacked him at all. She dropped her eyes to her lap, undeserving of his happy face. "I thought you forgot I was here," she said with a small voice, his neglect still fresh on her mind as the urge to leave pushed her to stick with her new plan. There wasn't much time to spare.

"I would never forget about you. I just thought you needed some space—you were super pissed at me that night," he said as he approached the bed. He smelled like that fresh body wash and warm blood. Not at all like weed or that heavy cologne he liked to wear.

"I'm really sorry. I don't know what came over me. I—"

He shushed her. "Like I said, I could never stay mad at you. And if you absolutely need to hear it, then I accept your apology." He sat on the edge of the bed and motioned for her to sit down. When she did, he laid his head on top of her crown and put an arm around her waist. She tensed.

"Still, I'm really sorry," she said. "And yeah, I was pissed, but this is really hard for me, Steve, and I—" Before she could stop herself, the words flowed like vomit, "I need to go."

He lifted his head and looked her in the eye. "I understand," he said. "I hope you get the help you're looking for. I feel like shit because I wasn't able to help you figure anything out." His expression was a portrait of rage, not guilt. "I really wish I could have helped you."

She nodded eagerly as nectar cascaded. "I know," she mumbled, hiding her fangs that were sliding out of her gums, hungry to take a drink.

Steve planted his knees on the floor and inserted his body between her legs. He leaned in and rested his head on her breasts. He hugged her so tight that her breath caught in her throat.

"I don't want you to go, but I understand if you need to," he said.

She sniffed, ready to let the tears fall into his hair. Even though he'd scared her, leaving her alone and confused, her heart ached for him. She returned the hug and planted a kiss on his forehead, careful to keep her mouth closed, careful about letting him see what his presence was doing to her. Before, her gluttonous intentions were easy to tame. But now her mouth was so wet that she could drool if she dared utter a word around him.

She went to break the embrace, but he beat her to it.

He stood up and looked down at her, a smirk playing on his lips. He let out a sweet sigh, then said, "Smoke with me?"

Vicky shook her head, an irritated jolt tearing through her body.

"Well, at least take a night walk with me before you go. Like we used to?"

She blinked. There were many opportunities to pretend like things were the way they used to be. Why now, after he'd ignored her and treated her like a stranger living in the basement?

When she didn't reply, he said, "Please, V?"

"I—"

"I won't take you to get anything to eat. I'll smoke by myself. All I want is to walk with you. That's all. We'll walk the property like old times. That's all I wanna do."

"Okay," she mumbled, careful to keep her lips tight.

***

The night was darker than Vicky remembered. The shadows fell together, blinding her to anything that wasn't a few feet away. The naked trees seemed to go on forever on the large slab of land. The frosty grass crackled under the combat boots Steve had gotten her, and the stars glistened brightly. Once they had gone outside and the smell of fresh air and pine needles filled her senses, her fangs retracted, and her hunger pangs went mild, only partially reminding her that she was starved. Even though she could not feel the chilly air, she could see the frost encasing Steve's breath as he walked alongside her. They walked for a while, following the narrow makeshift path that started at the road and stretched through the wooded land.

"Grandma wanted to reserve the land," he said, his face growing cherry-red as the cold nipped him. He was only wearing a dark hoodie and jeans, so there was no wonder that he was cold. He didn't show it though. He pulled out his cigarette pack full of joints, and a lighter. He lit one. After exhaling, he held it between his lips and wrapped his arm over Vicky's shoulders, pulling her close.

"How big is it?" she asked.

"Big enough that I'm sure there are parts of it that you haven't seen."

"*Tsk*. What is there to see? Everything looks the same."

He smiled and landed a kiss on her forehead. She was grateful for the breeze that came in, carrying the smoke away. "You'll see." He turned right at the fork in the path; left would have led them to the road if they were walking to the store. She'd never gone this way before. She imagined there were more trees, especially if his grandma held on to her wishes of reserving the land. But that could mean something other than what Vicky wanted it to mean.

When they came to a clearing, Steve released her and stepped ahead, putting a small distance between them. She hurried her steps, and as she did, she smelled something in the air. Something foreign but familiar. Something raw. Something red.

The clearing wasn't empty. There was a small wooden cabin that could pass for an oversized shed. It almost looked manmade and withered with age as if it were the original house built there before his family constructed the farmhouse that was closer to the road. The shed could have been teaming with life; yellow light shined around the edges of whatever was covering the windows.

"You like it?" Steve asked as he pinched the end of his joint, eradicating the smoldering cherry.

"I mean, I guess. What is it? Our new home?" She chuckled as she looked around. The smell of blood saturated the air. Maybe there was an animal nearby? Her fangs emerged as her mouth watered. She shivered at the thought of a body lingering somewhere close, envisioning herself sinking her teeth into fresh flesh. *Stop it*, she told herself.

Steve looked over his shoulder and waved her along. She followed him until he stopped and crouched along the side of the shed. She approached to get a peek at what Steve was studying. The black grass didn't show much at first, but she noticed wet fur. Its small face twisted in angst where its neck was snapped. The gash where the bone pierced its throat was sleek and covered with thick liquid. The animal had been split down the middle, its life pouring out of every crevice.

She closed her eyes and quavered, lost in the smell. Taken by the need to pick the thing up and lick every ounce of blood, feeding her belly, easing her pain. She parted her lips, and venom dripped from her fangs. Would it be enough?

It was only then that she noticed the other smells. Musk and meth. Sweat and weed. The smell that was so strong sometimes that it penetrated the floor, finding her in the basement. The smells that hid underneath whatever food or women they'd picked up.

She and Steve were not alone.

Vicky looked over her shoulder, searching the darkness, only to find more night and shadows.

"V," Steve said as she looked for faces that she would barely recognize.

"What?" she asked absently as she pulled her attention back to him. He was still crouched over the squirrel as if he were investigating its murder.

He pointed at it. "I saw your face when you saw it."

"Saw what?" she quipped.

He pointed to the dead animal. "When you saw that. You didn't scream, gag… You looked intrigued."

She shook her head, mind racing. *Did he plan this? Did he…* "You're disgusting."

He glared at her. His eyes grew serious as his brow dropped. "Eat it."

"What?" she shrilled. "No—are you serious?"

"You have to eat something," he said, insistent as he stood tall.

"I'm not eating that!"

"It's been almost two months since you've eaten anything."

"So?! Don't play with me, Steve. You're scaring me!"

"What the fuck do you mean? You need to eat something. And you and I both know that you want to eat this!" he barked.

"No, I don't!"

"Bullshit, Vicky. I see how you look at me. How you smell my neck." He ran his hand over the side of his neck where she had rested her head when they cuddled. "The look in your face when you saw those pictures the other day. When you saw that video. Your eyes were imagining. Your mouth was pretending to taste. Your fangs are out! And you need to eat."

"Fuck you! No!" Vicky took a step back.

"Then what then? Do I have to—" Steve grabbed the carcass off the ground and rushed for Vicky before she could run. He grabbed the back of her neck, pressing his fingers into her flesh.

"No!" she screamed. "Stop!"

Steve stuffed the rancid, bloody thing into her mouth. It was unpleasantly hairy on her lips. But the smell of blood engorged her senses. The fur hit her tongue first, but then the blood didn't taste too bad. It tasted too good.

She swung wildly at him, then shoved him with unexpected strength, sending him crashing to the ground.

When she turned to run, she froze; they were indeed *not* alone. His friends stepped out of hiding.

A metallic click made her turn back to Steve. He was still on the ground, aiming a pistol at her. She heard clicks around her, the other men joining in on her potential firing squad.

She spit fur out of her mouth and wiped her lips with the back of her hand. "Stop pointing that gun at me," she snarled at Steve.

"Not until you calm down," he said as he stood up.

"You just shoved a dead animal in my mouth!"

"Because you need to eat."

"No, I don't!"

"Yes, you do—you look half fucking dead!"

The world fell apart around her, sinking her into dread. Steve wasn't playing fair. How could he... *But why wouldn't he?*

"It tasted good, didn't it?" he asked, baring his teeth.

She didn't respond, because he was right. It tasted better than water, the only thing she could keep down. It tasted better than any food that she could remember. It was like a warm bath for a broken body. Meatier than any meat, and lighter than any fruit. It felt good on her teeth and tongue and enlightened her body as it flowed down her throat. She needed more. Had to have the whole thing...

"I bet you'd feel better if you had more. Like a whole person. I can get that for you, you know that don't you?"

Please, yes. It was better than sex, better than love, better than...
"You're crazy," she cried.

"Vicky, look at yourself. You have fangs, you're strong, the temperature doesn't bother you, and the sun burns your skin. You're undead. You're a *vampire*. It's alright to admit that. It's alright to *be* that."

The proper noun stung.

"I can get you some human blood. That's what you need, baby."

"Stop."

"I will take care of you. I swear. This is fucking brilliant. Don't you *see*? We can help each other."

"You're sick," she said.

"Vicky, hear me out." He called her Vicky again. Not the lovable V, but transactional Vicky. "I have someone who might be at the end of their rope here soon. Remember when I told you about Danny?"

No.

"I think she'd be perfect for this. I'll get rid of a problem, and my girl, the love of my life, gets to eat."

"I'm not your girlfriend," Vicky said, having known as much since she decided to leave. But she had a feeling that her exit wouldn't be so swift. Not anymore.

Steve's friends chuckled. They had been so quiet that, if not for their smells, she would not have known they were there.

Steve raised a brow. "Yes, you are."

"Fuck you."

Steve and his friends—Vicky counted five of them comfortably—laughed hysterically at her answer. She bristled. "Where else are you going to go?" Steve asked once he calmed down enough to form full words.

Vicky didn't answer. Instead, a fiery blast erupted, and a burning pain tore through her gut.

CHAPTER 27

He Shed

When Vicky arose from the confines of the bloody lake, she couldn't remember passing out. She could barely remember her own name, but her struggle to orient herself was interrupted by a petite woman crouching in front of her. The woman's dark hair was pulled back into a bun, and her smooth, almond-toned skin made her appear only slightly older than Vicky. She smelled fresh and fruity, her perfume tart but pleasant. Her baby-blue scrubs looked pristine, though her latex gloves suggested she'd just completed a difficult task. The doctor's blood smelled even better than Steve's—cleaner, without the spice that tainted his.

Steve. Vicky cringed.

The woman was focusing on an area that was underneath Vicky's left breast. The area was numb, but Vicky could feel string tugging at her wound, knitting it shut. The woman picked up a cotton ball from a small silver table and doused it with rubbing alcohol; the abrasive smell took the room. The wound stung when the woman pressed the cotton ball against it again.

Vicky winced.

"Shhh," the woman said, her dark eyes intense, her hands steady.

Vicky's head felt like a balloon full of hot air, light on her shoulders. The dim lights danced along the sides of her periphery, daring her to look around the room, to search the corners that were so foreign that the sparse light could play tricks on her. The place looked like a lab with two adjacent counters full of glassware, coffee filters, handheld propane tanks, and plates. There were also funnels of different shapes, several Styrofoam coolers, a twenty-gallon water dispenser, and a few tote boxes. Across from Vicky's corner was a pile of old furniture. Her backpack was propped up against the pile.

Grogginess wore on her face, forcing her to press her eyes closed again. It was only then that she noticed that her shoulders were numb. Vicky jostled her arms to get her blood flowing, but her movements stopped short. Her wrists were sore, pinned, held in place, strung up above her head. The cord nearly bit into her wrist as it held them together. She followed the orange cord. It was wrapped around a pipe in the ceiling and was tied to a pole nearby, forming a makeshift pulley. She sat in a wooly armchair with her ankles bound to its stubby wooden legs. The aroma of moth balls wafted from the flannel seat.

Vicky peered at the woman, who drew back when she saw Vicky staring at her. She stood up, a look of concern (*or fear?*) adorned her face.

"Why can't I feel—" Vicky cleared her throat.

"Take it easy," the woman said. "You were shot."

No shit.

"Here, here." The woman rushed over to the counter and pulled out a bottle of water. When she moved away, the smell of cat piss and old eggs took hold.

As the woman put the spout of the water bottle to Vicky's mouth, she turned her face. Water wouldn't help. Blood would.

The woman screwed the cap back on the bottle and asked, "Do you know where you are?"

"Who are you?" Vicky asked, remembering that the FBI was looking for her. Then she remembered the local police were also looking for her. And so were her family and friends and…

"Dr. Gonzalez."

"Do you have a first name," Vicky asked, her voice cracking.

"That's not necessary. Uh. Anyway. I checked your wound and it's healing very well. I was able to pull the bullet out and—"

"How long was I out?"

"A few hours, I think. At least that's what Steve told me."

Steve. Vicky remembered the smoking barrel of his pistol after he shoved a bloody carcass in her mouth. "Did he tell you what happened?"

"Oh, I don't need to know everything." She pulled her surgical gloves off and picked up a white rag from the pocket of her scrub bottoms. "I, uh—I removed the bullet and the fragments. You should be good to go in no time." Dr. Gonzalez spoke carefully, choosing her words, knowing that her loyalty did not lie with Vicky.

Vicky pulled her ankles away from the chair's stubby legs and jostled her arms.

"Untie me!" Vicky said between hurried breaths.

Dr. Gonzalez looked at her, a question strewn across her face. She put the water back in her purse and zipped it.

"Please?" Vicky asked. She clenched her teeth, pulling her wrists, willing the pipe to give, but it didn't budge.

"I only cleaned the wound." Dr. Gonzalez said, moving her eyes to the floor.

"You only cleaned the *gunshot* wound, you mean," Vicky blurted, reminding the so-called doctor that she was working on a victim of a crime and refusing to release them from captivity.

Dr. Gonzalez cleared her throat. "Yes, *gunshot* wound. After I removed the bullet, which was really close to your left kidney. That's all I was—stop before you open it back up!"

Vicky grunted and kicked, but her legs remained bound. She pulled against the restraints, but the cable held firm. "You can't leave me here!" she shouted.

The door flung open, allowing daylight in. Vicky was too far back into the shed for it to touch her, but her heart fluttered at the sight of Steve shutting the door behind him. He looked unfazed at first, but then he smiled as he walked over.

"Look who's finally up," he announced.

Vicky froze, hoping her stare made his insides boil.

He looked at Dr. Gonzalez. "And?"

"Uh, yes. She's, she's definitely different," Dr. Gonzalez said.

"I told you, Doc." He put a hand on her shoulder. She flinched. "You gotta have faith in me sometimes."

Dr. Gonzalez pursed her lips. "Can I go now?"

"Yeah, go ahead," he said, not bothering to look at her.

Dr. Gonzalez complied, hustling to gather her things and shutting the door behind her.

Without warning, Steve pulled on the cord that had been hoisting Vicky's arms up. Her body flung up, forcing her to her feet. She screamed as her flesh tore, snapping stitches as she involuntarily stretched, her weight shifting upward. She moved her middle, fighting the restrained. "Help!" She screamed.

Steve glared at her. "You sure you want to do that? You think anyone would help *you*?"

"Fuck you!" Vicky shrilled.

"Oh, calm down." He wrapped the cord around the post, leaving her in the stand-up position, the recliner pressing against the backs of her legs. "It can't hurt that bad."

He went over to one of the counters and pulled a stool from underneath it. He positioned it in front of her. "You know, this could have gone a lot different for the both of us." He picked up a black bundle from the counter. "If you just ate like I asked you to, then I wouldn't have to open you up and figure it out for you." He opened the pack and showed it to her. The surgical kit consisted of a knife, scissors, tweezers, and a scalpel. "I got this one especially for you— brand new!" His eyes glistened like a child's on Christmas morning.

She curled her lips as her mind raced. "Please. Please don't…" Her plea a mere whisper.

"Ah, ah, ah," he sang. "Stop that. There's no time for pleading and crying. Not now. Not when you had a chance to make a different choice." He set the surgical set on the small silver table. "Now I have to make the choice for you."

Steve picked up the scalpel and sliced the remaining stitches free. Wet blood fell down her torso, soaking the waistband of her underwear. She wasn't sure where her pants had gone. Maybe in her bag that was only a few steps away from her makeshift prison.

"Please," she blubbered, the pain stilling her screams. "Stop, I'll do what you want. Just please."

"I want you to stop moving," he demanded through bared teeth. He shoved the blade into the wound and drove it up. She squealed and hollered as the wound ignited.

"Now, say that again," he shouted, baring his teeth. His once caring gray eyes darkened, daring her to speak.

"Stop!" she shrilled as she forced herself backward, the nerves in her torso screaming and writhing, erupting in hurt.

"*That's* not what you said." He pulled the blade from the oozing wound.

She shrieked, losing the words to plead for help.

"Now, what did you say?" he asked slowly.

She shuddered and breathed, willing the pain to subside. But it brightened.

He tossed the scalpel onto the table and grabbed her face. He tilted his head. "What did you say?"

"I–I'll d–do any–anything."

"Anything?"

"Y–yes," she wailed.

"Good," he said. He kissed her mouth, his tongue tasting the blood that surged up her throat. When he pulled back, his lips stained red, he paused and cocked his head, mesmerized. "Your eyes look so sexy when you're mad. They look bloody hazel… I wonder what they look like when you eat. When you're full."

With that, Steve stepped back and unwound the cord from the post. She plummeted down, her body falling back into the seat. Pain wrapped her middle and shot through her legs.

Steve wiped his hands onto his hoodie, the blood invisible on the black cotton.

Passenger

Vicky was unsure about what day it was or how long she'd been acquainted with her new prison. The smell of spoiled eggs and ammonia was prominent, but more welcomed than Steve, because when he showed up, she passed out shortly thereafter, her head dangling and her arms still held up. The strain in her shoulders had gone numb, accepting that she'd never lower her arms again. Her muscles slacked and her blood seemed to abandon her arms, flowing down and out of the wound that was reopened time and time again. Steve would tear it open and pick at her insides, and Dr. Gonzalez would show up to close it again, much like she was at that very moment.

Vicky winced as Dr. Gonzalez stitched her up, the pain fresh and her skin stiff under dried blood.

"Twice in one day, huh? I must be lucky," Vicky said, her throat sore from screaming and her head weary with exhaustion.

Dr. Gonzalez offered a wry smile. "I don't think that's very lucky, Vicky. I think that's shitty."

"Oh, come on, it's not *that* bad," Vicky teased, bloody spittle leaving her lips. "At least you get to see me before and after you go to work. Right?"

Dr. Gonzalez chuckled that time. It seemed like she was warming up to Vicky. Vicky preferred waking up to Dr. Gonzalez because she was a healer, a healer who Steve left alone with her patient.

"You're right. It could be worse. But it's not. I saw you eleven hours ago. I stitched you up and everything was alright. But now, you got some new cuts that look like they had been bleeding pretty bad…they are healing slowly, but—"

"What kind of doctor are you?" Vicky asked, wanting to know more about the woman, tired of hearing about her own anatomy. She was a monster—she understood that. Steve only talked about it nonstop as he cut into her and used his fingers to spread the wound open. *You have tissue and visceral fat like everyone else*, he said, before pulling the blade up to her rib cage, metal scraping bone before she passed out…

"A medical examiner," Dr. Gonzalez said, her stitching pattern making it up to Vicky's ribs.

"What made you want to do that?"

"I–uh…" She sighed. "I grew up poor. My parents were farm hands, making half of the minimum wage. Luckily for me, I like science, and I used to hang out with the farmer's granddaughter, whose mother was a doctor." She paused, ruminating on something. "He can't keep you here forever," she mumbled.

Vicky chuckled. "He'll never let me out."

Dr. Gonzalez caught Vicky's eye. "Steve is, uh…"

"Poetic?" Vicky blurted.

They both laughed, their joy cut short when Steve rushed in with his phone in his hand.

"I was just—" Dr. Gonzalez started, but Steve cut her off.

"You ready to give me what you owe me?" he asked Vicky.

Dr. Gonzalez looked bewildered as Vicky said, "Yeah."

"Good. Danny will be here shortly. He'd be honored to help you with your eating problem. You up for it?"

"What? You can't be—"

"Nothing to do with you, Doc."

"I—" Vicky started.

"Don't have a choice," Steve said. "Trust me, you'd be doing him a favor."

Vicky searched for the words, a way out. A way away. And as he texted, fiddling with his phone, her mind raced. She looked at the doctor, who was just as perplexed and terror-stricken. Vicky knew why Steve held *her* captive, but what did he have over Dr. Gonzalez?

His phone buzzed, and then he lifted it, screen facing Vicky. "You know who this is?" There was a picture of a license. Long black hair, pouty red lips. Round eyes. But it didn't look pale. The woman in the picture looked fair-skinned, almost in her forties.

DOB: 10/1/1986

The woman in the picture…

Patricia Weston, 550 Fallon Lane, Lakeshore, MI, 49523, DOB: 10/1/1986, Height: 5'10.

Vicky shook her head.

"Hm," Steve said. "What about this one?"

Vicky's eyes widened at the photo of a woman who was chained to a bed. The room surrounding her looked clean and bright. But her nose was busted, and her eyes…they looked red. Angry. Monstrous. Vicky's heart thudded in her chest.

Patricia Weston, 550 Fallon Lane, Lakeshore, MI, 49523, DOB: 10/1/1986, Height: 5'10.

They caught her. They finally caught her. But how? Vicky caught the name of the person who had sent the picture: *Barbie.*

"Do you?" he asked.

"N–no."

He sighed. He texted. "Well, whatever it is, Barbie's not responding." He grunted, impatiently and bothered. "Fucking weird if I had to say so myself. Fuck it." He put the phone onto his face, calling someone. "Yeah, Lou. We're going to scoop her up. See if Troy can meet us at the 7-Eleven first… Yeah. Okay. Tell him I'll give her a bag… Alright."

Steve hung up. "Looks like I have to go get them myself."

Them? Vicky thought. *Danny and… Patricia Weston, 550 Fallon–*

"Sit tight, Doc. I shouldn't be gone too long. Be ready though." He looked Dr. Gonzalez up and down. "I'll grab you an apron or something. Don't want you to get your pretty scrubs all dirty." He winked, then left.

Dr. Gonzalez frowned. "He…he isn't serious, is he? He's going to kill someone and—"

"Make me drink their blood, yes," Vicky said, sounding more nonchalant about the situation than she thought she should have.

Dr. Gonzalez put a hand over her mouth as if this was the hardest thing for her to hear. But Vicky knew that the woman had seen worse things. Her tone made it seem as if her loyalty to Steve didn't exist at all.

"He's going to drain Danny. I don't know what he's going to do to…" Vicky trailed off.

"What did he show you on the phone?"

Vicky blinked. "A woman," she said. "He's going to make you do something to her too."

"I can't…I can't do that," she said. "No! This is where I draw the line."

"What do you mean?"

"I…" Dr. Gonzalez raised her hands in a calming gesture, as if she could somehow regain control of the situation. "He said he needed me to wait around until he brought his friend back, but I hope he doesn't think that I am going to harvest someone's blood and help him feed it to you! Is that what he wants? No! That—that's sick, man. I'm—" She grabbed her purse. "I'll take the loss. Deport my father. I don't care. Hell, I'll go back with him. I'm not a murderer. That's not me!" The doctor turned on her heels, nearly running for the door.

"Wait! I don't want this either. Please don't leave me here. I— At least let me out!"

Dr. Gonzalez's face turned beet-red. "Let you out?! So you can go kill people? You are all sick! Is this some kind of game or something?"

"No. No…it's not." Vicky shook her head. "I swear, it's not. That woman in the picture…she did this to me. She… It's all her. It's…"

Dr. Gonzalez narrowed her eyes. "You told Steve you didn't know who she was."

"I lied. He…he doesn't—"

She shook her head and turned for the door.

"You see what he did to me! He… You think I like what I am? You think I like being tortured? You think I want to starve? I can't eat food. I can't—but I don't want to drink blood. I'm not dangerous. *He* is. The woman in the *picture* is. Not me." Vicky's voice cracked. "I want my family; they are looking for me. They think I'm dead! Let me out. Let me go back home."

Dr. Gonzalez's phone rang, and she looked at the screen with disgust. She put it on speaker.

"What?" she said softly.

"Yeah," Steve said. "It sounds like our friend ran into a problem. It might take more than an hour to deal with but be ready to start as soon as we get back. Alright?"

"Okay."

She hung up and looked at Vicky. Dr. Gonzalez's eyes moistened and her fist shook as she gripped her purse strap. "Where do you want to go?"

"She—there was a problem?" Vicky asked, panic nipping at her chest.

"Where would you go? What would you do?"

"Did the woman on the bed get away?"

"I don't know," Dr. Gonzalez said sharply. "Now answer me: Where would you go? What would you do?"

"I–I would go home. I would. I would go to…Lakeshore."

PART 5

The Set

CHAPTER 29

Consider a Car

November 7, 2024

Trish couldn't stay seated on the couch for long. She set her laptop aside and stood up, beginning her restless circuit around the first floor. Darwin watched from his placemat as she paced from the living room—where he sat watching a colorful cartoon—through the foyer. She cringed at the black tape covering the bullet hole in the door, then continued around the kitchen table and through her office. Sometimes she'd pause to smile at him, knowing he was only mildly entertained by her predictable route. With clenched fists, her anger pushed her forward, denying the need to stop. Her jaw clenched as she schemed.

Victoria would be back. Yes. She wouldn't be serious about her threat if she didn't actually return. "I'll leave, but you *will* change me back." Her words were abhorrent, as serious as a deeply held promise.

But Steve could have also been to blame for the blood on the Jeep, left for the neighbors to see.

"Fucking foul," Trish growled once she stopped in her office, too afraid to lift the shade and study her yard. It felt like a sin to engage with the defaced lawn that had been embarrassingly plastered on the news. She ground the backs of her teeth and spun around, willing the conclusion of the fight to form in her head, paving the way for the inevitable disappearance of three people: Steve, his driver, and Victoria.

Thirty more seconds, Trish thought. All she'd needed was thirty more seconds, and Victoria would have died that night in Chad's room and Steve would not be out looking for Trish.

Or would he? The burning question left her stuck. With or without Victoria, Trish may have ended up at Toby's house. She may have still run into Barbie—Steve would still be a problem.

But those thirty extra seconds would have removed Victoria completely, Trish thought. Thirty more seconds and she would be like the others. Not turned, but dead. Not elusive, but missing—forever. Now, Trish wasn't sure how to get rid of Victoria. How could she kill Victoria when no one had been successful at killing Trish? Her heart rattled in her chest. "Dammit," Trish growled. She wanted to shriek, wanted to tear her own hair out.

But she sighed. It didn't matter how annoyed or confused she was; the damage was done, and it was time to clean. She pursed her lips, praising the positives. Randel was out of town until next Tuesday. It was only Thursday. She had time. She relaxed. Pita was going to grab Darwin tomorrow afternoon, giving Trish space. "Okay, family safe," she reasoned.

She felt her face lift as hope rushed through her. She would lure Steve and Victoria to the house…

Separately, of course…

Get rid of them…

Need some firewood for the firepit…

Clean, and everything would be—

She snapped her fingers and slapped her forehead. "The damn cameras," she said. How could she forget about the installation? She bit the inside of her cheek. "Fucking sabotage," she mumbled. She'd have to tear the wires out and blame it on the squirrels…the raccoons. *You really think that'll work twice?* she thought, risking the rehashing of something that worked on the old bat next door. She tsked, feeling as if her head were on backward.

Trish's house didn't need a security system—she knew exactly who had vandalized her car. Her family's vehicle, the means of getting her son around, had been deliberately targeted.

If anything, other people needed a camera, not the other way around. She was the reason people locked their doors and upgraded their security measures. Trish was the reason people had guns and slept with one eye open. Not Victoria, some scared kid, or Steve, a drugged-out wannabe Dr. Frankenstein.

She circled back to the living room and found Darwin bouncing on his short haunches to a sing-along. A happy lady wearing a striped train conductor's overalls with a neon orange short-sleeved shirt brushed her teeth with a toothbrush the size of a wine bottle.

If you are the scary one, why didn't you hear Victoria coming? The thought gnawed at the edges of Trish's mind as she envied the carefree happiness of the woman on TV.

Trish had not heard Victoria coming, but she vowed to be the last one to see Victoria at all.

She flopped down on the couch, put her laptop on her lap, and opened the search engine. They may have slowed her down, but Trish wasn't out of the fight. First, she needed to fill the gaps, and no plan would work if she didn't have a way to dispose of her newfound problems.

She searched *used car lots near me.*

C H A P T E R   3 0

Across the Street

At night, when the abandoned shed felt cramped, Vicky thought of Steve, and those thoughts led her to find a worthy distraction. She set out, looking for ways to disturb Patricia's life again. Vicky jogged, not leaving much time for anyone to see her if they were looking out windows. The neighborhood could have been on curfew or a shared bedtime, because the sun had been down for a while, and no one was out. Vicky heard an engine start in the distance every now and again, but there wasn't much activity.

When she reached Patricia's house, the Jeep was gone. Vicky giggled, suspecting the police had finally taken it away. She hadn't been sure they'd care enough to act over some animal carcasses, but apparently they did.

Good, Vicky thought. Their eyes would be on Patricia for a while.

Vicky continued on toward the opposite end of the block. She stopped six houses down where a purple minivan sat on the curb in front of a ranch-style house. It was quiet, and the yard stretched far enough for the inhabitants to remain blissfully unaware that their family van was under attack. Mom used to drive one of those vans. Vicky and Moody used to call it the big-back spaceship and took all the credit when Mom finally traded it in for an SUV. Still, the purple eyesore reminded Vicky of what it was to be young and safe under her parents' watchful eyes. Life was nothing like that now.

She plucked the back tire on the curb side, jamming the tip of the flathead screwdriver deep. She snatched it out and was met with a satisfying hiss as the air escaped.

A couple more houses down, Vicky shoved the screwdriver into the driver's side front tire of a cherry-red Mustang that had been in someone's driveway. She'd probably never have one like she planned. As she made her way closer to Patricia's house, she gripped the screwdriver tight, wanting to knock on the monster's door and shove it in her eye.

Then she'll turn me back, Vicky thought. *Then she wouldn't have a choice.* And Vicky wouldn't accept any other outcome. Patricia was a vampire, *is* a vampire. But somehow, she looked normal. She didn't have fangs, pale skin, or rosy eyes. No. The Patricia on Fallon Lane had fair skin, dark eyes, and a baby. "A whole-ass kid," Vicky proclaimed. That monster, that liar, that wolf! She's human? Does she use the kitchen in her house? Is there food and juice and water in there? Or were there jars of blood lining the shelves? Did Patricia pull them out and heat them up in a pot on the stove? *What the hell does her kid eat?*

Vicky's chest burned at the thought of Patricia pretending, and lying, by telling her neighbors that she didn't know what happened to her Jeep. Telling them that she was a victim and that someone was probably out to get her. Vicky had heard the sirens; she knew the police had been around. What did Patricia tell them?

Regardless of the sick charade happening inside Patricia's house, Vicky needed to be back to her old self, the person she fashioned and grew proud of. The person that she molded, crafted, and had plans for.

As Vicky got closer to Patricia's house, she stopped two houses down, frozen in place by a familiar smell. Vicky backed up and crouched next to the brush that lined the perimeter around one of the many ranch-style houses. She looked around, eager to guess where the smell of fried chicken and collard greens was coming from. It smelled like Granny's house on a Sunday or Thanksgiving back home. It smelled like Auntie Ty's house in Atlanta, or Jazzy's Soul Food on Fenkell.

But who is cooking like that in a neighborhood like this? she thought.

She arrogantly cocked her head under the veil of the dark night and walked slowly up the street, scrutinizing every house, every car.

The house across the street from Patricia's was awake on the sleepy street. The door was being held open by one of the patrons. "What?" a short woman said over her shoulder as she shouted into the house. She held the front door ajar as she looked inside. She pointed something at the minivan in the driveway, and it started, the red taillights illuminating the concrete. Vicky heard small mumbles from inside the house. It sounded like the woman was talking to a man.

"Hold on!" she said, as she let herself back inside, closing the door behind her.

Vicky backpedaled and crouched, stopping behind a car that was parked in Patricia's neighbor's driveway. Now she was hidden from the front and the back. She almost hated her new position. The smell of nicotine-infested smoke clogged the space, almost completely blocking out the savory smell of soul food. She looked through the car windows, which offered a clear view of the house across the street.

The couple spilled out of the house. They were older; the man was bald, tall, and slender like Daddy used to be before he packed on a beer belly, and the woman was petite with thick hips like Mom. The sight was unsettling because the couple looked like her parents might in ten years.

They laughed like happy people as the woman climbed into the passenger seat, and the man closed her door for her. They looked dressed up, as if they were headed to Thursday night mass or the opera.

Vicky almost wanted to run to them, beg them to take her and fix her. Beg them to take her to church—maybe the pastor would know what to do? But the more her legs pleaded for her to run, to do something, her mind threatened her: *They'll turn you in to the cops. They'll call the FBI. They'll trap you in the basement and make you a slave.*

She swallowed the lump in her throat and watched them leave, driving in the opposite direction. She stared at their house for a few minutes. *Who are they and why did they choose to live there? Did they go to college? What do they do for a living?* As thoughts swooned her mind, she felt herself stand tall and jog over to their house.

Did they grow up here? Do they have kids? How long have they been married? Can they help me?

The closer she got to the house, the more intense the smell. Vicky imagined grease popping from a hot skillet over a naked flame. She frowned as a smell that used to make her mouth water made her stomach twist and cheeks tingle. Luckily, there was nothing to vomit, but that never stopped her from heaving and her diaphragm from pulsing, pushing up nothing.

She walked the perimeter of the house, this one a lot like the others in the area. They didn't have a fence sectioning off their yard, only a hilly backyard that descended into a row of trees separating them from the houses around the corner. The house looked like a tri-level with two floors in the back, a patio off the upper floor, and a walk-in entrance on the ground level behind glass patio doors. Vicky focused on the second-floor patio, which was supported by wooden posts. A table and chairs sat on the deck, and next to the sliding door was an open window that let the smell drift into the neighborhood.

Empty Nest

After scaling the length of one of the wooden columns that held up the second-floor patio, Vicky stood on the patio ledge and reached over to the screenless window. She lifted the window high enough to let herself in. She stepped into the empty kitchen sink, leaving the window open behind her. The space was pristine aside from the three boxes that lined the kitchen walls. They had the word *kitchen* on the side of them. The people must have moved in recently and felt safe enough to leave a window open, even if it was merely cracked.

Vicky pursed her lips, realizing that she was probably one of the few people in the world to go through such lengths to get inside someone's house. The couple looked like they were well-off judging from the glass dining table, glass china, white couches, and modern sculptures. They definitely had money to spend on portraits of black women wearing the American flag or rocking round afros while holding up a balled fist. Yes. If Vicky were there to steal, she would leave with those very things. But that's not why she climbed into their window. That's not why she nonchalantly assumed that they lived there alone and that the dark house was all out of inhabitants at that very convenient hour.

It was a feeling that took her there. It was the longing nostalgia that dragged her inside like that dog on those cartoons she watched when she was a kid. The smell of pie had its own personality, beckoning the dog to break the rules, daring him to snatch up that fresh, hot treat.

"Vicky, go wash up. You got school tomorrow," she heard Mom say, voice as loud as it's ever been, playing in Vicky's ears. She looked down at the couch arm, so clean and white. Unblemished and maybe never sat on. Vicky could see Mom's freshly pressed navy slacks and black button-up laid out over the arm as she rushed around getting ready to head out for third shift.

Vicky went on, finding the top of the steps that led to the lower part of the tri-level house. The walls were lined with more portraits. Not pictures of the couple, but pictures of rhinos and elephants, some abstract and some made up of blocky prints. She could almost hear Daddy's heavy feet as he walked around after a long day at the shop. He'd head to he and Mom's room, which was the largest one in the bungalow, and the only room on the second floor.

"Y'all need anything?" Daddy called down the steps as Vicky and Moody sat in their rooms on the first floor. He always asked them if they needed anything before bed, and it usually consisted of a glass of water or advice.

"No, Daddy," she used to say to him.

Depending on the job that Moody had at the time, either cooking at a restaurant or bartending at a bar, he'd come in reeking of burgers or vodka. He'd stop by Vicky's room and say the same thing every night: "Good night, big head." Her night was never complete without the words of her family. Even when she went to Miller, they would text or call every night, letting her know that they were thinking of her and rooting for her success.

She frowned as she took the first step. Vicky imagined herself graduating from law school and passing the Michigan Bar. Then, she'd practice constitutional law and become a civil rights lawyer someday. Maybe even become a federal judge and move up to the Supreme Court.

She cleared her throat, suddenly aware that she was alone in a stranger's house. She listened intently to the sounds of the night outside and the whisper of air through the ventilation system, hyperalert for any sign she might be caught.

Once she reached the bottom of the steps, she found the master bedroom. The door was open, and the room looked clean, with the bed made and their citrus cologne and flowery perfume lingering, consuming their personal space.

She went to the next room, betting it was a guest bedroom since they didn't seem to have children. She looked at the crevice underneath the closed door. There was no light. She put an ear to the door and was met with nothing. No breathing, no tossing and turning. Nothing.

The room felt like it was set in the deepest part of the nest: farthest from the front door and without a neighbor's window glaring at it. It faced the enormous backyard. She stared at the door, thinking about how she and Moody fought over the room that was farthest back in the house. Whoever called it first got it, but they had to remain open to bribes for thirty days. If they took a bribe, they forfeited their rights to the room. Moody made up those rules after Vicky won the first room. She then went on to win the second time they moved, and both times she never took a bribe.

Vicky wondered why the room door was closed. The bathroom across the hall was open and so was the master bedroom. She opened the door, expecting to find another bedroom ready for guests to come spend time with the older couple, or a space waiting for their adult child who was away at college or in the Army. But that's not what she found. In fact, the space wasn't for guests at all. It was an office with oak furniture, three monitors, and photos everywhere: on the walls, scattered across the desk, and lying on a blue loveseat. There was also a whiteboard with small magnets holding the photos in place.

Vicky put a hand over her gaping mouth, her heart slamming against her ribs. The photos on the whiteboard captured glimpses of recent carnage. A mugshot of a woman sat next to a photo of someone lying on the floor, wet blonde hair caked with blood. The skull was covered in deep gashes and missing eyes, nose, and lips. The name "Barbara 'Barbie' Webb" was scrawled in red underneath the gory image.

"Barbie," Vicky whispered, her heart lurching at the memory of the dead woman's text to Steve. She'd sent him a picture of the monster—the monster who had gotten away.

Next to that was a Miller University College ID. Vicky teared up, recognizing Jason 'Tay' Thompson, a junior she'd seen at Steve's house before Patricia turned her into a monster. His crime scene photo showed him lying face down in his own blood. Red clots had pooled in front of his mouth as if he'd coughed up his lungs before dying.

The next mugshot showed a blond man with blue eyes who looked mean and drug-addled. His name read "Daniel 'Danny' Knocks." The corresponding crime scene photo showed him on a bed, neck twisted, face blank except for death. Danny was going to that night no matter where he ended up. Trish did him a favor.

Finally, there was Dr. Tobias Webb's Miller staff ID. Vicky hadn't taken his classes, but Teresa had told her about a pass he'd made. They weren't sure if he was flirting when he winked at Teresa, but they'd laughed it off, knowing Teresa preferred guys their age. His crime scene photo showed him on a carpeted floor, face blue, two bloody holes in his neck, and a laceration on his left pec. Vicky touched her own neck where she had been bitten.

Tears slipped from her eyes, falling onto the plushy carpet. But she didn't care. This couple wasn't a well-to-do black family that reminded Vicky of herself and the things that she was going to miss out on. No. This couple was tracking someone.

That's why no pictures on the walls, she thought. *That's why no kids.*

They were after the person in the picture that sat in the center of the whiteboard, her name written in blue marker: Patricia Weston. In the photo, she was standing in front of her porch, a look of deep concern on her face as if she was mid-sentence, talking to someone. The photo was a little blurry, as if it had zoomed in to see her face, but not from too far away.

What else do they know? Vicky thought as she rushed to the desk. On it was a map of Miller University; the Beta house on Frat Row was circled, the very house where Trish had bitten Vicky. Her heart lurched when she saw what was set beside it: a photo of Chad, his trombone to his lips as they protruded out, ready to blow more air into it. Then there was the picture of him dead in bed. She froze. Her missing person's photo was next to the crime scene, Mom's cellphone number scribbled below Vicky's smiling face.

Her breath caught and her hands trembling, Vicky pulled open the drawer. Inside was a stack of folders with "top secret" stamped across the front. She opened one from the middle of the stack and found an email printout addressed to Agent Peter Morgan.

CHAPTER 32

Security

"What?" Trish asked. She'd heard Randel clearly the first time, but she wanted him to feel her contempt.

"How is the install going?" he asked again, his staggered breathing evidence of his time on the treadmill. He was active, running ten miles at least five times a week, taking full advantage of the gym at whatever fancy hotel his company put him up at.

"Loud," she said, putting a hand over her exposed ear and pushing the phone closer to the other. The banging from the worker mounting cameras along the outside of the house was driving her nuts. A pale man with long scraggly hair had shown up, asked for a signature, put in some earbuds, and got straight to work.

Trish sat back on the couch and watched Darwin, who pulled himself on his tippy toes and searched the window for the security man. He was so curious about the stranger that he fussed whenever the man left his sight.

"It shouldn't take too much longer," Randel said, his breath turning into hollow puffs.

"It's unnecessary," she heard herself say as she looked at the blueprint that the service man had given her. All the cameras would be outside, which was promising; Randel wasn't interested in what would happen inside. She was also pleased with the blueprint, because it was comprehensive, saving her time from deciphering. Once the security guy was gone, and Darwin left for Pita's, she was going to turn some of the cameras, creating blind spots. And if Randel called, noticing that he couldn't get a feed to his phone, she'd fix it and tell him that the wind or an animal must have knocked it out. Having the blueprint also helped her solidify the plan for later that night when Victoria or Steve would inevitably return.

When Randel sighed, she wasn't sure if it was due to being frustrated with her, or if he'd reached his runner's high. "Trish, this is for the best. I can't be there all the time, which we both knew before we were married," he said matter-of-factly, as if she had asked him to stay home. As if she had asked for security. He went on. "Clearly, someone is out to get you. You can say that it was some pissed off kids all you want, but it looks more personal, if you ask me. Until the police figure it out, I don't feel comfortable leaving you and Darwin there without some kind of..."

"Oversight?"

"Don't say that. You know it isn't like that. What if they come back?"

They will.

"If they do, we would have them on camera. It'll make it easier for the police to find them, don't you think?" he asked.

She curled her lips, holding her words in. The police were not going to find something that didn't have DNA. The police didn't know who or what Steve was either. Apparently, that deranged lunatic ran his town under the behest of a corrupt-ass sheriff—or at least that's what Danny had said. Who's to say that the police wouldn't simply let him go? Trish was the only one who could deal with the threat. She didn't need the police to witness that—she didn't need anyone to witness that. But here they were.

"You don't have anything to say?" he asked, his quickened breath passing through her ear.

"No. Like I said before, it sounds like you have your mind made up. The cameras stay, even though they are outside only. What if they come inside?"

"That's what the guns are for. You remember the code to the safe?"

"2-3-1-7," she said. He knew only of the gun hidden deep in their closet, not the pistol in her office safe. She could never be too prepared for a real threat…a lot like the one she was currently dealing with.

"Good. Hopefully, it never comes to that."

"Hm," she said.

He sighed again, and she pictured his chest heaving as he gasped for oxygen. Annoyed, but undeterred, he said, "I'm really trying."

"Well, try *less*," she spat. "You're overreacting and wasting money in the process." She tucked her bottom lip, full of regret. Randel didn't deserve her rage. He wasn't the one who trashed her car or threatened to hunt her down. Victoria and Steve were. Randel had been nothing but supportive, trusted her enough to allow her to lead an independent life full of false solitude. She didn't need him to pry now, and the cameras were only that: a mechanism of nosiness. They would make it harder for her to eat, harder for her to be a mother. Harder for her to truly protect her home the way she always had, and that included the time well before Randel was born. "It's nothing to worry about, okay?" she said, softening her voice. She gave a shy smile to Darwin, who had abandoned his post at the window to turn and glare at her when he noticed her tone shift. "The cameras are overkill. We're fine here."

Really?" Randel growled a little that time. His breath sounded like it slowed, as if he wasn't running anymore.

"Yes, they are! It just feels like you want to watch me. Like you don't trust me with our son or something. I just— I–it just feels like people act like they don't already have enough to worry about."

"So, what the hell do you want me to do, huh? It isn't just about you! It isn't just about how *you* feel. Not only do you not *tell* me shit, but you are also so damn *secretive*. I'd be lucky to find out what the hell you're up to all day. It's like sharing is a damn chore for you!"

She shook her head. "Whatever," she said. "I'm not secretive; you're just being paranoid." She pictured him cringing.

"Look, Trish, I feel like you've been distant. You don't talk to me as much and you seem so standoffish since Darwin. I want my wife back. I want us back."

"What are you talking about? I'm not—"

"There it is! Right there! You're blowing me off. I'm telling you that you've changed. I'm pleading with you to open yourself up to see how I'm thinking and feeling, and you just blew me off! You're making me look like the asshole. Don't you get that?"

"I'm standoffish because I'd rather push people away than to risk having them hurt our family?" Her tongue froze, and she winced. She wanted to take the words back, but it was too late—they'd already reached Randel's ears.

"Okay. Okay, now we're getting somewhere. You are bothered by what happened yesterday. I am too. That's why the cameras. It's not that I don't trust you; it's that I'm worried about you. That's all. Can I not worry about my wife and son?"

"Yes. Yes, of course you can. I just—when you start to worry, I get—it makes me feel worse. You know? Like I fucked up. Now you want to put up cameras and I—" Her throat tightened, and she couldn't stop the tears before they came. They rushed down her face, and her son's curiosity turned into worry as he pouted.

"Trish, I'm putting the cameras up so that you can sleep easy when I'm not there. So that you and Darwin can feel safe. If those people come back, we'll catch them. I am only doing this to keep us safe. That's all. I'm not angry with you. I'm upset at myself for not getting a security system sooner, and I'm angry at myself for not being around more. I'm so pissed about it."

She wanted to tell him that he was wrong. That her greediness and carelessness was what dragged them into a bloody situation. She wanted to tell him about the used Honda Accord that she'd bought for disposal purposes and that it was in their garage at that very moment. She wanted to tell him that she was over one hundred years older than him, and that she had stopped counting bodies a century ago. She wanted to tell him that she would kill his kind again and again so long as she lived long enough to watch her son grow into a very old man and die. She wanted Randel to know that she planned on telling Darwin the dreadful secret behind her very own existence because Darwin would ask why his mother looked fifty when he himself was seventy. But she couldn't share any of that. She could only say what she always said to Randel: "I love you, and you're right."

C H A P T E R   3 3

The Set

Trish stood on the patio, plastic bags in hand. The camera faced away from her, its lens reflecting the white gate and copper leaves that dangled from a bare maple tree next door. Trish knew the family as the Pauls—a married couple with one teenage kid. He never came outside. In fact, she rarely saw any of them, assuming they lived elsewhere most of the year. She wasn't worried about them seeing anything anyway, with the tall fence and trees shielding her yard from theirs and Pepper's.

Nowadays, cameras were battery-operated and connected to the owner's phone via an app or Wi-Fi—something Trish realized after reluctantly skimming the manual. So, to evade *that* hurdle, she begrudgingly used her laptop to log into the security system app, Security Plus, and clicked on a few buttons, feigning ignorance. She changed the color of the display to black and white for the cameras in the front yard, and disabled night vision. She turned the motion sensor lights off, trapping their house in darkness. Then, she *accidentally* turned off the cameras in the backyard and cut the audio feed to all the cameras surrounding the house and locked the parameters, making it impossible for Randel to change them. Or so she hoped. Then, she changed the password to override the lock, making up lies as she went along:

I'm sorry, Randel. I thought it was asking me to make up my own password.

Oh, I'm sorry, Randel. I thought the lock button meant to lock the camera in place.

Maybe I should undo all the cameras, she thought. "No, no, no," she said aloud. Deception deserved subtlety.

She was sure that Randel could fix those very things from his laptop if he figured out what she'd done. She hoped that he wouldn't log in until the morning, when Victoria and Steve were less likely to show up. Trish was surprised that they hadn't shown up the night before, but she didn't expect to be so lucky for a second night in a row.

Trish put her bag of newly purchased goods on the patio table and inspected the metal traps as she pulled them out. Spiked prongs protruded from the traps' openings, making it look like a metal mouth full of sharp teeth.

Randel had every right to claim Trish was standoffish or friendless, but it was for his benefit. His and Darwin's. He was better off not knowing what she was and the atrocities that she was ready to commit. She'd hoped Randel would have seen her as bashful and careful, like those people who were so paranoid that they overreacted to every situation with quiet awareness. But Patricia's personality quirks were not working this time around, just as they had failed a couple times before.

Jonathan Feldman, her third husband, had been of the more aggressive variety, making her seasonal escapades a memorandum of his misgivings. But he hadn't always been that way. When she met Johnny at a dive bar at the foot of the rolling hills in the capital of Kentucky, he was enamored with her dark lips, pants, and tank top during a time that most women wore long skirts and button-up shirts that could have choked the words out of their throats. The 1950s town of Frankfort wasn't ready for a woman like Trish, but it welcomed her with open arms. Because why wouldn't they? She sat alongside them in the pews at First Methodist every Sunday and served whiskey and moonshine every other day of the week. With a little flirting here, and a little prayer there, it was enough to stay within the good graces of the men that mattered in town. They had no idea that she'd been responsible for the multiple murders and disappearances that occurred around the state since she showed up the summer of 1952.

Johnny had been her favorite customer, having come in fresh off work as the only mechanic in town. He looked so much like Josef, the boy who fawned over her until she left West Virginia as a monster. He was tall and slender, tanned from working in the sun all day, and wore a boyish grin. Every day at quitting time, Johnny sat on the same stool, and they'd laughed at the town's hypocrisy— Pastor Douglas' "Do as I say, not as I drink, smoke and take whores" attitude—and Johnny got off on watching Trish shoot down anyone who flirted with her except him. It was like she was his long before they made it official. He liked her company and contrarianism, and she liked his predictability. Johnny ordered the same thing, *whiskey and Coke, please*, and requested the same song, Johnnie Ray's "Cry," on the jukebox. He'd order the same liver and mashed potatoes with onions and tell Trish that he'd marry her one day. Luckily for him, that had been the plan. Trish already knew the importance of an alibi, and men provided the best ones.

She didn't realize that his nightly drinks and sense of togetherness would turn into obsession. He courageously took to turning the bottle up and waiting for her to come home; but he never followed her out. Every four months, Trish stalked and killed as she was required by her very nature. But she'd return to a very self-conscious, very drunk and sweaty Johnny who'd spew a few "cheating whore," "spiteful cunt," and "ungrateful sluts" her way.

Eventually, like all romantic stories, Johnny stopped designating his drunken rants to her seasonal outings; he graduated to going after her every day after work once he himself had been laid off. Johnny had degraded into the town drunk by going out to whatever bar just to spend whatever money Trish had given him. Every night, she'd talk him down with a bottle of pain killers and play big spoon as she lulled him to sleep. But when Johnny decided that punching Trish in the nose was the next best thing he could do to keep her under his watchful eye, that was his last day as a married drunk. They never found Johnny, and the last time Trish checked, his family was still hoping to find them both. Rumor around town was that he'd pissed off some people at the bar and they followed him home, which ended in them killing he and Trish. But that was far from the truth. Johnny was in the Kentucky River, but she was fine with going along with the fake lore. It was much more interesting.

Trish doubted that she'd have to go through such lengths with Randel. Not only was he not a drunk, he was also her son's father. But as she kicked the leaves around the patio, making room on the smoky gray wooden planks that they'd painted that summer, a nagging feeling pulled at her gut: *What if Randel changes? Becomes obsessive?*

After making enough room to lay out the various rodent and bear traps, she grabbed the first device, a galvanized spring-action trap that snapped closed if the plate was grazed by a rodent.

Or a foot, she thought.

She placed the trap on the patio table and removed the safety clamp. The metal jaw snapped closed, barely missing her fingers. Then she carefully disengaged the jagged jaws and laid each side flat. She pulled the trigger across either side, setting the trap. She repeated the same process seven times with the smaller traps and four times with bear traps that she altered with box cutters and fast-drying metal glue. Working quickly, she laid the traps around the yard, finishing by 6:30.

She studied her homemade map. There were eight traps in total: three against the fence to the right of the patio and two along the path to the patio. There were three buried beneath small piles of leaves against the foot of the patio steps.

Then she stopped. *What if, by some stupid miracle, no one shows up?*

Then I'll clean the yard up and try again some other way.

"Hm," she said aloud. Surely one of them, Steve or Victoria, would come around that night. They both wanted something from Trish; whether it be personal or complete nonsense, they *wanted* something.

How will you lure them to the backyard?

To that thought, she sneered. If Victoria destroyed Trish's vehicle, she did it in the cover of night.

The girl knows to stay hidden, Trish thought. After narrowly escaping a gunshot, she doubted Victoria would ever dare approach the front door again. Trish had to replace the door because of it.

And shooting her won't kill her anyway.

Trish needed to get Victoria inside and saw her to pieces. *It's the only way…*

But if Steve shows up, I'll shoot him on sight.

Trish took the remaining tools to the garage. She put them in the trunk of her much smaller car and headed inside. Then she killed all the lights and waited by the back door. If Trish couldn't smell Victoria, then she was sure Victoria could not smell her. She would instead watch the girl and then deal with her once she was down.

Trish fastened a silencer to her pistol and set it in her lap.

Steve wasn't in his own jurisdiction anymore and, according to her search history, he took full advantage of his turf. Many of his *friends* had gone missing. There was a guy named Cooper who, according to his Facebook page, was missing more teeth than a six-year-old. He was last seen at a 7-Eleven near Steve's house a little over four years ago. Then there was Samantha Allhart who was the typical partying twenty-something, with ruby-red hair, big green eyes, and took pictures wearing clothes that left little to the imagination. She was last seen leaving her apartment, heading to Steve's house. Trish was sure there were others. She searched *missing persons flyers in Miller*. Of the eight from the last fifteen years, six of them were thirty and younger, one of them was Victoria, and four of them were in social media pictures with Steve.

This would be alarming to anyone who wasn't a monster, but the information was insightful.

"Uh huh," Trish said as she sat in her chair eyeing the darkening backyard through the patio door. Perhaps it was a good thing that they, Victoria and Steve, were on Trish's turf. They had indeed found what they were looking for, and Trish was going to give it to them.

CHAPTER 34

Jag

The night felt young as Vicky went along the streets, hoping Patricia was ready to change her mind because "I can't" would not do, not when there was a federal agent in the vicinity. She wondered if Patricia knew about her neighbors at all, and if she didn't, maybe Vicky could trade that bit of information to be turned back? Vicky spent most of the day thinking about how that conversation would go, and something told her that it would end with she and Patricia fighting to the death. Death was better than existing as she was. Vicky couldn't go another day with her disgusting urges; she berated herself for licking the bloody stump of the racoon's body that she smeared all over Patricia's Jeep. But destroying Patricia's property was much easier than Vicky thought it'd be. The alarm did not go off because Vicky's bony fingers only lightly pressed the mangled animals' bodies onto it. The racoon's blood ran like rain; she couldn't help but taste it.

Until she figured out how to approach Patricia again, she wanted to up the stakes, starting by damaging more of her neighbors' things. Not only was it hurting the people who oh so carelessly shared a street with a monster, it could turn them all against one another, making them all look at each other differently, including Patricia. Petty, yes, but that was all Vicky could think of as she took her lonely stroll.

Vicky circled back around to Patricia's street; it was lazy as ever for a Friday night. It was close to midnight, and she didn't hear any party noises or smell anything outside of damp leaves and burning wood. She pulled the screwdriver from her bag, ready to put it to use once again.

She approached a Jaguar that was parked at the edge of a driveway as it had been the night before. A sedan and a Mini Coupe took up the part of the driveway closest to the house, leaving the bumper of the Jag to barely hang out into the street.

Probably leaves for work first, she thought, hearing Daddy tell Moody to move his car up to the garage. He left at 7 am every morning, and didn't tolerate anyone blocking him in. It was stupid to leave such a nice car that close to the dark street, far back from the house which had a motion-sensor porch light: she'd run by the place twice in the last two nights and it lit up without fail.

Too bad, she thought, pushing off the oncoming guilt for what she was about to do. It wasn't fair how this household, this undisturbed family, got to live normal lives, concerned with the minimal shit like inconveniently having your car blocked in. But now, no one was going anywhere.

The small car's silhouette was a mere shadow in the night save for the small gleam on the hood from a porch light a few houses down. She crouched as she got closer and blew nervous air between pursed lips. Before piercing the tire, she looked over her shoulder, then froze. A car crawled up the street with the urgency of a taxi driver searching for a pickup location. But the headlights were off. From where Vicky was hiding, it was difficult to decipher the car's color and type, but as the build of the bulky sedan formed in the shadows, it was unmistakable. Her heart dropped from her chest and her body quaked.

That…that can't be… She knew he'd find her, but not so soon. Not before Patricia changed her back. Had Steve taken care of the monster already? Was Patricia already dead? Or was she in the trunk?

Vicky contemplated taking off, knowing that they'd already seen her; she wondered how long her back had been to them? The car stopped behind her, and a telltale *click* sounded as someone let themselves out.

Fuck, fuck, shit. She dashed across the yard, grateful that the many people in the neighborhood did not have fences. The car revved angrily as it took off, following her up the street.

The yards were so unnecessarily massive that there seemed to be no end in sight. But she kept running, jumping over yard toys and bikes. She ran for a maple tree that stood in the darkened corner of the yard of a house that looked much bigger than the others. It could pass for a brick mini-mansion that she'd seen in a movie once. She couldn't think of the name of the movie or who was in it, all she could do was praise the very tall, very thick tree as she leapt and grabbed onto the lowest branch, dropping the screwdriver in her haste. She traversed the tree's limbs, pulling herself higher and higher from the ground. Before she could reach the top, her body seized, stealing her breath and hypnotizing her muscles as they jerked. The electric current rode her nerves, sizzling her senses and gripping her in place. Once the shock ceased, she lost her footing and watched the yellow leaves rush toward her face.

Electrode

The fall from the tree was hard and the thud against the grassy ground made her bones knock. She landed on her shoulder, surprised that the fall wasn't accompanied with a righteous *snap*. Stunned, she forced herself to roll over to her back just to find Lou, or Vodka Tony, standing over her, his meaty head and hooded brow hiding his beady eyes. He hefted her to her feet with more grace than she anticipated and put one of her arms over his shoulder as he held her side, much like a friend would if their companion had a broken leg or foot. She limped, leaning her body against him, too stunned to realize defeat or search for new options. Dizziness and pain did not allow a fight.

Steve helped Lou slide her into the back seat, seating her right next to him. She pictured herself snatching away from his gentle hands. But instead, she slowly turned away from him—*Is he fucking kidding?*—as she fought to ease her staggering muscles. The light dimmed and the passenger cabin went dark once Lou got into the driver's seat.

"I've been lookin' under every rock wondering where my girl went," Steve said. The flicker of a lighter before the skunky aroma suffocated the car.

Vicky's shoulders involuntarily jumped as sparks rode her extremities. When she didn't say anything, Steve went on. "Why'd you leave me like that?"

It was weird seeing him ride in the back seat. She'd always only seen him in the front seat, driving. But then she realized that the back windows had been tinted and that the seats were leather.

Easier to clean, she thought. *Once he gets his way.*

He must have noticed her looking around, because he said, "Yeah, I bought a motorcade for this operation." He inhaled smoke and blew it out. "How are you feeling? I hope you're not in too much pain."

She wanted to scream. But her jaw felt stuck. She shuddered, neglecting to look at him.

"You know Lou hates running around, right? You made him chase you for no reason at all. All I want to do is talk."

Her legs and arms jerked and her abs clenched, forcing her to lean forward.

Steve sighed. "So, you not fucking with me no more? I thought…I thought we were more than that." He pulled on the blunt again. The cherry made small popping sounds as he fed it more oxygen. He blew the smoke out, filling the cabin and making Vicky's eyes water. "You left because you wanted to meet her first, right? Warn her that I was coming?"

She felt her muscles relax, finally turning control over to her.

"I did a lot for you. I took you in when the government was after you. I found the person who turned you into *that.*"

Her lips jerked as she turned her head. "Oh yeah? What else did you do?" Her throat shook, almost making her swallow the words. She sniffed, failing to hold back tears.

"When everyone said, 'fuck you,' I was like, 'Well, let's figure that shit out. What are you? What makes you tick?'"

Her sobbing intensified as her thoughts became her own again. *How could he say that? Are we from the same damn timeline? We were at the same farmhouse for the last couple months, right?* To be sure, she let him go on.

"I tried to help you. All I asked was for you to give me time to make everything make sense. Then you up and fucking left. You—"

"Fuck you!" she finally shouted. "You fucking psycho!"

"Ah, there she is. My V, not taking shit from nobody."

"I left because you hurt me!"

"Hm. Is that what happened? I thought I gave you a place to stay. I tried to feed you, but you wouldn't let me."

"I told you no!"

He dropped his eyes to his lap. "Then you were gone, right after I showed you Patricia Weston's license. It was almost like you had no use for me anymore."

"I could say the same about you. You got bored with trying to figure me out and moved on to trying to kill me."

He scoffed.

"Look at what you did to me!" She pulled her hoodie up to her chin. Welts crisscrossed her torso, starting just below her breast, ending just beneath her navel. They stretched from the mess of bruises and raw skin around the bullet wound. Her stomach expanded and collapsed as she breathed heavily, trying to forget the slicing and stabbing.

"Wow. You healed up really fast. You know how long it takes a living person's incisions to heal, to turn into scars? About a month. And I... Wow."

She shoved her sweater down. "You're sick."

"You did that to yourself. All you had to do was eat."

"No!" she screamed, wanting to tear his head off. But she knew the moment that she reached for him, Lou would use the taser again. She pressed her back against the door instead.

"Wow. You are angry, huh?" He chuckled. "Lou, it looks like I really fucked up this time, yeah?"

Vicky watched Vodka Tony in the rearview mirror. He lifted a thick brow.

"Look, I fucked up. I know—and for that, I am sorry." Steve bowed his head.

"Sorry?!" she growled. She'd seen what he was capable of when he was amazed and simply studying. She didn't know what he would do if he was chopping and slicing to kill. She used to buy pot from the man. Flirt and sext all summer with him. Hoped to make him her next college sweetheart even though he wasn't a student. She fantasized about waking up next to him in the morning and heading to campus just to come back to his house and sleep with him that very night. Now, she wished she'd never known him. But she did. And he knew everything about her. He knew about her escape from the hospital. He knew who had bitten her. He knew that her family was convinced that she was missing and in trouble—maybe even dead. Even from the pictures they chose to share of her as a happy college kid, going to create a new future for herself and her family, it was all destroyed, and Steve knew all about it.

He glared at her through the billowing smoke that made her stomach turn. "You a deserter?"

"You're high. Let me out, now."

"No. No, see, you lost your opportunity to make demands or tell me what you are going to do. See, just as you may or may *not* know, it will not be easy to get inside Mrs. Weston's house with all the cameras along the outside of her house. Have you seen them? Have you been over there at all since this afternoon?"

Vicky felt her face crumple in bewilderment. *Cameras?* "No."

He tapped his blunt out in an ashtray that had been sitting on the center console. He pointed to her. She flinched when he did.

He narrowed his eyes. She could not tell if he was high or skeptical.

She held his scowl.

"Why do I feel like you are lying to me?" he said quickly.

"I—"

"Don't lie, because I will cut your tongue out."

"I didn't. I just came out…"

"Does she know you're nearby? Does she know that you are here?"

"Yes."

He raised his brow and then smiled. "Good. You can go up to her door and ask her to come outside."

"What? No! That's not gonna work."

"She knows you, right?"

"Our meeting didn't go well."

"Hm. What happened?"

Vicky didn't answer.

He sucked in a deep breath. "Welp, looks like you are in a tight spot. Either you go and get her to come outside, or we put you in the trunk and take you back. And I'll make sure you don't get out. Your choice."

Vicky wanted to ask about Dr. Gonzalez. She wanted to know if Steve knew the details about her escape. But she decided that it was best not to bring it up. It was best to pretend that Dr. Gonzalez and her father were far away from Michigan. "How do you know that she won't just call the police?"

"Because you are still alive and walking around free. And since you said that it didn't go well, and that those cameras were not there when you first arrived, it looks like she's waiting for your inevitable return."

"What happens to me when I lure her outside? You're not going to stun me again and put me in the shed anyway?"

"You saw the shed. Shit, you can see this car. There is only enough room in there and there"—he pointed to the trunk behind him—"for one subject." He sighed as if casually discussing torture was boring. "I have a bigger issue with her right now. Not you. I'm sure we will meet again under better circumstances." He touched Vicky's face and the smell of burning cigar leaves encased her nose. "You know I will always love you, right?"

Her nostrils flared. His lie would have been convincing to her two months ago. But now, she wanted out of his car. "Okay."

Steve winked and smiled at her. "You know, if we get her, I'll let you go back to the basement. You can even help me with her… We can figure this all out together." He leaned in, his lips ready for a kiss.

But Vicky turned away. "I want you to stay far away from me when this is over."

He sat back and smirked. Then he tapped the back of Lou's seat.

They drove around to Trish's house and Vicky spotted the cameras. Even in the dark, the one on the garage was not inconspicuous. Maybe it was there to purposely scare Vicky and Steve away. That's if Patricia Weston knew that Steve was after her.

The house was dark and the driveway was bare.

"What if she isn't there?" Vicky asked. They stopped a few houses away from the monster's yard.

"She's there. Her car is in the garage," he said. "Get out and walk. We'll watch from here, and Lou will be ready to stun her when she comes out onto the porch."

"What if she doesn't—"

"Make her." He sounded annoyed. "Or you are going in the trunk. Got it?"

She went to protest but stopped, already planning her approach in her head.

Don't plan, she reminded herself. *Just do, because if you just do things, no one, not even you, will know what to expect.*

She nodded stiffly.

"Go," he said, the clicking on his demand.

Vicky got out of the car and jogged along the flattened curb.

Once she approached Trish's house, she passed the garage, noticing that the camera was not following her. Steve was not going to let her go, with Patricia in his custody or not.

She ran past the porch and past the windows, which appeared dark behind the drawn shades. Steve's arrogance clung to the inner workings of her mind. Lies rolled off his tongue like papers rolled joints.

Quickening her pace, she approached a fence that separated Patricia's house from the neighbor, waiting for her body to ignite in white shock, ready for Vodka Tony to subdue her again. Her heart thudded as she imagined all the curse words that Steve must have been calling her in that very moment. But instead, she heard tires burrowing into the ground, screeching before taking off.

Knowing that Vodka Tony was heading her way, itching to maul her body with heavy tires and hardened aluminum, Vicky took off, top speed, and hopped the fence, landing in Patricia's backyard.

CHAPTER 36

Teeth

Vicky's feet hit the ground with a thud, and she winced as pangs tore through her abdomen and bruised shoulder. Light on her feet, she limped slowly, trying to take the backyard in. She saw what could have been a sandbox or a pen for those colorful balls that they had at Chuck E Cheese. Next to that was the silhouette of a jungle gym. The swings moved slowly in the night as if some invisible kids were merely sitting on them and chatting, not actually swinging. There was also a toddler-sized slide set; the gray of night peeped through the holes that made up the ladder for a small child to climb.

She felt her own feet press against the grass as she took small steps and listened for Steve as he rode around, coming up with another plan. She also listened for Patricia, who she assumed wasn't home. The house was dark.

There was a patio to the left full of lawn furniture shadows. She could not make out the colors because, surprisingly, Patricia's motion-sensor lights were not active that night.

You know I will always love you, right? Steve had said with that look in his eye. It was the same look he had given her when they lay naked in bed. That subconscious feeling of *Am I too cold?* wore off in that moment, when he moaned and groaned inside her.

But now, as she stood in the dark with her face contorted in fear and sadness, she realized the truth. His invitation to keep her in his basement, his insistence on keeping her hidden from everyone else in the house, taking her phone, training her to stay away from her family—she wasn't hiding out. She was being held captive. Willingly at first, until it was time for him to experiment. Time for him to force her to eat after months of refusing. Their physical relationship had only fulfilled the fantasies of a necrophiliac.

"She has to turn me back," Vicky said, compelled by the mission to be rid of such madness. Once she turned back, she would catch a train home and get a lawyer. Then she would go to the police. Vicky tucked her lower lip. She'd turn Steve and Patricia into the authorities for ruining her life, and ending many others.

Then something dawned on Vicky. If she warned Patricia about Steve, would she turn Vicky back? Would she be open to a favor for a favor? Vicky was still going to report the monster, but the monster did not need to know that. In that very moment, she and Patricia had a common enemy. Vicky would even throw in a warning about the agent across the street.

Maybe they could help each other?

Vicky's steps quickened as she decided to go for the back door on the patio. She stopped when she stepped on something that didn't feel like the mix of soft grass and dead leaves that had carried her from the fence to the foot of the patio steps. Her mind was caught in the metallic throng as it announced her misstep and bit down on her calf. Her mouth dropped, but the pain muted her screams, and her breath was harsh as her lungs forgot how to inflate. Teeth penetrated her leg, shredding her calf and taking her down to her knees. Only then did she feel around. The metal mouth chewed her calf and snapped her ankle in the process. When she tried to separate the teeth to set her leg free, it seemed to sink in deeper, turning her muscles and tissue into mush. She fought the urge to cry out. Steve would hear her. The neighbors would find her. She swung her busted leg out front and stuffed the side of her hand into her mouth. She hissed and let out a guttural cry.

Vicky was sure Patricia could hear the low pained screech in the yard.

And she did. As Vicky blinked back tears, she watched the thin frame of a woman with long hair step out onto the patio. She wielded a tool. As she got closer, Vicky made out the barrel of a pistol.

"About time you showed up," Patricia said, voice a whisper but as clear as someone shouting into Vicky's ear.

"H–he's coming," Vicky said, terror and exhaustion harsh on her tongue. "He's coming to kill both of us." Before she could say anything else, her eyes grew heavy as the pain encroached every inch of her body. Patricia advanced as white flashes and black spots lit up the darkness before Vicky's eyes.

Tatters

The girl had been beaten, and her leg was in tatters. If Trish disengaged the trap, Victoria's cry would penetrate the quiet night. Trish didn't need Pepper or any of the other neighbors peeking out their windows, wondering what she was doing in her own backyard.

Victoria groaned and sucked air through her clenched teeth. There was something tired and ragged about her breathing and crying. It reminded Trish of the time she was out in the sun before she'd gotten the ring. Before she'd gotten to know her new self.

Victoria's fangs weren't visible in her bared teeth, so she had probably eaten recently or was in too much pain to think about food. Trish made a mental note to ask later—if there was a later. Even in the darkness, Trish could see that Victoria's once-youthful, even caramel complexion was mottled with bruises. It might have been dirt, since it certainly wasn't a sunburn. She needed to get the girl inside quickly—there was clearly more damage than what Trish could see.

"Scream into your hand," Trish instructed. "I'm going to take this off."

The girl didn't answer, but she did as she was told, as if opting for secrecy on her own accord.

Trish pulled the pin, and the trap loosened its jaws. She detached the metal teeth from Vicky's calf, one side at a time. The wet sounds of crushed sinew accompanied the removal. Vicky screamed and whimpered like a baby, squeezing Trish's shoulder as she shouted obscenities into her own hand.

"I am going to carry you now. Alright?" Trish said.

Through heavy breaths, Victoria grumbled, "Mm…um… uhmm." Horror etched the frightened grimace that crossed her face.

"What?" Trish asked.

Vicky dropped her hand into the grass. "A–are you going to k–kill me?" she stuttered.

"No," Trish said. "I'm going to ask you some questions."

"Okay. I don't want to go in your house. You—can–can ask me out h–*here*," Victoria said. Her speech slowed on the last word, as if she had to make sure Trish understood the word *here*.

Trish shook her head. "No. Can't chance anyone seeing you like this. Can't chance anyone seeing you at all."

"No, I—"

"Victoria, I—"

"Vicky."

Trish scowled. "What?"

"My name is Vicky," she blubbered.

"Okay. *Vicky*. We need to go inside. If—"

"Steve's h–he's here. He—" Vicky swallowed. "He brought me over here. He wanted me to lure you outside."

Trish felt her heart reel at the mere mention of him. That batshit-crazy asshole was closer to her house than she thought. Thankfully, Darwin and Randel were out of the house.

"So, you expect me to believe that you came here to tell me that? To tell me to beware. Why should I trust you?"

"Because I'm scared," Vicky wailed. Her dreadful whisper was low enough to hide her from the neighbors, but loud enough to make Trish shudder.

"We need to go inside."

"I…" Vicky grimaced.

"You don't want Steve to see us out here, do you?" Trish's plea made her feel like she was trying to convince Darwin to eat his peas. Vicky shook her head, a new layer of seriousness overtaking the sorrow on her face.

Trish squatted, sliding one forearm underneath Vicky's knees, and another behind her back. She lifted her, noting how heavy she was for her stature. She looked like she weighed 80 pounds, but she felt like she weighed a little over one hundred.

Bone density, Trish thought. She carried Vicky into the house, making a note to clean up whatever blood they'd tracked inside. She felt Victoria's, or *Vicky's*, heart shudder and throb, beating hard as she was carried, cradled in Trish's arms.

Trish crossed through the kitchen and down the hallway, past her office and the front door. She led them into the garage, kicking the door closed behind her. Her Honda sat inside, undisturbed and protected. She rounded the vehicle and headed for the door at the back of the garage. The storage room was well lit, its shelves covered in labeled boxes. Everything from Christmas decorations to unwanted gifts—Trish could swear Randel's parents had bought them a slow cooker three years running—sat neatly against the walls. Gardening tools like the rake and lawn mower lined one wall. The tool bench sat against the adjacent wall. Randel never used it; he only mowed the yard. But Trish had used it. It was the longest tool bench she'd ever seen, and being metal, it was easy to clean.

As she laid Vicky on the bench and studied her face, her intentions shifted so much that she needed to change course. The plans that she had laid out so carefully, getting rid of Vicky and Steve, abruptly changed.

He's here, Vicky had said. Her limbs shivered and her teeth clattered. There were bloody scrapes on her face, and her hoodie was filthy. Her eyes looked sunken, and her sweatpants were covered with bits of orange and pink leaves and blood.

Trish went to reach for Vicky's bloody pant leg, but Vicky leapt up, sitting up fast and grabbing Trish's shoulder. She dug her bony fingertips into Trish's flesh, making her tense. "Please, don't."

"I have to see it," Trish protested, pulling her shoulder from Vicky's grip. "Can't just leave it like this."

Vicky sobbed. "But it really hurts."

"It'll heal. But I have to see it. Alright?" Trish looked around, searching for something to distract the girl, much like she used her keys to distract Darwin when she needed to clean a new boo boo. She pulled the *Christmas Decorations* box down and opened it. Shimmering crimson garlands wound around newspaper rolls sat at the top of the pile. *Will have to do*, she thought.

"Here," she said, handing it over to Vicky.

Vicky stared at it, tears still rolling down her sunken cheeks.

"Bite on it, because this is going to hurt."

Vicky shook her head. She laid back. "Just do it."

Trish stuffed the garland back into the box and headed back to Vicky. "Don't scream. Hear me?"

"Fucking do it," Vicky said before putting her forearm against her lips, wincing the entire way.

Trish rolled Vicky's pant leg up with ease, thanks to the fact that Vicky was wearing sweats. Vicky shrieked into her arm and banged a balled fist into the workbench top. Pink flesh dangled from bone, as the blades had embedded deep gashes into her leaking calf.

Trish tilted her chin up. "Sit up."

"W–why?"

"Take off that nasty hoodie."

"Again, why?" Vicky growled that time.

"Do you want my help or not?" Trish yelled. "I need to see what I'm dealing with."

Slowly, Vicky used the hand that she banged against the table to prop herself up. She lifted the hoodie halfway but then stopped as she shuddered.

"Here," Trish said, impatience begging her to change her mind. She reached for both sides of the hoodie and pulled it off. Her eyes rested on a cacophony of terror that was drawn into Vicky's torso. Her right shoulder was blackened with a prominent bruise. Her ribs pressed against her skin, making her look frail and sick. Scars expanded from a dime-sized patch just below her left kidney. They looked like a brown spider web, and the ill-treated gunshot wound was the epicenter.

Trish thought about her own trip through the woods as she crossed over into Pennsylvania. How Ally gave her the ring. How Trish could have suffered greatly if not for his help. How she didn't choose this life for herself, and how some hungry creature made the decision for her. How she went and did the same thing to— *No*, she told herself. *No. You are still getting rid of her. You have to—*

"Did he do this to you?" she heard herself ask.

Vicky sobbed.

"Did Steve do this to you?" Trish felt herself going manic, desperate to know. Desperate for Vicky to tell her *no*. Begging for a reason to stick to the original plan.

"He–he found me," she said, sulking in a tormented stupor. "He's gonna kill us both. There's no getting away."

"Stay here." Trish rushed out of the garage and into the house. She ran past her office and into the bathroom, reeling as Vicky's flesh riddled her mind. Steve had mutilated her. How? Vicky was stronger than Steve, and she was hungry. How had she not drained him dry?

Because you didn't give her a manual when you turned her. She grunted once she snatched the linen closet open and grabbed a bottle of iron supplements. She had eight bottles in stock, all neatly lined up next to Randel's cold medicine. All unopened, waiting for the inventory in the medicine cabinet and kitchen cupboard to be depleted. She grabbed one of the first aid kits—this one small enough to fit into Darwin's diaper bag—and a baby-blue beach towel with small pineapples on it. She'd have to explain what happened to it, because once this one was gone, there would only be three left and Randel would surely notice. After deciding to worry about her future lies later, she rushed back to the storage room.

She set the first aid kit and towel on the shelf next to the box full of decorations and handed the iron supplements to Vicky. "Take ten of these," she said.

Vicky's eyes strolled over the words. "Iron pills?" Her voice sounded hoarse.

"Yeah. It'll help you heal just a little faster. I'm assuming you haven't been eating…"

A look of shame wore on Vicky's features.

Trish left Vicky alone in her feelings as she headed inside to grab a needle and thread from her office. She'd only had one use for it: to fix holes in clothes. Then she went back to the bathroom and grabbed the peroxide. Vicky was covered in dirt and exposure. She'd benefit from a little sanitization; it would only speed up the healing process.

When Trish returned, she set her homemade surgical supplies on the counter.

"He shot me," Vicky said, an absent expression on her face as she stared at the shelving unit. "He tied my arms together with an extension cord hanging from the ceiling. He had someone close the wound, just to re-open it up, poke around, then close it. I don't know how many times he did it—I lost count."

Trish ripped the beach towels into rags and soaked four of them in peroxide. "Did he take anything?"

"No. I don't think so." She let out a wet chuckle, then her face fell into a frown. Vicky winced and stopped herself from drawing back when the wet towel hit her skin.

"The doctors wanted to experiment on me just like the FBI and my own boyfriend. I'll be dead before this is over," she said.

FBI? Trish didn't call attention to that. Instead, she said, "No one is killing anyone." Trish was something to be afraid of. Not Steve. Not some human. Trish picked up the needle and then stopped. "This will hurt."

Vicky shook her head. Her nose flared. "I don't think you get it. Steve's crazy. His uncle runs the sheriff's department. He's—"

"First off, Miller's Sheriff's Department has nothing to do with *here.*"

"Not if he knows you murdered Barbie."

Trish felt her heart skip a beat. How could she forget that very inconvenient fact? Steve knew what had happened that night. Even worse, now he knew where she lived. "How did you find me?"

"The picture of your ID."

"Hm," Trish said, confirming her suspicions. "And he showed it to you?"

"Yes," Vicky said. "C–can you change me back?"

"I told you, I can't."

"Yes you can, please, I—"

"I can't do *shit* if nut bag is out there chasing us around," Trish barked. "Any word of what his plans are if he does catch me?"

"The shed."

"Yeah?" The shed meant nothing to Trish; she didn't even know what that was. But she didn't care. "And what is he going to do with you?"

"He said he'll leave me alone. But I don't believe that. He's going to kill me."

"If he can figure it out."

Vicky raised a brow. "What do you mean?"

Trish bit her tongue, wishing she could take it back. She wasn't there to tell the girl secrets about what she had become. She wanted to learn everything Vicky knew about Steve.

"Hello?" Vicky asked. "Did you say that I can't die?"

"I don't know." Trish threaded the needle and readied herself to start stitching. "Once I'm done stitching this up, the dead skin should fall off overnight, and your ankle should be usable by the morning, so long as you eat the iron pills. I need you ready because we have work to do."

Vicky peered at Trish, stunned. "Work to do…what exactly?"

"I'll help you get better, if you help me get rid of your boyfriend."

Vicky stared, her expression blank but engaged.

"Sounds like we have a deal," Trish said. "Now hold your breath."

CHAPTER 38

Garbage

Trish spent the midnight hours cleaning the patio and floors, raking the leaves in the backyard, and spraying the grass underneath the bear trap that snared Vicky's leg. It was around 6 am when she progressed inside and found some solace until she looked at the front door. The black tape taunted her, tightening her gut. *Get a new door*, she reminded herself yet again. Buying a new door and installing it wasn't as easy as replacing a broken glass; it was a whole thing that she didn't have time for.

There were a few things that needed to happen before Randel got back, namely evicting the vampire who was lying up in the garage, because Vicky hadn't left. Trish checked on her a few times throughout the night. She hadn't acknowledged Trish since they'd talked, but that was fine. Trish was too busy cleaning and thinking up a plan.

Because of her newfound perplexities, it took her longer than she thought to pick up the traps and put them in the trunk of her very small car.

She drove over to Burger King just outside her neighborhood and tossed the garbage into the dumpster full of old food. Although she wiped the blood off the trap and, if Vicky was anything like Trish, there was no DNA to track, her heart sped up. There were people searching for Vicky. The Feds were out there actively looking for her. Not the police like the YouTubers had been saying, but the Feds. And the doctor at the hospital had studied her. Some of those studies required blood. Trish didn't know what came of it, but she had a feeling: they may have detected biomarkers that weren't necessarily DNA. There were no identifiable antigens to name it A or AB blood type. Trish's blood was of the inconclusive variety.

But who was to say they couldn't match what they took at the hospital to what they may find on the traps or at Steve's house?

Fuck, she thought. She dug through the dumpster and retrieved her garbage bag full of traps.

Once she made it back home, she made two piles: one with the bloody trap, and another with Vicky's disgusting bloody worn clothes. The latter would be burned.

Trish rushed through the garage and into the house, heading to the kitchen for a lighter. In her haste, her foot kicked the leg of a maple end table that was against the wall in the foyer. The pink vase full of fake black roses toppled over, slamming onto the hardwood floor. Randel's mom had gotten the flowers for them once Trish moved in. The cluster of fake black roses scattered across the floor, interspersed with pink glass shards. As she scooped up the glass, she grunted, knowing that she'd never hear the end of it because buying an imposter dozen roses and an imposter vase was far down her list of… She stopped when she stepped back, her foot crushing a rogue shard. She hurriedly lifted her foot to stop the glass from penetrating her cleaning house shoes. But what she found wasn't a plastic rose or a piece of the busted vase. She picked up the cracked case. It was the size of her index fingernail. Although flattened now, it was once a cylinder. The round glossy lens was split, a silver crack riding down the center.

"Are you fucking serious?!" she asked the crumpled mess.

Her face flushed as rage kicked her chest. Had she messed up that much to where her husband had cameras in the house that she didn't know about? A chilling panic made her shudder at the idea of Randel becoming Johnny. Next thing she knew, he'd come into the house with his breath reeking of alcohol and popcorn from a night-long stint at the bar. No, no, that wasn't happening, not with a child to raise. Not with Darwin around. If she needed to deal with Randel, she would. But right then wasn't a good time.

When is it ever a good time? she thought.

Never.

Then why and when? How long had he been watching her? "Dammit!" she spat. *Not you too, Randel.*

Her world had turned against her.

She crushed what remained of the camera in her hand. Then her phone rang…

She looked at the caller's name. *Of course*, she thought. What else would Randel do if his camera had been compromised. What had he seen?

"Did you know that the cameras were disconnected?" Randel asked over the phone. It sounded like he was walking around, in a rush that marked his everyday life.

"They are?" she said, holding back her ire, wanting to check him about the mini-camera. But it wasn't the time. She had other matters to address. "I must have done that when I played around with the controls on the laptop. Sorry about that. How long were they out?" she asked. *Or are you concerned about the secret feed that I just found?*

"Well, I checked them this morning, so hopefully not too long. Last time I checked was around four in the afternoon yesterday, they were all on and working fine. Be careful with that next time, alright?"

"Yeah, it was an accident," she said, her frustration slipping into her words. *How could you be watching me like that?*

"Hm," he said.

"People are allowed to make mistakes," she said. "I mean, I know I do."

"I wonder if I can lock it," he said.

She tilted her chin, knowing that he could lock it, but knowing that she could not tell him that. "What do you mean by *lock it?*" she growled.

"Well, I know how to use it and clearly you don't."

"Excuse me? It was an accident. It's not like somebody broke in last night."

"I know, I know. But I can't risk that ever happening because you accidentally turned the cameras off. And the cameras in the front are showing black and white. I can't see anything from last night. It's all black."

Trish sighed. "Okay, Randel. Do what you want."

"Look, I'll teach you how to use it when I get home, alright? I just want you and Darwin to be safe. That's all."

She pinched the bridge of her nose and clenched her eyes tight. *No, you don't. You just want to spy on me…* "Okay," she said.

CHAPTER 39

Favors

The new scabs on her calf twinged as Vicky held her knees to her chest, wishing she could lull off into a deep sleep in the tight space. For a second, she wished she hadn't bothered with Trish's Jeep, because the Honda's trunk offered little to no space for Vicky to stretch as she waited and listened. For once, she beckoned her blood-coated dreams to drag her underneath, to hide her from the pain and misery of that day, the night, the last two months and change. But it didn't. She was left aware—awake—to deal with the damage.

Before she was chaperoned to her new hiding spot, or the awaiting chariot to her final destination—who knew?—she took some time to look herself over. Sucking down ten iron pills seemed to do something, because the topical webbed disturbance on her torso started to fade, with the minor aches from the bullet hole rendered numb or nonexistent. Her ankle only barely held her up straight as she limped over to the trunk, but her ragged skin was cut loose and her bones were reattaching, regenerating like a lizard's appendage. Her ankle was still swollen but not broken, and her skin was raw as it grew a new layer. Still, she imagined she'd feel less stiff and rid of the small creeping sensations of pain if she could stretch. But no, she was stuck in the fetal position.

She listened for a while, hearing the normal banter between a mom and her kid, him babbling and her speaking with a patience that she could not picture on Patricia—or Trish, as she had told Vicky earlier when she led her over to the trunk.

Vicky heard furniture move, maybe a chair, and water splashing. She even heard the baby laugh. She couldn't imagine the woman who had turned her into a monster—the same woman who had trapped her with a bear trap, which was batshit insane—making an innocent baby laugh. Making *anyone* laugh.

Shortly after the sounds of a normal family doing normal family things, she finally heard Trish and her son talking, or cooing, to some woman, or girl, named Maggie.

"I'll be back in a few hours," Trish said, her voice getting louder as she drew closer to the garage. "I'm going to the dump to drop off some dead leaves—that it took forever to get up this morning—stop at the gym, do some shopping, and stop by my friend's house for a while. She wanted me to help her decorate her living room."

Lie, lie, lie, Vicky thought.

Trish sounded so real, so innocent, that Vicky thought she had confused the monster for an actual living person. She never outright admitted to turning Vicky into a vampire. *Did she?* Trish never mentioned Chad. She never admitted to anything. She only asked questions. And now, as Vicky lay in the trunk, Trish was actively lying to *Maggie* about her afternoon plans.

The situation was so surreal that, for all Vicky knew, she could be hallucinating in Steve's shed, not having found Trish at all. Vicky could still be sitting in that old chair with her hands tied over her head. But a quick throbbing ache shot up her leg, igniting the mild pangs in her side, reminding her that her current situation was very real. She'd found the monster, and for the third time as her new self, she was being held captive.

"Bye, baby," Trish said as the garage door closed behind her, or so Vicky thought. Then the latch let up and the trunk flung open. Trish was wearing a leather jacket with gray jeans. Her raven hair flowed past her shoulders and her lips were nude and glossy. Her eyes were hidden underneath square sunglasses that were too big for her face. Vicky didn't mind it though. She'd seen pink irises in the monster's eyes when she was feeding. She was fine with not knowing what the monster looked like when she was living out her lies in the daytime.

"Get out," Trish whispered, handing Vicky a black comforter. It was as thick as the comforter that Vicky used every winter night when it finally got too cold to sleep with the fan on. Trish opened the back passenger door. "Lay down and cover yourself. Wait for me to tell you to move."

"Where are we going?"

Trish let out an exasperated sigh. "Let's get past this part first, yeah?"

Vicky didn't answer. She climbed out of the trunk, wincing as she placed her right foot onto the ground, the shoes that Dr. P and Nurse Cammy had gotten her still in play. Trish had cleaned the blood off them after realizing her feet were bigger than Vicky's by about 3 inches. She nearly tripped over the too-long hot pink yoga pants that Trish had given her, but she liked the heather-gray zip-up hoodie. It fit snuggly and was thick enough to keep the sunrays off her arms if she encountered it. Vicky limped forward, grabbed the blanket.

"Get on the floor," Trish said so low that if no one was listening, no one would hear. Vicky used her left arm to help lower herself onto the floor. Then she began to cover herself but stopped when Trish took the blanket and finished the job. Garbage bags swooshed and rattled as Trish set them on the back seat, covering Vicky in the process. Then they were on their way. The mechanical gears squawked as the walls vibrated around the car while the garage door rolled up. The car jostled once Trish let herself inside.

The new car smell barely covered the scent of smoke, stale French fries, and carpet shampoo as Vicky inhaled, picking up bits of lint in her airway. She coughed to clear the itch forming in the base of her throat.

"Was Steve alone?" Trish asked.

"No," Vicky said, her answer clipped. She didn't ask to go along with Trish's plan; she was forced.

"Who's with him?"

"Vodka Tony."

"What?"

"Lou."

"Hm. Do you know where Steve lives?"

Vicky paused, her heart fluttering at the idea of where this could be going. *Why does that matter?* The last place she wanted to be was at Steve's.

"Vicky?" Trish asked, snapping her fingers. "The more questions you answer, the more I'll be able to help you."

"Yes." Vicky listened to the blinker as they came to a stop. When the car began to move again, Trish went on, as if taking the time to think about what she wanted to say. "I don't have a reason to think you're lying, do I?"

"I don't have a reason to lie," Vicky said. But she did have a reason to hold certain things back, like the fact that Trish was being investigated by Mr. Minty Fresh, Agent Morgan, who lived across the street. That the government was on to Trish, and that no matter what happened, she was going to answer for what she'd done to Vicky and many others. No. Vicky kept that to herself because, just as everyone in Miller knew, Steve wasn't beholden to the law. The only way he was going down was if something *different* had intervened. Something *otherworldly.* Something like Trish.

Once Trish's car seemed to pick up speed, uninterrupted by stops for about ten minutes, she said, "Was there anything else to his grand plan? Other than having you bait me?"

Vicky cleared her throat again. "No. He sped off once I hopped the fence."

"Hm. Well…I was in and out of the house all night and this morning, and I hadn't seen him. So, seems like he may've gone back to his lair. Maybe looking for a different approach."

"Maybe," Vicky mumbled.

"So I guess *maybe* we need to go to him."

Vicky sighed.

"What?" Trish asked. "You don't like my idea?"

"You don't get it. He's not some scrawny college kid that you can just throw around. And his property is big… Going there will make it easy for him to catch us."

Trish scoffed. "Sure."

"I'm serious. He really—"

"—thinks he's a monster hunter. Huh? Has he caught the Chupacabra? Sasquatch?" She snickered. Her taunting giggle made Vicky recoil, making her rethink the entire situation. "He should stop snorting his own shit—maybe he'd stop seeing colors."

"You laugh, but he isn't entirely wrong for what he's doing. He'd be doing a service by catching us—by killing you. You caused all of this," Vicky snapped.

A short pause. "Okay, well, I'll just drop you at his doorstep. Is that what you want?" Trish's matter-of-fact tone was dismissive and disappointed all at once.

"No. I'm just stating the obvious. He's right."

"Monsters don't have a special anatomy. You can be human and still serve as the biggest threat to your own species. Ever heard of Hitler?"

Vicky didn't respond to Trish's obsolete statement. A monster describing another monster didn't give the monster a pass, no matter what its physiology was.

Trish changed the subject, probably noticing how ridiculous she sounded. "How does your leg feel? Looks like the bleeding stopped. That's good."

The reminder seemed to give Vicky's leg permission to pulse, letting her know that it had gone through a new trauma recently. "It hurts."

"Ah, when you decide to eat, it won't hurt anymore. In fact, it'll only take a few hours to heal completely," Trish said. "That roadkill trick you pulled on my Jeep came with a special serving for yourself, didn't it? But those little rodents won't do it for you. Nope. You need the real thing. A full person."

Is she gloating? Trolling? Either way, Vicky wasn't falling for it. "I can't stay like this," she said, a deep grovel in the base of her throat.

"That was your handiwork, wasn't it?" Trish asked. "My Jeep?"

Silence.

"Yeah. I figured. The slop job at the end of the night. The blood on the side of the Jeep facing the neighbors. That was clever. Way too subtle for Steve. He did what I figured he would do…wait for me to come outside and ambush me."

Vicky held onto her secrets, seeing no point in confessing.

"Doesn't matter, I guess. But if you want to fully heal, you need to eat a person. A whole adult. There's no way around that."

"You're lying."

"Those small fucks that creep across the yard at night won't do it. You need a full-grown human," she repeated. "I learned that the hard way, and trust me, nowadays, it's much harder. With cameras and GPS and the internet…it's super easy to get caught."

Silence.

"It's the truth," Trish said.

"You don't know shit," Vicky sputtered.

"Yeah, I do," Trish said. "You're dealing with pain that no living human can ever feel. It's beyond death itself…and guess what? You don't starve to death. You just starve."

"All thanks to you."

"Yeah? Well, what are you going to do right now? Huh? Not eat? Heal much slower than you need to? You're going to eat one day. I promise you that."

"Why do you care, huh? Change me back or just let me out here! The sun will kill me now!"

"Nope and no. No to both of those things. Can't have them circling back to my house if they find some strange being on the side of the road and I get caught on camera driving away. I told you… cameras are *everywhere*," she said, the end of her statement sounding strained as if she was looking over her shoulder. "And I can't change you back. I told you that. But I can take care of our Steve problem, with your help of course. Nope. I'm afraid you are staying with me until we deal with your boyfriend, my dear girl."

PART 6

Store and Go

CHAPTER 40

Cigarettes

Vicky looked around from her cozy corner, an entire life surrounding her. The walnut dresser was so long that it took up an entire metallic wall. There was also a clothing rack that doubled as a shoe rack. She assumed Trish used all the clothes that she stored in her unit as costumes as she cosplayed as a normal person. Vicky cringed, wondering if Trish recycled her clothes or burned them after every kill. There was a mirror that reflected the back of the garage-style door, and a small filing cabinet that Vicky leaned up against as she sat on the hard floor. The inside of the storage unit looked a lot like Granny's garage. When Vicky, Moody, and their cousins, Tanya and Justin, played hide and seek, Vicky always hid in the garage. There were stacks of old boxes that were filled with memories that no one seemed to have any use for. Cobwebs built up in the narrow spaces between them. The light bulb was never changed once it had gone out; it got so dark at night that everyone was too afraid to search for Vicky in there, making her the champion of most of their manhunts.

Or did somebody change the light bulb, and it never worked?

She wrestled with the memory, but family lore buried the truth somewhere in her early life. Maybe she was five or six when they gave up on putting light in the garage. Vicky's side ached again, reminding her that the iron pills weren't enough for her to recuperate and heal. Her new bruises and gashes—*Thanks, Patricia Weston, call me*

Trish—reawakened all Vicky's aches, reminding her nerve endings that it was time to start the pain all over again.

As she sat in the unit, stored away from the world, she pondered the many things that she could ask Trish. Or was this the beginning of her impending death? Did she plan on letting Vicky roast in the sun? Would she even melt in the sun?

You don't starve to death. You just starve.

But still. Why did Trish care? Why was she helping her at all? Or was she micromanaging Vicky until she figured out what to do with her? That's how Mom was when she was mad at Vicky or Moody. If she had given them a chore and they half-assed it, she would stand over their shoulder until every bit of dirt was wiped clean from the wall. She'd even add on more chores and make them harder than necessary: wash out the oven with a toothbrush, clean the bathroom floor with Lysol and a bath towel. Throw the towels out and use your allowance to buy replacements. It was egregious and pointless, but they cleaned things right the first time, most of the time. Is that what Trish wanted?

"Stay here," Trish said about an hour or so ago.

"You're *leaving* me here?" Vicky said, sheepishly.

Trish looked around. "I have to go get some supplies." She headed over to the filing cabinet and opened it. She pulled out a blank sheet of paper and a pencil and handed it to Vicky. "Draw me a map of Steve's house and property, then I can come up with something when I get back." She turned, but then stopped, doubling back. "And come up with some places where we can dispose of him and whoever else is over there—you're from Detroit, right? I'm sure there are some places between his house and there." A conniving smile crossed her face.

Vicky drew her head back as if she'd caught the stench of rotting meat. "We?"

Still wearing that smile, Trish said, "Well, yeah. Did you think—" Trish chuckled. "You're funny. No, I'm not cleaning this up by myself. He wasn't only following me; he was also after you."

"Yeah, but this wouldn't be happening if you didn't bite me."

Trish held Vicky's eyes for a while, her smile fading. It was impossible to tell what she was thinking or planning outside of the very stupid idea of raiding Steve's land, the last place Vicky wanted to be. Then Trish turned and left.

Vicky's mind wavered as she grew dizzy. Then her stomach growled, the noise reverberating off the metal door and walls. She hoped no one had heard it.

Who would? The lonely man manning the front desk across the parking lot?

Vicky hadn't seen him herself. Once the car had stopped, Trish unloaded it, closing the door behind her. It wasn't until all the bags that had been covering Vicky were removed when Trish said, "Before you get up, cover yourself. There's a man in the office on the other side of the parking lot. I don't think he will see you, but just in case."

Vicky raised on her haunches and winced as a fiery light licked her cheek.

"Oh, and the sun's still out. Thought you knew that." Trish didn't sound apologetic, but she also didn't sound combative. "Here."

Trish handed Vicky her sunglasses. She slid them on and wrapped herself with the blanket. Then she followed Trish to the door of a white building that had no windows. The clunky red letters on the side of it read *Store and Go*. They climbed a lot of stairs before they reached the top floor. Roll-up doors lined either side of the hallway.

Even though Vicky hadn't seen the man, just knowing that he was alone pushed her to fantasize about who would miss him if he were to die. She'd never see herself starving to death, and the thought of living another day in such a frail state made her sick. Her body had already fed on itself, making her bonier than she had ever been, making her nauseous and crampy in the interim. Would her body go for her heart muscle next?

"No," she said.

You only starve, Trish had said. No death in sight.

Vicky's lips tremored. Even though the urge to leave was tempting and there was a whole man nearby, and no one else, she could not kill another person. She would not eat. She'd rather starve. She'd rather dream. She'd rather…

Her gut fluttered again, but this time, it wasn't from hunger.

Footsteps fell upon the concrete floor, marching up the steps and then up the hallway. She perked up as nicotine gripped the air, suffocating her, making her weak at the knees, pinning her in place.

It wasn't Trish on the other side of the door. No. Trish smelled like her son: apple juice and baby shampoo. She smelled like her house: coffee, aftershave, and rose hips. Well, at least that's what she smelled like when she looked a little older, had more meat on her bones and rocked a few gray streaks amongst her silky raven mane. It's what she smelled like when she was masquerading around like a human, playing pretend with the very real people in her domain.

No.

The person in the hallway was a human. Like a *human, human.* Steve's basement and shed kept them safe from her. Trish's garage and her storage unit kept Vicky safe from them. But now, there was nothing—no barrier, no stops, no nothing. Only her and her reality.

She stood up and headed for the door. She pressed her ear against it and listened to the steps as they grew closer. What if it was someone else storing their things?

She pulled her head away from the garage door as if the metal had burned her face.

What if it's Steve?

No. Save for the nicotine, this human smelled too clean—too good. Like fresh lilacs from strong soap that they'd probably used every day since forever. It was someone that she hadn't sensed before. Something new. *Someone* new.

The steps passed by the door and continued until they stopped. Then the sound of a metal door rising.

Vicky's stomach moaned. Her gums burned as her fangs grew and her spit sweetened her mouth. She bent at the waist and clutched the handle of the garage door. They were alone on the floor, except for the cameras that did not point at the storage unit. She knew that from earlier when Trish led Vicky *around* the cameras.

Still, her heart told her to resist. Not to kill an innocent person. Not to gorge on human blood or to pierce human flesh. But her fangs leaked, and her lips quivered, and her stomach stirred.

She pulled the door handle up.

Visitors

When Trish pulled into the storage facility, she cocked her head, having noticed that Earl was not posted up in the window doing his normal thing: watching TV. She looked at the clock on the car radio: 5:36 pm.

He should be there. *Maybe he went to the bathroom.*

Still, not knowing made the alarm rise in her chest. He had no reason to go to her storage unit, did he? But then she relaxed a little as she noticed three cars in the parking lot. Two were parked against the tower, possibly unloading things into a storage unit, and the other was parked close to the single-floor building where Earl spent all his time.

Not a big deal, she thought. She and Vicky would just have to wait. Trish had spent the last couple hours getting supplies from different places: tarp, duct tape, rope, and filling up three gas cans. Each place, Walmart, Lowes, and Speedway, were situated up and down the coast of Lake Michigan.

She looked at one of the cars parked near the tower again. It looked like the car that she had seen Steve inside of as he waited at her son's daycare. She shook her head. How many white sedans had she seen while she was out and thought they were Steve?

Eleven, she thought, kicking herself. Paranoia only made things worse.

She parked near the tower door and headed inside, giving the white sedan the side eye. There was no one inside, and there was no one around. The place was as quiet as it always had been. Even though the cameras were in their normal spaces, scoping out the doors on each flight, she still moved with awareness, listening and looking.

Once she made it to her storage unit, she unlocked it and let herself inside. After sliding the door closed, she fastened the lock on the inside. It was funny the Earl allowed such a thing. So long as she bought the lock and hasp from him, the tenants were allowed to slap ten locks on their units, inside and out. She set her purse on the dresser. "Did you finish the map?"

When Vicky didn't reply, Trish looked at her. The girl was sitting against the wall, her gaze fixed on the back of the door.

"Hello?" Trish asked. "Did you—"

"How do you do this?" Vicky asked.

Not fully aware of what Vicky was talking about, Trish took a guess and said, "I don't know. I just do it."

"I–I don't want to be like this," she said. Trish took a step toward her. Vicky's face was drenched in exhaustion.

Trish inhaled and stepped back. Then she remembered the cars outside. "Did you hear anyone in the hallway?" *If they were on another floor, we could leave sooner…maybe.*

"Yeah. I was going to open the door to–to see who it was, but it stopped. It was locked. You locked me in here."

Great, she thought. "I'm going to take a walk," Trish said. "I need to see where they are."

"Why did you lock me in here?" Vicky asked, finally moving her eyes to Trish.

"You didn't hear me fasten the lock on the outside?" Trish raised a brow. "Why would I not?"

"Why do you care if I got out? Huh? Isn't that why you change people? You want them to kill!"

"Stop yelling," Trish said, her patience wearing thinner than it already had been.

"You want me to suck blood, slit somebody's throat and let the red curtain fall down their neck! You want me to lick it up until there ain't shit left! You want me to be a killer, just like you! That—"

"Keep your fucking voice down," a sharp whisper. "You wanna know why I locked you in here? Wanna know why you are going to show me how to kill your boyfriend? Because you were supposed to die that night. Just like Chad. But no. No. Your meathead mates decided to infringe on the party. You would be in the ground right now if it were up to me. But now, I have to figure out how to get rid of your deranged boyfriend, and then we will deal with whatever the fuck we need to do with you because, guess what? You can't die and I can't turn you back. And if I could, I would have turned you back and killed you by now. Get it? You understand now? You understand how much of a pain in the ass this all has been for me?"

Vicky didn't say anything. Her eyes moved back to the door; a look of terror crossed her face.

Trish watched Vicky's throat pulse with every heartbeat. "You ignoring me again? Y—"

"He's…he's here."

"What?" Trish spat.

Taps on the garage door, followed by the voice that put ice in Trish's gut. "I knew I'd find you here. Are you going to let me in?" Steve asked.

C H A P T E R   4 2

Duck

Trish looked at Vicky, who balled up in the fetal position in front of the mirror, right across from the door. She shook her head, mumbling what sounded like, "I'm not going back there. I'm not going back there."

Trish wanted to shake the girl. Why didn't she understand that she was stronger than any human? She could kill Steve with her bare hands. But then Trish remembered the state of Vicky when she showed up last night. Her leg had been shattered but was healing. Her hoodie was covered in blood from her old gunshot wound which doubled as an incision sight. Then there was her damaged shoulder and the old burns on her ankle. Her transition hadn't been easy. It would be abnormal for her *not* to be afraid.

"Ah, don't get quiet now," Steve said. "I thought I'd come in and join the discussion. Share my thoughts."

"How did he find us?" Trish asked under her breath.

"Patricia, is Vicky giving you a hard time?" Steve asked. It sounded like a genuine question, as if he *knew* her.

When she didn't answer, he went on. "Yeah, she gives me a hard time too. Stubborn as shit." He chuckled.

She and Vicky looked at one another.

"Oh, come on, ladies. I know you want to see me just as much as I want to see you. You don't have any questions or…at least a bit curious about what's about to happen?"

"I'm not going back," Vicky cried, burying her face in her arms.

Trish pulled a pistol from the bottom drawer of the dresser. It was loaded. "Vicky," she whispered. "Get over there." She nodded at the space between the file cabinet and the clothing rack, the farthest away from the door. But Vicky didn't move. She cried in her arms. "Vicky," Trish hissed.

"Okay, I get it. And you're right. I need to be fair about divulging information. Maybe I can start by telling you how I found you," Steve said.

Trish's ears perked, curious by his moot point.

"My friend followed you here," he said. He laughed. "No sneaky tracker, no GPS, no insider at the NSA. Nah. Just old-fashioned following with an inconspicuous car."

Trish thought about how he could have been in any car anywhere and she would not have noticed.

"Now, I know you may have firepower in there, and if you're the type of person I think you are—the type who would stow a vampire away in their storage unit, who can shift into something else when you're not busy sucking people's blood or committing mass murder—then you'd have guns everywhere. In your house, in your car, and in your storage facility."

No answer. She rushed over to Vicky and grabbed her arm. Vicky snatched it away.

"Move!" Trish whispered. "He is going to shoot through the door. You wanna get hit?"

"I don't fucking care!" Vicky shrieked. She cradled her face in her hands.

Steve sucked air between his clenched teeth. "I told you she was stubborn. A damn firecracker. That's why I love her so much. You know she's my girl, right? Vicky? Vicky, baby, can you hear me? Tell her to open the door."

Trish looked at the girl, then back at the door. She couldn't let Vicky get incapacitated in the unit; if the Feds tracked her there, Trish would never shake them.

"Now, this only ends one way: my trunk full of bloody bitches. And neither of them is on this side of the door."

"Don't be stupid, Steve. The police will hear the gunshots," Trish said, not caring for the threat. It sounded venomous coming from him.

"Oh, it feels *so* good to hear your voice again," he said, fake relief coating his words.

Trish pursed her lips, hating to have graced his ears.

"Well, sounds like you don't want the police to come around here. Does that mean that you are open for negotiation?" He sounded hopeful, but slick.

She looked at Vicky, who hadn't changed or moved. "What do you want?"

"What do you think I want?"

Silence.

"Oh, you're no fun," Steve teased. "Alright. I want you *and* her. Come out here, and you get to ride in the trunk unscathed. I'd even put you both in separate cars. How does that sound?"

"Or what?"

"Excuse me?"

"You heard me."

He chuckled. "You won't like the alternative."

"Try me."

"Darwin."

Her heart dropped as she closed her eyes tight. How did he know her son's name? And what did her kid have to do with what happened between him and Vicky? Him and Trish? The trade didn't seem fair. What the hell was he going to do with her kid anyway? Steve was batshit insane if he thought she or her kid was going anywhere. *Did he follow Pita too?* She didn't ask aloud. Instead, she allowed him to go on.

"After we followed your Uber, I let you go into that school and disappear inside the classroom. Then I approached the teacher who was on her way into an office. I asked her for an application because I wanted my little girl to go to that very school. But she was in such a hurry to speak with you that she promised to see me the next day. I went back the next day, hoping to get your kid's name somehow, and it was way easier than I thought. Those little cute pictures on the classroom wall showed me what I needed to know." He paused. "I couldn't mistake those dark eyes and hair. He looks a lot like you. Darwin. Darwin Weston, like Patricia Weston. Right?"

Trish's breath was drained out of her chest. The one place that her kid should have been safe turned out to be a red zone.

"If you don't give me you, then I'll just take your kid. Maybe I'll raise him to be my own. Or…or maybe I'll just kill all of you? I could open a museum in you guys' names, and it'll make me rich. No one protects monsters. I mean, or I could get rich off your head, sell you to the FBI as a bundle in exchange for a clean record. It'd be fun too."

Trish chuckled at his nonsensical ambitions.

"You think it's funny?"

"No. I think it's stupid how dumb you are. You think my husband and my kid are vampires?"

"How else would—"

"I've been trying to figure that very thing out myself," she said. "Steve, you are worse than I ever could be. You've killed so many for sport. At least I kill to eat. You kill for what? Money? Drugs? To appease the sick voices in your head? There isn't anything special about your brand of monster. There are so many out there just like you."

"Oh yeah?" His voice softened. "Are there?"

"Yeah. Most of them have mommy issues, but the others are lost. Are you lost, *Steve*?"

An impatient chuckle. "Vicky? We had a deal. Come out here and claim your end of the bargain."

Trish's nostrils flared.

Vicky kept her head down.

"Open the door, give her to me, and you go free," Steve said.

Nothing.

"Vicky?" His voice groveled as if he were seething. "Vicky!"

Still nothing. Vicky didn't even look up.

He sighed. "Okay. I guess I'll just have to let myself in then."

He went to raise the door, but it stopped.

"You honestly thought the door was unlocked?" Trish asked. "What the—"

Bullets tore through the door, sending sparks, metal shavings, and debris flying.

CHAPTER 43

Where?

Trish scrambled, crouching off to the side of the door as a barrage of bullets tore through metal. Vicky screamed as she crawled, her flattened hands pressing the concrete floor as she moved toward the left side of the door, next to Trish. The shots didn't sound like loud fiery pops; the chorus of firepower was evidenced by slicing wood and mangling metal furniture. Steve wasn't alone with a pistol. The sloppy spray of bullets ate up the storage unit much too fast for the assault to arise from a single gun, but from several rifles as they ate up the entrance.

It felt like forever before the bullets stopped. New holes decorated the space, ripping Trish's dresses that hung on the clothing rack and shattering the body mirror, reducing it to a holey cardboard backdrop.

The smell of gunfire, weed, lilacs, and nicotine was strong as it wafted in from the hallway. After a pregnant pause full of gunpowder combustion and settling scrap, a boot stepped through the mangled opening as someone pulled himself inside.

Trish aimed up from her crouched position next to the opening and shot the intruder in the head. The bullet pierced him, drawing a hole into the side of his dark peach-fuzzed skull. His big body collapsed, shaking the storage unit underneath his bellyflop. Scrambling footfalls dispersed in the hallway, ducking for cover.

"Are you hit?" Trish asked as she leaned into the hallway, looking around. The gang had gone, leaving the area outside the door clear. Trish didn't know how many more people Steve brought along. How many more threats lingered in the tower…how many more bodies she'd have to lay down…

"Vicky?" Trish asked, stealing a glance at the girl who had been trembling next to her.

Vicky didn't say anything. Her eyes were plastered on the man on the floor. The puddle around him had grown into a pond as the angry hole in his head leaked profusely. His eyes were plastered in shock as they peered at Vicky. "That was Vodka Tony," she said.

"Okay…" Trish said, uninvested. "We're going to go look for them now," she said, trying to be instructive, but condescension rolled off her tongue instead. Now wasn't the time to get Vicky to follow along. Now wasn't the time for an *Aw, there, there* or condolences. They needed to get moving.

But Vicky did not move.

Trish sighed, and in a calm, easy voice, she said, "They will come back for you. And based on what Steve did to this door blindly, knowing that you were in here, he will shoot you first, and then take you back. And I'm telling you right now, I'm not going anywhere with them. Come or don't come, but I'm going."

Vicky got up as Trish stepped out into the hallway.

Aiming her pistol, Trish stepped easily, scrutinizing every unit. Then she tensed. The door to the unit across the hall, three containers down, was open.

"Wait!" Vicky said. She rushed out of Trish's unit.

"What?" Trish said, eyes trained on the open door, mind racing, expecting someone to jump out at the sound of Vicky's voice as she gave away her position with her shouting. But no one hopped out.

"That's where one of them went earlier," Vicky whispered, not nearly low enough. It was too late anyway. Trish was sure their position was blown.

Trish headed up to the opening, pressing her back against the right side of the door. She quickly leaned over, peeking inside. "It's empty."

"What?" Vicky asked, exhaustion weighing on her question.

"Empty," Trish said as she peered at the other end of the hall-way. She felt herself bristle, finding nothing there. The tower had two more floors, and the property was a hefty size; Steve and his friends could have been anywhere. "They can't be far. Come on."

Each floor looked the same—all the storage units were closed, and there was no sign of Steve or anyone else. They stepped out into the darkening evening empty-handed and met with the same four cars that Trish had seen earlier, including her own.

"They're still here somewhere," Trish said. Vicky said nothing. She only limped along with her arm crossed over her belly. She looked alert with her eyes darting around, but she didn't seem to have much to say. Nothing to add. Trish wondered what was going on in Vicky's head. *Trauma*, she thought.

There weren't many places for Steve to hide aside from the wooded area that took up a huge slab of land across the dead road. There were rolling acres that made up the background of the property, making the parking lot and office building the only places for them to hide.

The office building's door was wide open, and Earl wasn't watching TV. In fact, on approach, the building seemed eerily quiet. Trish peered through the window next to the door. The lights were off, and Earl was nowhere in sight.

"Shit," Trish said, frowning.

"What?" Vicky whispered.

"I think they killed Earl."

Guilt cross Vicky's pained expression. *Empathy will be your downfall*, Trish thought. Or maybe there was more to Vicky's expression…say, if Steve had followed her to Detroit instead of Lakeshore…

"Look in the window," Trish said, waiting for a reaction. Empathy or no, Vicky had a choice to make, kill or be exposed and scoping out her surroundings was key to her continued survival. *If that were still on the table at all*, Trish thought.

Vicky's guilt morphed into panic as her eyes widened.

Trish sighed. "I don't think they're in there unless they are held up in the office or bathroom. Both of those doors are open, so I doubt it." Vicky cocked her head, inquisitive.

"You aren't going to look for yourself?" Trish asked.

Vicky blinked.

Trish smacked her teeth. "Just—come on." Still on her haunches, she went inside. Once Vicky cleared the doorway, Trish closed it and flipped the lock.

"What's the point of—"

"So that we can hear them coming," Trish said, amused that Vicky chose to speak on something so trivial.

They passed the counter and headed for the office. Inside, the office chair was on its side. The leather sopped up a pool of blood that spread, creeping into the retail space.

Trish turned to the counter where the TV had been. The screen was black. Next to it was an open binder, a telephone, and an old, clunky computer. The binder stored a list of names and their assigned storage container numbers. Trish's name was the fourth one down.

Grinding the backs of her teeth, she shoved the page from the book in her jacket pocket. *Burn this too*, she noted to herself.

Trish picked up the phone. "Line's down." She hung it up and scoffed; the line had been cut. She tapped on the keyboard; the old computer didn't come alive.

"Can't we just leave?" Vicky asked, a tremble in her throat, her eyes fixed on the blood on the floor.

"No, because there is a dead body in my storage unit," Trish said pointedly. "And Steve won't just *go away*. We need to deal with him. Now."

"Then what are you looking for?"

"Them," Trish snapped.

Vicky said. "He's clearly not in here."

"The same cars are in the parking…" Trish wavered off, bored with the conversation. Vicky didn't listen, so why the hell was Trish explaining anything to her?

"He could have a car up the road. He probably left because he isn't protected here like he is in Miller," Vicky reasoned.

Trish looked at the blood on the floor. "Sorry, Earl," she said under her breath. She stepped over the puddle, leading them into the office. There were a host of monitors with black screens and a console; none of the buttons were lit in the dark room.

Trish pulled her phone from her pocket and shone the flashlight on the console. It wasn't until she saw chunks of pink viscera on the buttons that she realized that her hunch was correct: Earl was dead.

"We need to get out of here," Trish demanded, her heart doing backflips in her chest. Steve had the upper hand. He'd been through Earl's office…he'd seen the layout of the tower…he'd taken the time to get to know the storage unit. He had the drop on Trish, and retreating was, indeed, the best course of action.

"Okay, and—" Vicky started.

"Now," Trish said before she headed for the door. She turned to Vicky, who hadn't moved from her spot behind the counter. "I don't know what Steve has planned, but we need to regroup. I don't—"

The window shattered, littering the tile floor with glassy shards, and Vicky's shoulder jerked, pushing her back with an invisible force. The girl let out a guttural scream as she bent at the waist, holding her shoulder.

Trish pinned her back against the wall underneath the window next to the door and waited. When bullets stopped, Trish aimed at the silhouette in the parking lot. Between Vicky's cursing and screaming, and the gunman's exposure, Trish returned fire, aiming at the man's head.

There was a loud grunt, then nothing.

"Come on," Trish said as she crouched next to Vicky. She grunted as she put Vicky's arm over her shoulder and stood up.

"Ah!" Vicky shouted.

"You have to walk," Trish said, beckoning Vicky to move her legs, to take steps.

"H–he shot me…again," Vicky said, finally taking a step, holding onto her arm to relieve the weight on her shoulder.

"That wasn't him," Trish said as they headed into the parking lot, the lights finally kicking on, polishing the dark gray ground in a white glow. They passed the body. He lay splayed out, his gun sitting on the other side of his hand, his blond hair dyed red in his blood. Vicky looked at him, but she didn't say anything. *I guess he didn't get a weird nickname*, Trish thought.

Vicky hacked up blood, nearly falling out of Trish's support. Her body trembled and she looked frail and weak, as if that last bullet undid her healing from the night before.

"Don't close your eyes," Trish demanded.

Vicky chuckled. "I thought y–y——" She slurred her words.

"You can't die, but you can go into a coma," Trish said. That was the last thing she needed, a comatose vampire with nowhere to store her until she woke up.

Trish pulled the door to the tower open, only for metallic dings to slam into it. Gunfire rained upon them.

"Fuck!" Trish said as she used her free hand to close the door behind them. She hefted Vicky up again as she slid down Trish's side.

"Ah, stop! It hurts," Vicky cried.

"You have to—fuck it!" Trish sat Vicky on the first set of steps. Her body stretched across the height of the flight of stairs.

"No." Vicky coughed up blood. "No, y–you. What are you d—" She choked on her plea.

Trish said nothing. She took off up the steps, leaving Vicky behind.

It wasn't long before the tower door opened, and Steve let himself inside.

CHAPTER 44

Boyfriend

"Vicky." Steve's voice was as soft as it had been when they lay in bed, him holding her. Him kissing her. Him loving her. But now, she could hear the menace in the word as he spoke. Had that menace always been there?

"Did your demon leave you here?" He leaned against the railing and glared at her, a smile playing on his lips. "All you had to do was stick with the plan. You would have had the basement suite to yourself, not lying here, bleeding." He looked up the staircase. "She seems like the type to work alone."

Vicky struggled to sit up, her hands sliding in her own blood, forcing her body back down onto the steps. She breathed hard, watching him move, waiting for him to take her back. Waiting for him to shoot her or knock her out. Anything to make the pain stop. Anything to make the fear subside, if only for a little bit.

"You know, I really do love you," he said.

Vicky recoiled, wanting to shout at him, hit him, kill him for torturing her. But she couldn't. The pain in her ankle ignited, joining in with the throbbing in her shoulder and chest, pinning her in place. The belligerent pangs made her feel as though the incision had burst open.

He slowly climbed the steps, inching closer to her, but holding onto the railing. "You know when people say that their first love will forever live in their heart?" He put a hand on his chest. "That's how

I feel about you. You unlocked something in me that I didn't know existed. You showed me something that nobody has ever seen—nobody has ever had. I got to spend time with a myth. I got to kiss and love a vampire. I got to fuck a monster. I even got to see what you looked like on the inside." His eyes darkened. "You bleed like a normal person—scream like any other woman…you… But you don't die, so I get to try again, and again, and again. I bet I could take your organs out one by one before reinstalling them again and again. No one could ever give me that. But you can. And you did. And you will."

Vicky coughed, failing to stop the abhorrent shiver shooting through her body as she took in his sickening words.

He leaned over and picked up her chin. His eyes were glazed but focused.

"I can't wait to get you home, my love." He sighed, his soft breath playing in the blood on her mouth.

The look of concern in his eyes was so genuine that she thought Steve was someone else. His gaze was so intense that she thought he would kiss her, and if he did, she was ready to muster up her last bit of strength to spit in his face. She hoped it would be enough to turn him into a monster like her, like that bitch upstairs who was probably waiting for Steve to take Vicky away so that she could head back to her family. Her son. Her house, her fake life.

I will find you again, Vicky thought. She escaped Steve once, and she wouldn't hesitate to escape him again.

He ran his thumb over her wet lips. His eyes held onto sick dreams starring her. She remembered what it was like before, when he texted her all summer. She was happy to see his face on video call, and eager to read his messages. They were supposed to be happy together. Not her being miserable and him acting out fantasies that no human should have. "When we go back, you don't have to worry about Dr. Gonzalez filling your head with possibilities of a better life outside of what I offered you because there is none. No better life, and no Dr. Gonzalez."

"W–what did you do to her?" she asked, her heart sinking deeper into her gut.

"Ah. Don't give me *that* look. You're the one who got her killed, not me. All she had to do was help. That's all."

"You wanted her to bleed Danny! You wanted her to help you *force-feed* me," Vicky cried.

"Yeah. Yeah, well, and Dr. Gonzalez forgot who she worked for. She forgot whose family gave her a job when no one else would. Who got her and her family jobs, citizenship on speed dial, and places to live. I even taught her how to hide that accent. I trained her to be an American. She…she forgot all of that." His face crumpled in disgust. "All she had to do was her *job*. But instead, she fell for you. Fell for you like I did."

His eyes softened as he watched hers.

"You need me," he said. "You need me just as much as Dr. Gonzalez needed me. And I can help you. I can help you accept your purpose. I can make you your best. All you have to do is come back with me…"

Vicky swallowed the lump in her throat. "No."

"I'll take you back to the shed—"

"No." Her plea came out a little louder than a whisper.

"—and I will heal you. Get you better."

"No." Her gut jerked, forcing the declaration out louder.

"I can get you some food, and when we aren't playing in the shed, I'll let you back into the basement."

"No!" she blurted. Her strained shout encased them, reverberating around the staircase.

Steve sucked in a breath. His eyes widened and his eyebrows arched as he reached around, patting his back. He stumbled back onto the stairway railing, sliding down, leaving a trail of blood. Deafened by her slamming heart and bewildered by his subtle change in demeanor, Vicky tried to push herself up, but the bloody steps stole her grip, forcing her elbow down to the floor.

She could barely make out the sound of footsteps coming down the staircase. Trish stopped next to Vicky, looked at her, then pointed the gun at Steve's face. He raised an arm, shielding himself from the blow, but he didn't speak. The stunned look on his face seemed to hold in any words or screams, pleads or threats.

Trish put a hole in his forehead.

Die

Trish placed Steve's lifeless body on the floor of her disheveled storage unit. Blood and bullet holes riddled the space. Her mirror was shattered and the clothes hanging on the clothing rack were reduced to shreds. The dresser adopted new scrapes and splinters, and black holes were carved into the metal walls. Even the light bulb in her lamp had been shattered, leaving her to depend on the light in the hallway to see what she needed.

Vicky lay on the rug, her limbs stretched out as she bled. Her eyes were low, staring at the crimson face of the man who acted as her captor. A man that raised the alarm, forcing Trish out of a place that she'd called a second home for over eight years.

But she wasn't carrying anyone or anybody out of there. Not even Vicky. No. The only things Trish was carrying back down to the car were her belongings, not the dresser or cabinet. Not the busted mirror. But the clothes within the dresser and the history of important papers in the file cabinet.

She pointed to Steve. "Eat," she said. "Now."

Vicky struggled to push herself to sit upright. Somehow, under all that blood and snot, spittle and tears, she managed to look concerned. Whatever she was feeling, Trish felt her face get hot. She didn't have time to convince Vicky of anything, but she couldn't leave her behind. The Feds were already looking for Vicky; Trish didn't need them to come after her too.

"Or should I take you to the hospital?"

Vicky grunted and looked at the dead man on the floor.

"It's the only way you'll feel better. The only way to be one hundred percent. Here."

Trish bent over and grabbed Steve's shoulders. She pulled him over Vicky's lap, stopped when his waist was just over her knees.

She knew Vicky wanted to cry out in pain as her face pinched.

"The only way he's moving, the only way you are leaving, is if you eat. That's a promise."

Vicky's jaw quavered as Steve's skull leak modulated to a steady spill.

Trish pursed her lips and rolled her eyes. "You better hurry up before you end up lapping it up off the floor," she said. "Eat while I pack." Trish pulled the drawer open and pulled a box of black garbage bags out. She opened one and shoved her jar of teeth, clothes, and shoes in. "You have ten minutes, and I'm out of here."

Vicky didn't respond. She only let out a low wail.

Trish tied her first bag and tossed it out into the hallway. Then she pulled out another trash bag and began stuffing more items inside. "Why won't you eat?" This girl was worse than her damn toddler.

Vicky shook her head, her chest heaving.

"Vicky, if you don't eat, you won't die. You'll just starve—"

"I know! You said that already!" she snapped before falling into a coughing fit.

"So, what am I missing? You need to eat so we can leave."

"I don't care!"

"You don't care if the police come?" Trish lied. She had a feeling it would be a while before that happened.

"No!"

"You sure about that?"

"I don't fucking care!" Vicky screamed so harshly that her throat growled.

"Why? Why won't you eat?"

Vicky stammered, then cried.

Trish moved on to throwing her boots, shoes, and folders into the bag, even the ones that were tagged by bullets. She tied the bag and then tossed it out into the hallway. She opened another trash bag.

"I–I just can't. I can't. I'm—"

"Did you feed on those racoons that you spread all over my car the other day?"

"A little…"

Trish paused, stunned at the open admission. "A *little* as in a few licks just to see what it tastes like? Or a little as in a few big gulps to get you through for a few days?"

Vicky didn't answer. Trish stuffed clothes that were hanging up inside the bag, then moved on to her papers again.

"You know, an animal can only hold you over for a couple days, and that's if you don't have any injuries and no sun exposure, and haven't been strung up and tortured in some freak's shed, or been caught in a bear trap—"

"Thanks to you!"

Trish shrugged. "You became a pain in my ass. Had to be done. You're lucky I didn't shoot you in the face. Don't think you would have died, but you'd be down."

"Then what? You'd turn me over to the government?"

Trish shook her head. "Oh no. So that you can tell them how you turned out like that? Like a vampire? No thanks. Would've had to handle you myself."

"Is that what this is?" Vicky asked, her voice wet and raspy. "You helped me just to keep me around…so that you can handle me y—" She stopped talking to cough.

Trish stopped packing and looked over at the girl. She crouched, Steve's body serving as a centerpiece between the two women. She gripped the bag in her hand tighter. "You are my fault. You should be dead, not turned. You should not be lingering around, harassing me and my neighbors. Not running away from the Feds. So, instead of trying to kill you, instead of cursing your name and hoping the sun kills you, I'll teach you how to survive. I'll teach you to get far away from me so that you can risk getting yourself caught. Because if you know how to survive on your own, you'll understand why it's important not to end up in some government lab. Not to end up in some freak's basement. If you care about living, then I have less to worry about once I upend my family and start over somewhere else far away from you. You get it? You get me? You knowing how this existence works keeps us both free. I can't leave it to chance. I can't risk anyone ever finding you dead because they will start looking. They will start wondering. And I know what happens when they figure out what we are. They are dangerous. So listen when I tell you that you can survive this. Things aren't all fucked like you think. But you have to listen. You have to be receptive. Consider this the first lesson. Do not starve. It'll slow you down. Make you stupid and irrational. Vicky, you have to eat."

"No." A low grumble, one that was very familiar. Trish had made a sound like that before, but it wasn't to say no, it was to prepare for something very necessary. When her fangs elongated, squirting sweet venom into her mouth, ready to subdue. Ready to…

Trish licked her lips. She softened her face, made her tone easy. This wasn't her toddler who refused vegetables and sometimes even fruit. This was a vampire, and she was hungry. "I know you can smell it. The blood. That moist, warm, meaty, fleshy tinge across your tongue. The nourishing metal floating through. It tastes the way that you think it does too." She dropped her gaze to Steve. "Why should you be denied the right to a real meal? The chance to heal? He sure helped himself to your mind and body. Taunting you emotionally by making you think he cared about you. Fucking with you mentally by shooting you, tearing pieces of your beautiful skin to run his botched experiments. None validated. All senseless. It was torture. It was a sick game." Trish raised a brow. "But he's dead now, and he's not coming back. Let him actually help you this time."

Vicky's mouth opened, and red drool fell onto Steve's jeans. "W–what about the others?"

"Earl is divorced with no kids. There aren't many people who store here or come here very often. At least, that's what he told me. One day soon, the police will find these bodies. But they won't find us. They never do, and they never will if you listen to me."

"I—I—"

Trish pointed to the base of his neck. "His heart isn't pumping blood anymore. You better hurry."

"It's wrong."

"For them, it's wrong. But for us, it's food. It's medicine. It's hydration."

Vicky looked down at her ex. She opened her mouth, exposing sharp canines, and plunged them into Steve's neck, slurping heavily.

She breathed frantically, desperate to get it all down. Trish wasn't sure if it was excitement or fear. Whatever it was, she'd finally gotten through: the first step to acceptance was to drink. As Trish continued to shove things into a bag, she thought about how she would document the night. She'd start a new notebook called *Vicky*.

CHAPTER 46

Friends

They drove in silence, the highway empty of all traffic. Vicky sat in the passenger seat, gawking out the window. She seemed relaxed, but not at peace as Trish thought she might be. Vicky had used her teeth for the first time. She sipped bashfully, but once she allowed herself to fall into it, she moaned and slurped, filling herself up on Steve's blood. No doubt Vicky was high. Her eyes were low, and Trish knew that euphoric pulse was thumping alongside her sick heart. Blood never drowned out unresolved emotional strife. Nothing did.

Trish sighed, and said, "I remember when I had to kill my best friend."

Vicky looked at her.

"Yeah, I did. Melody was my girl. We were inseparable. And that was back in the days when hitchhiking was dangerous but still cool. I mean, how else were you supposed to get to a Janice Joplin concert?" Trish smiled. "We…we lived on the road, hopping from gas station to gas station. Van to van."

Vicky sucked in a deep breath.

"I used to worry about how we'd get money. But Mel had an answer for that: steal it from some guy we seduced." Trish chuckled. "Can you believe how lonely some men were back then? I mean, they were married, but they never hesitated to take the family van out to the sticks to pick up a lot lizard or two. I–I didn't mind it because…"

"You were killing them," Vicky said.

"Well, yeah. Not all of them, and Mel certainly didn't know about it. I'd wait until she had her turn with them in the bathroom, and then I'd go in last to finish him off. By the time anyone found them in a hotel room or rest stop bathroom, we'd be long gone. And Mel had this thing against listening to the news or watching TV. She said it dampened the imagination. She was so high that she never knew what was going on."

"Sounds like you loved her."

"I did. She was my escape after I had gotten a dirty divorce."

Vicky raised her brow.

"I killed my ex-husband and then went on the road. I started in Kentucky, then…" Trish trailed off, hearing Mel's hypnotic laugh. "She was a beautiful soul until she wasn't."

Silence.

"It was kill or be exposed," Trish said. "I don't know why I told you that. I just thought maybe—"

"The people across the street are investigating you," Vicky said. Her words were so flat that Trish drew her head back. The girl, the girl she saved, the girl she had tolerated for the last twenty-four hours, delivered a gut punch.

"Are you sure?" Trish threw glances at Vicky, failing to focus on the road.

"Yeah. I went inside their house."

"Why? Why would you break into my neighbor's house—any-one's house?! You know how risky that is?"

"Do you wanna know who it is?" she asked, suddenly willing to offer up information.

"Yes!" Trish shouted.

"The bald guy and his wife. They live right across the street from you. They drive the minivan."

"Peter?" Trish spat, trying to remember his wife's name. They had just moved in the other day. Trish met them, up close and per-sonal. "H–how do you know? What did you see?"

"Pictures of dead people: Barbie and two guys. Then there was a picture of you, standing in front of your house."

Trish's lungs tightened as the air left her body.

"My missing persons flyer was in the desk, and Chad's pictures were there too. They're onto you."

"And how long were you going to wait to tell me?" Trish sped up, leaving the highway. She clipped the curb when she turned onto the main road which led to her neighborhood.

"Now. I was going to tell you now. You helped me, so I helped you." The words were laced with venom.

"You call this helping? What the fuck, Vicky?"

"Yeah. Actually, I do."

"You should have told me sooner!" Trish said as she turned onto her street.

"Uh-huh. Right. Then what? Would you have taken care of the agents?"

"You're damned right, because guess what, baby? They're not only after me! They'll be after you, and when Steve's uncle finds out that his nephew is missing…You think his friends don't know about the vampire in his shed?!"

Vicky turned her head away.

"No response?"

Nothing.

"Unbelievable." Trish snorted. How was she going to deal with that? "Ugh!" She shouted, slapping the steering wheel. "I guess we… Damn it!" Nothing came together. No plan. No options. She was stuck on nothing. But she needed to do something. There was an agent across the street, and yelling at Vicky wouldn't change that. It did nothing. It…

When Trish pulled into the driveway, all thoughts of what happened that night faded to the back of her mind as she listened to the distressed cries coming from her house. It wasn't a cry for food. It wasn't a cry for a diaper change. It wasn't a cry for attention.

"Stay here," Trish said as she ran for the shrills of terror.

C H A P T E R   4 7

Little One

Trish ran up the short staircase and rammed her fist into the door. "Darwin! Maggie!"

Nothing but his cries filling the house. Nothing from Maggie.

Trish pulled her keys out of her pocket and fumbled with them, shoving the correct one into the handle, cursing Randel for being against key code doors.

She pushed her way in, letting his screams out onto the quiet street.

"Darwin!" She ran past the office, the door open.

"Maggie!" Trish ran into the living room and her eyes widened. Cold with shock, she felt the blood drain from her face when she found what she was looking for.

Darwin sat on the couch next to Maggie, who stared back at Trish, her eyes lifeless as she lay slumped over. Blood caked her neck, a mess of it pooled onto the leather couch.

"Oh no!" Trish yelped. She ran over to Darwin and picked him up. "Oh no, Darwin! Are you hurt? Are you..." She looked on his back and legs. There were no scratches or cuts. She looked in his mouth. She froze, her heart skipping a beat, palpitating, deafening her to her baby's screams.

My son...

He reached out for Trish, his tearful eyes begging her to tell him what to do.

My only child…

His plump cheeks were sticky with blood and his thick dark hair was glossed with it.

My baby…

His fangs were short and sharp, lethal enough to tear Maggie's jugular open.

"I'm sorry," she said. She held him to her shoulder and rocked him, but he kicked and cried, his tantrum full of bloody slobber.

"I'm so sorry," she said to Maggie. No signs of life came from her as she lay there, still bleeding from the holes in her neck.

This is my fault.

Maggie wasn't going home. Her family would never see her again.

"It's all my fault," Trish whispered.

She held her son the way she had when he was born, cradling him in her arms as they sat in the tub, the warm water encompassing them both.

"He's beautiful," Pita had said as she washed her hands. It was odd to see her in her nurse's uniform, but there she was, making a house call. "What's his name?"

"Darwin," Randel announced. He'd finally taken paternity leave, and anxiety over Darwin's birth forced him to grow a short goatee.

"Darwin," Trish said, trying the name on for size. Randel proposed the name, and Trish had taken to it instantly. It made her think of Charles Darwin, and how it was a miracle that she was able to procreate with a human at all. It made sense. Darwin smiled at her. "I think he likes it." They all laughed.

But instead of happiness and beauty, she was staring grief, terror, and sadness in the face. His beautiful skin was painted in gore because he'd given in to his true nature. He wasn't like his father at all. He was his mother's child.

EXCERPT FROM
BOOKS 3:
WATCHER

C H A P T E R   1

Gone

Darwin's screams strained his throat, making him raspy as blood dried around his lips. Blood clotted on his tongue as his uvula trembled, drenched in red. Trish turned, her hand on his side as she positioned him over the kitchen sink.

"I don't—" she said as she turned on the faucet, fighting to adjust the lever with her free hand, hoping for a little hot, a little cold. Her fingers shook, threatening to drop the spray hose before she could pull it long enough to rinse Darwin's gums, his teeth...his fangs. They were small but thick, surely going to be replaced with adult ones, a more resilient pair. Her chest thudded as tears fell into the sink. "I got you. I—" She stifled a sob.

Darwin twisted, somehow screaming louder as she moved closer with the hose. Then she dropped it and used her free hand to collect some of the running water from the faucet. She poured it on his cheek, and it slid past his mouth, collecting blood and carrying it to the drain. Her breath hitched, a cold prickle ran down her spine, and the world seemed to shrink around her. His teeth had retracted into his top gum when the warm water hit them, as if knowing it wasn't blood. Snot flowed from Darwin's nose, mixing with the drool on his face. He shrieked, shouted, cried, kicked—blamed her. "No!" he yelled as his small body jerked. "No!" Drool dripped from his mouth as he slapped Trish's hand away.

She tried to steady him by pressing him against her belly. "Darwin, please," she said.

"No!" He twisted and kicked. "Mama, no!"

"I have to—we have to clean you up, baby." She collected more water and tried to get him to drink it. But he didn't. He slapped her hand away. "I—"

She wanted to tell him to gargle and spit it out, to swish it around and dispose of it. But he wouldn't understand her. He'd only just started calling her mama and using the word 'no.'

Trish held him upright and watched him weep. Fury and sorrow radiated from his little body, begging her to make it all stop. But she could only think about herself—how she'd ruined something so beautiful and innocent. The curse in her cells, her blood, her atoms had transferred to her son, bloating his being with darkness he didn't deserve.

Time slowed, and Darwin's cries grew quieter. "How?" she whispered to the person who could not answer. "You can't," she said, her throat strained. Darwin had never reacted to his vaccinations. And he loved food—normal food.

But normal babies didn't kill their babysitters. They didn't drink blood. They didn't have fangs.

"I don't care," she said, the declaration breaking through the fog in her head. She met Darwin's eyes. "Once you rolled into the world and cuddled up to my chest—needed me in a way that no one else ever had—I was devoted."

Trish pulled him close and rocked him. "Shhh," she said. "Mommy will fix it. I promise," she whispered. "It's okay. Shhhh."

He rubbed his face into her neck, his cries tapering.
"You are mine," Trish said. "And I will do anything to protect you. It's going to be okay."

She swayed, and he eased, allowing his body to shudder from the fading panic. "I know you couldn't help it, baby. I know. I'll fix this. Just please stop crying. It's okay."

As Darwin's cries simmered to small groans and stumbling breaths, Trish closed her eyes and thought about Maggie—no, the body in the living room. There was no doubt that Maggie had been paralyzed and then killed by Darwin. The way her head hung, those dead, vacant eyes...

Trish pressed the sides of Darwin's stomach, noticing it wasn't hard, only slightly bloated. Was his stomach big enough to hold a grown woman?

She turned to find Vicky standing in the doorway wearing the clothes Trish had given her the night before: hot pink yoga pants and a now bloodied gray hoodie. Luckily, the bullet slid out of Vicky's collarbone, and she was standing on her injured ankle without leaning against the door frame. Steve's blood had indeed healed her.

"Vicky," Trish said evenly, hiding the urgency that could disturb Darwin's settling calm. "Check for a pulse."

Vicky didn't move. Instead, she stared at Trish, her once-hazel eyes now dark and exhausted. Then they flashed with accusation: Darwin was another innocent life that Trish had corrupted.

"Victoria," Trish said. "Vic-tor-ria," she growled. She wasn't in the mood to deal with another child.

"I don't want to touch her."

"Check for a pulse," Trish spat.

"I—"

"Remember our deal." Trish swallowed hard, burying the rising fury in her chest. "You listen to me, and I will teach you to go your own way. Now please," she hissed.

Vicky turned toward the living room just off the kitchen. The bloody scene on the couch was hard to miss.

Vicky turned back to the kitchen, her eyes wide. "She's gone!"

Preorder Book 3: https://mybook.to/trishwatcher

Sign up for updates, advanced review copies, and book recommendations from K.T. Rose:
https://www.kyrobooks.com/subscribe-1

**Netted- A Serial Killer Thriller and Fast-Paced
Suspense Book 2
Inside Out**
Is it possible to escape a cult that feeds on fear?
https://mybook.to/bKRr

**Netted- A Serial Killer Thriller and Fast-Paced
Suspense Book 3
The Crash**
When time runs out, bodies will fall.
https://mybook.to/aeMfHJ

Trinity of Horror- Macabre Tales Volume 2
A normal summer day…drenched in blood.
https://mybook.to/Fqsg

**The Haunting of Gallagher Hotel- A Chilling
Haunted House Horror Novel**
*Pride and greed infect the soul, trapping
the dead in Gallagher Hotel.*
https://mybook.to/FbYFj

Stay connected with K.T. Rose by visiting:
https://www.kyrobooks.com/subscribe-1